BLOODMOON
AT CABIN CREEK

To Henry & Martha—
Best wishes and warm regards.

[signature]

June 2007

Gean B. Atkinson

Also by Gean B. Atkinson

Pilots of My Soul
Internal Invasion

WYNDHAM HOUSE
B O O K S

ISBN: 1-58961-476-3

For information address:
PageFree Publishing, Inc., 109 South Farmer Street, Otsego, MI 49078

Dedicated to Eunice Brook Atkinson

The first Cherokee in my life.

PROLOGUE

The man turned the corner in his Cadillac and suddenly felt strange. Almost instantly, he weakened and his stomach surged suggesting nausea was not far away. At first, he only felt a slight discomfort and then it struck him. He was diabetic and that feeling always heralded the onset of low blood sugar. The recent excitement he'd experienced must have caused his adrenalin to mask it.

His first thought was to measure his sugar level but then remembered the test kit was back at the motel. He'd have to listen to his body and, unfortunately, it was screaming he wasn't far from slipping into a diabetic coma.

He began to experience sight failure. Small pockets of blindness obscured his field of vision. He had to move his head around radically to achieve a complete picture of what was in front of him. He wasn't totally successful as the car bumped against a curb with a scraping noise.

Should he stop the car to prevent having a wreck? No, then his six-year old son who was riding with him would be helpless.

The man reached for his glucose pills but to his horror those, too, were back at the motel. Experience told him he didn't have much time. He was terrified about his situation and that anxiety was no doubt worsening his condition. He knew his boy thought something was wrong but was afraid to say anything. *Maybe this small town had a drug store but where?*

"Daddy, what's wrong?" asked the child, his small voice trembling.

"It's okay. It's okay," he mumbled but knew it did little to assuage the child's fears.

He looked ahead, his sight deteriorating with each minute that passed. He thought he saw a small roadside store. Pulling the Cadillac in, it slammed against the concrete parking stop, jumping back with a protest of sounds. He opened the door and felt his way to the front of the car and, without saying a word, stumbled into the store. There was staleness in the air, found in many stores of that type that lack regular cleaning. The disinterested clerk did not acknowledge him.

"You got any glucose tablets?" he said with a thick tongue. It wouldn't be long before he passed out. The clerk probably thought he was drunk. He estimated his blood sugar in the low 30s.

The clerk looked at him dumbly. "Got what?" she said.

"Glucose—never mind," he replied and turned. Before him was a merchandise rack. His breathing was coming in short gasps now and drops of sweat peppered his forehead. He didn't have long before he would be fodder for the paramedics. If the paramedics came so would the police and the police were the last people he wanted to see.

He knelt to the floor to keep from falling down.

"Hey. Are you okay?" yelled the clerk as she tenuously began to move from behind the counter.

He knew he wasn't far from unconsciousness and just as he looked up through murky eyes, he saw it. He knew it might be his last chance to save his life. But whether he could pull it off, he wasn't sure.

CHAPTER ONE

CLOSE TO BAXTER CREEK, KANSAS
143 YEARS EARLIER
SEPTEMBER 1864

The First Sergeant slowly pushed the high grass back from his face so he could see. His strong, slender hands were sweaty from crawling on his belly the fifty yards to the top of the ridge. The tiny teeth on the blades of grass tore infinitesimal chunks out of his palms that stung as perspiration met them.

Blistering heat from a lingering summer brought insects that swarmed his face and gnawed at his neck and arms. Though their bites smarted, he dared not slap them. He was close enough to see the enemy and that meant they could see him if he compromised his concealment.

The soldier watched as the blue-coated troops below scurried about, preparing horses and wagons for the continuation of a journey. Tons of supplies bound for Fort Gibson, he suspected, were frenetically being re-secured aboard the mule-powered supply train. It was important to count the type and number of the troops so he could make his report. There were over a hundred wagons and hundreds of mules guarded by, what looked like, nearly a thousand Union soldiers.

Gus—full name Charles Austin Augustus Rider—edged his six-foot-one inch frame back from his vantage point and got to his feet. Crouching, he began to retrace his concealed steps back to the safety of the Confederate camp, a long ride away. After only a few yards, his heart stopped. Thrashing in the bushes, the clatter of equipment and the sound of voices ahead gave him a short warning. He quickly snuggled inside the nearest thicket of brush and tried to blend into it.

The commotion rapidly escalated and within minutes his position was swarming with Yankee soldiers taking a break as their unit halted before moving into the camp. Gus had no choice but to remain motionless, hoping they wouldn't detect him and simply pass him by.

His slouch hat and ragged homespun butternut jacket were soaked with sweat from the heat. Holding his breath, he watched through the brush as the men sat and cursed. Some were rubbing their feet and others spitting tobacco. They all appeared to be well-fed and clothed. A few moved away from the group and relieved themselves in the undergrowth.

Gus knew what would happen if they discovered him. Torture, for sure. Death probably. The urge to bolt and run was strong but he knew he wouldn't make it fifty yards before they caught him. No, he only had one option. Actually, two. Stay frozen and pray.

In a few minutes, the Union commander called for the troops to re-form. Grumbling, they congregated in two rough lines twenty yards to Gus' left. On their lieutenant's command, they began to shuffle toward the supply camp.

As soon as the last of them disappeared from view, Gus carefully crawled out of his hiding place. Staying low, he kept them in sight as he hurried through the trees to distance himself from the columns. Moving quicker and quicker, he was about to break into a run when he was stopped in his tracks.

With his back facing him, a Yankee soldier stood silently in the process of urinating. Gus froze. There wasn't time to consider the situation. His Cherokee instincts took over. Reaching into his belt, he pulled a 17-inch, razor sharp "D" Guard Bowie knife. The man turned and horror flashed in his shocked eyes as he saw Gus, set to slam the blade up and into his back. The trooper frantically fumbled for his pistol but his unbuttoned pants and holster dangled helplessly from his belt beyond his reach.

As Gus was ready to stab him, the soldier threw himself into a ball and rolled forward, knocking Gus off his feet. He hurled himself onto Gus and began to bite the back of Gus' neck. The pain was excruciating but Gus could not cry out without alerting the Yankee camp.

The two men rolled around with Gus trying to stab backwards and catch the man any way he could. The rasping sounds that came from the Yankee were those of a frantic caged animal not a combat soldier. He could feel the man madly straining for his pistol but it was just out of his reach. If he couldn't stop him before he grabbed it, Gus was dead.

The Union camp was a hub of frenetic activity. Troop formations moving in and out, sergeants and corporals yelling at soldiers; horses and mules tugging at their handlers, whinnying all the while. Major Henry Hopkins, U.S. Army, was also as animated as his subordinate had ever seen him.

"By God, when those bastards come at us—and they will, mark my words—we'll have this ready for them," he said as he leaned over the drawing on the table in his tent.

"See here, Captain, this flips down and then these flip up." His spindly fingers pointed to the diagram of his secret weapon as he talked, his black, wavy beard moving up and down.

I know there's a mouth in there someplace but I'll be damned if I can see it. Just of bunch of whiskers with a sound coming out of the middle, the Captain thought as he stared at Hopkins' bizarre beard.

"Excuse me, sir, but won't this be awfully heavy?" he asked as he leaned over the plan to comprehend what his superior was talking about. "These wagons are made to carry supplies not six heavy men and hundreds of pounds of rifles and ammunition."

"Good question. See these reinforcements? The axles have been strengthened to support the extra weight. Understand this, Captain. One of the problems we have in defending these wagon trains is the massing of fire. If these—I call them 'security wagons'—can be placed strategically, each one combines the firepower of six snipers.

"Notice the loaders—here," he said as he jabbed his finger at another sketch. The drawing showed a wagon with six sharpshooters placed on platforms, three below and three above with heavy cover on hinged barriers. Behind them, panels dropped and provided cover and a tabletop for six loaders. The entire wagon was covered with a canvas top and looked like any other supply wagon.

"They load and load only. The loaders provide the shooters with freshly armed weapons. It increases the rate of fire to 25 rounds per man, per minute. Think of that, Captain. That's 300 rounds of deadly accurate fire from one small, movable platform," Hopkins continued with his diabolical plan.

"We know they're already reconnoitering us, waiting for our supply train to leave. They could be watching us right now. Someplace along the line they'll attack like they always do but this time we'll be ready. We'll kill those bastards in wholesale lots and that will make me very happy."

Most troopers fostered an animus for the Confederates but after four arduous and exhausting years of war, had accepted the notion that the enmity would probably fade once they returned to their families and homes. Not so for Hopkins. He'd despise and loathe the soldiers of the South every day of his life.

Hopkins pulled his thin frame to its full five foot ten inches. He straightened his blouse and walked purposefully across the dirt floor. With arms clasped behind him, he stared out the flap of the tent at the activities in the center of the encampment. He suddenly turned, his pale complexion more chalky than usual.

"Some day, Captain," he said solemnly, "we'll have guns that spit out 400, even 500 rounds per minute. They'll revolutionize warfare. But I don't have them now. This idea of the security wagons came to me in a dream. I believe it's Heaven sent. Just let those damn traitors attack our supply train."

He walked over to the table and again leaned over his drawings, supporting himself with both hands. "Their construction is already underway. I had the carpenters start on the modifications yesterday. Undercover, of course. They'll be ready for our supply train on Friday."

Hopkins was tiring of this conversation. He raised his head. His eyes were narrowed, full of hatred. "But you are a Captain and your job is to worry about making sure the train is ready to move out day after tomorrow. I do not expect failure. I will not tolerate failure. Understood?"

"Yes, sir," answered the Captain, detecting the change in the Major's demeanor. The Captain saluted and exited the Major's Spartan tent.

Gus reached behind with one hand and grabbed the man's hair. With a firm grip he jerked as hard as he could. The soldier let out a scream that caused him to release his bite on Gus' neck. That was all it took. Gus rolled over and was immediately on top of the Yankee trooper.

With one smooth stroke, Gus used all his body strength to swing the knife into the stomach of the enemy. He twisted the blade, grabbing the man's head and pushing it into his own shoulder to muffle any more screams that might alert his comrades. There were none. Only a momentary struggle and then warm blood coursing onto Gus' hand. The limp body slowly settled into the dry and cracked ground. He paused for a moment and was still. Apparently, the soldier's scream had gone unheard. But before long the man would be missed. The enemy would then know they had been penetrated and were under surveillance.

Damn, Gus thought. *So much for being undetected.* Wiping the blood from the knife, he replaced it in his scabbard. He had long since lost the ability to grieve after taking someone's life. With a quick glance behind him, he began to trot and then run toward his horse hidden nearly a mile away.

The Yankee soldier lay in a heap. He half-opened his eyes, his vision now foggy as his life drained from him. With one last ounce of strength he managed to drag the heavy Colt Dragoon pistol from his holster. Using his body, he forced the hammer back and then squeezed the trigger. The bullet furiously spurted from the gun as life grudgingly ebbed from his body. While the round struck only the dirt a few feet away, the loud report turned every face in the camp toward his location. Within seconds, men from his unit reversed their march and raced toward him.

Major Hopkins looked up and strode to the front flap of his tent. Pulling it back he could see the men all facing the ridge top and a number of them running toward it on foot and horseback. *Probably a Reb scout*, he thought. *If they catch him, they'll make him pay. What I do not see, I cannot condone or object to.*

He chuckled to himself and closed the tent flap then walked back to the diagrams of his pet weapon.

Gus crashed through the forest. He turned his head at the echo of the gunshot but didn't stop running. He knew what that sound meant. Now the Yankees would be coming for him. Sprinting faster until he had reached the greatest speed he could achieve, he realized he still had a half-mile to go before he could get to his horse. If the horse were still there.

The angry cries of Union officers and soldiers began to filter forward. Gus' lungs were on fire for more air and as his legs tired, he found himself falling more frequently. The bitter taste of bile unsettled him as he scrambled to his feet. He forced his legs to pump as he heard the sound of brush behind him being trampled by the people in fierce pursuit. Gus couldn't see them as he glanced back. He didn't need to. He could sense they were getting closer.

At twenty-five, Gus Rider was a muscular man. A farmer before the war, he knew physical strain well but this panicked running was taking its toll. His buttocks were burning. His vision was blurring and his heart was pounding uncontrollably. Gratefully, he spotted the horse he had hidden 100 yards ahead. He willed himself to reach it before the enemy reached him.

Exhausted, he got to the mount and leaned against him. He shakily reached for the saddle horn and, for just a second, rested his head on the stirrup. Before he could make his next move he heard a young voice bark a command.

"Don't move, Reb," a man said. "I'll blow your goddamn head off. I wondered who parked this fine looking horse and then left it. Figured I'd just wait and see. And look what I found."

Gus raised his head and saw a random Union soldier coming around the rear of his horse with a rifle pointed at him. *These bastards are scattered everywhere*, he thought. *This Yankee doesn't know I have a crowd after me.* He made a slight move toward the soldier.

Quickly, the young trooper jumped back, unknowingly putting himself not far off Gus' horses' flank. "Don't move. I mean it, Reb. I'll shoot."

"Now, there's no reason to get excited, cousin," Gus said, trying to catch his breath as he slowly turned and ran his hand down the side of his horse. Sweat poured onto his face and his breaths came in short gasps. "I don't want you to be shooting me and I'll bet you'd rather not do any shooting. Am I right?"

The soldier stood silently, lips pressed together tight and nervously grasping his weapon even tighter. His etiolated face was also covered with droplets of sweat and his hair matted to his head. Gus had been fighting with the Confederate Cherokee Mounted Rifles since '61 and could spot a veteran when he faced one. Confederate soldiers in Indian Territory averaged 26 — this young Yankee couldn't be much over 20. He was sure the uncertain, young warrior with his scraggly attempt at a mustache had never shot a man at all.

Gus wasn't worried about this youngster. He was pretty sure he could win a fight with him. But he was worried about the crowd that was on his tail and closing fast. Once the Union boys got in sight of them he had little chance of escaping. He only had one chance left and he decided to take it.

Camp Pleasant
North of Tahlequah, Indian Territory

Brigadier General Stand Watie was worried. The battle for the Trans-Mississippi Theater was not progressing well. The news from the East was that Lee was having a hard time with desertions — a sure sign that the war was not going the South's way. Even the soldiers that stayed and would be loyal to Lee to the end were starving.

Watie gazed out at his men as they went about the mundane duties of garrison. No one could tell what brave and gallant warriors they were from their appearances. They were a sad looking lot he had to admit. Their clothes were in tatters, some wearing boots with little sole and others attired in shirts that had no backs.

Many wore civilian clothes while some were dressed in the captured blue uniforms of the Federal troops. With Lee suffering close to the South's supply sources, he was not surprised that shortages were being felt in all the Confederate units west of the Mississippi. Clearly, the Federal supply train that he had sent First Sergeant Rider to reconnoiter had more importance to the command than just military strategy. The battalion desperately needed the clothing and supplies it carried.

With blinding speed, Gus jerked hard on his horse's cinch. Reacting instinctively, the skittish horse delivered a powerful kick with his back legs connecting with the chest of the youthful Yankee, sending him flying to the hard baked ground.

Gus leaped on top of him instantly and stripped the weapon from the groaning trooper. Even though he knew, someday, somewhere, he might have to fight him again, he had neither the time nor the inclination to kill him. He left the man writhing on the ground. Hurdling onto his horse he sped off just in time to hear shots behind him as the Union soldiers broke through the forest and saw him.

Gus rode at a full gallop until he thought he would kill the horse if he went any longer. Only then did he look back to see if he had eluded his pursuers. When he was certain he was out of danger, he veered off the main trail to a small stream and watered his animal. His face red and stinging with exertion, he doused himself with the cool water. After they had refreshed themselves, he remounted the horse and continued on the long ride back to his base camp.

Gus wanted to forget about the damn war and go home. He had a wife, Mary Ann, and a small son, Thomas Lafayette—"T.L."—whom he missed desperately and hadn't seen in six months. They were not far. About thirty miles to the east in Goingsnake District. *They may as well be a million miles away*, he thought.

The Yankee Captain's cheeks were stinging from the rebuke he had suffered from Major Hopkins as he strode across the busy camp.

What a harpy he is. But still, the Old Man may have stumbled onto something. He opens up on the Rebs with those security wagons of his and he'll break any charge they can come up with, that's for sure. They won't know what hit them and by the time they realize where the fire is coming from it'll be too late. They may figure it out after the battle and be able to spot them beforehand but the first few times it'll catch them totally by surprise. It'll be a slaughter.

This isn't about getting the supplies through with him. It's all about killing, he thought.

Gus loped into the camp and went directly to General Watie's tent. After announcing himself, he entered and reported to the legendary leader.

"Well, what's out there, First Sergeant Rider?" the stocky General asked as he interrupted a conference with the Battalion Executive Officer.

"About what we expected, although less than last time. I guess a thousand Yankees, mainly cavalry, some infantry, couple hundred wagons and maybe 600 mules," Gus said. "They've got tons of supplies and it looked like they getting close to being ready to move out."

"Any artillery?" the executive officer asked eagerly.

"None that I could see but you can bet they have some," Gus replied.

"Well, General, they know we're watching them. I barely got out with my scalp. Had to kill one of them and they chased me for three miles. We can beat them if we have enough men and they don't expect us."

"Thank you, First Sergeant," Watie said coldly. He turned his gaze to his desk, folding a piece of paper and handing it toward Gus.

"First Sergeant, take this to General Gano with my compliments. It asks that he move with all possible dispatch to augment our forces. Last time we were outnumbered. That will not be the case on this occasion," he said flatly as Gus reached for the note.

"Yes, sir," Gus said and turned and exited the tent.

A gentle breeze slipped through the camp as Gus leaned on a tree and stared at the distant mountains. His light complexion and blue eyes testified to the intermingling of white and Cherokee blood in his ancestry. The son of Austin Rider, a patriarch of the Tennessee Cherokee Nation, he was recognized by most as one of the young men who would lead the nation—the new Indian Territory Cherokee Nation—after the war, if he survived.

"First Sergeant?" the Battalion Executive Officer said as he walked up from behind. "Are you sure you're up to delivering that message? You just got in after a pretty grueling trip. We can have a courier take it just as easily." Gus turned and straightened up.

"No, sir, I can do it. I don't want it falling into Yankee hands. I'd rather do it myself," Gus replied. Everyone had heard the story of General Lee's battle plan that had fallen into enemy hands at Antietam nearly two years earlier.

"All right, I'll tell you what. General Gano is located about twenty miles east of the Martin House. You live around the east border of the territory, don't you?" Bell asked.

"Yes, sir. On Evansville Creek."

"Good. Ride hard and deliver the message to General Gano. Then spend the night at your house and get back here the next day. It's a might like a twelve-hour pass," the officer smiled.

"I'm much obliged, sir," Gus grinned.

"Tell General Gano you won't be back here until tomorrow night so if his reply is urgent, he can send a courier of his own," Bell said. "And First Sergeant, there are Federal patrols all around Gano, so be careful. Some of them are from those colored Regiments and they'd just as soon kill you as look at you."

All of a sudden Gus' fatigue left him. The threat of the enemy paled next to the exhilaration of the thought of seeing his family, even for a few hours. He began packing his gear—the same gear he had unpacked just a few hours ago. He was going home.

CHAPTER TWO

Gus sat down beside his cousin, Private Mitchell Harlan.

"Mitchell, how are you doing?" he asked.

"Aw, Gus, I'm tired. I need to be at my farm. They just can't make it work without me. Minta and the boys try but it's just more than they can do. When do you think this thing will be over?" Mitchell asked.

"I wish I knew. We're all in the same boat. Our families need us and we're here. But Mitchell, this is what they call a 'temporary inconvenience'. We'll be with our families soon and we'll have protected the Confederacy in the West. Plus, if we can keep Yankee troops tied down here then Grant can't use them against General Lee," Gus said.

"I guess you're right. How's your family?" Mitchell asked.

Gus smiled. "They're fine, thanks. Say Mitchell, how about trading horses with me for a couple of days? Mine's pretty well worn out. She needs some rest and I've got a couriering job to do. I don't think she's up to it."

"Sure, Gus. Take my bay, he's fresh," Mitchell said and rose to untie the reins and hand them to Gus.

"Thanks, cousin," Gus replied as he transferred his saddlebags and saddle to the new horse. "I'll catch up to you in a few days."

He struck out just as the sun reached its zenith, intent on reaching the Texas General's headquarters by nightfall. If all went well, he could be home before midnight.

He decided to take the faster but more hazardous route north of the Martin Home. He rode at a brisk pace but not so much that he would lose his horse. The jagged, hilly course through the Boston Mountains had sharp drop-offs. The trail became so narrow in places that he often had to dismount and blindfold his horse. He would then lead it over the precarious path to keep it from spooking and falling into the gorge.

He arrived at General Gano's headquarters as the setting sun began to shoot rainbow shafts of light to the sky, painting the clouds with generous strokes of pink, orange and purple. For a moment, he forgot about the carnage he caused in earning his daily bread. He reveled in the beauty of nature's signal of a perfectly completed day in his adopted but beloved homeland.

He rode to General Gano's tent and presented himself to the Adjutant who took the note and stepped into the General's tent for a moment and then signaled him inside.

"General Watie is ready to try them again, eh, First Sergeant?" the fully bearded General Gano asked as he looked up from the note.

"Sir, I reconnoitered the train that's coming down the road myself. General Watie believes if our forces are combined, and we have adequate artillery support, the supply train can be taken. It's a rich prize, sir. I've seen it with my own eyes and there must be a ton or two of supplies. Food, ammunition, clothing, all of it."

"I understand you'll not be returning until tomorrow so I'll send a courier tonight to advise General Watie we'll move out in the morning. Thank you, First Sergeant," General Gano said and stood, signaling the end of the interview. Gus took his leave and departed the tent. He refilled his canteen and got to his horse before someone might decide he needed to stay.

With darkness descending, he hurried to make as much time as he could before poor visibility slowed his progress. He guided his horse up the steep trail and straight east to his home next to the Arkansas border.

Major Hopkins ambled over to his second-in-command, a brevet major with the 1st Colored Home Guard. "Major, a word please," he said.

The Major approached, saluted and awaited Hopkins' orders. "I want to change our Order of March. We will bivouac here and then move out shortly after midnight. That will allow us to surprise the Rebels and get across Cabin Creek before they have a chance to prepare. I want to be across the creek before the sun rises. Inform the column and make sure the sergeants are ready to have the mounts move out on my command."

"Excellent idea, sir," the Brevet Major replied sincerely. He didn't think Hopkins was capable of such innovative tactics. "Sir, do you think there is any danger the movement will place us at Cabin Creek at the same time our chance of engaging the enemy is the greatest?"

Hopkins ignored his question as if he hadn't heard it. "I want the security wagons positioned midway across the creek to protect the column as it moves across," he said, obviously still formulating the plan in his head. *If the Rebs did try to ambush the column they would have a big surprise waiting for them.*

"Yes sir. I'll see to it," the Brevet Major said. He saluted, did an about face and headed for the column's First Sergeant to relay the order.

Inky darkness covered the mountain when Gus heard a low rumbling and reined back his horse. Listening intently, at first thinking it might be far-off cannon fire, he soon recognized it as thunder announcing the impending arrival of rain. He could smell the moisture and knew the downpour would be on him quickly. Driving the horse up the ascending trail until they reached the top, he stopped to rest.

He jerked when the first drop of rainwater pinged his hand and almost simultaneously heard the gentle pelting of the leaves around him. Urging the mount on, he began to descend the hill. Within a few hundred yards it was raining heavier and the resulting runoff was making the trail more difficult to navigate.

The horse began to slip and lose its footing. Gus slowed his pace to make the going easier but the soil of the trail was quickly turning to mud. The steep descent was proving too much for the struggling horse and he couldn't seem to stop himself. The frantic animal began sliding down the trail.

Gus had grown up on the back of a horse but for the first time in his life he wasn't sure if he could manage the creature on this terrain. Suddenly, the horse gave a loud whinny as its rear legs buckled underneath him. The animal fell to its side, throwing Gus off.

He frantically rolled away to keep from getting pinned by the thousand-pound mount and felt himself tumble through puddles of water and mud. The hard surfaces and pointed edges of stones jabbed him in the side. Abruptly, vertigo overcame him and he realized he was falling.

Branches slapped him hard as he fell. After what seemed like an eternity, he slammed to the ground with an audible thud. He lay face-down gasping for air, wondering if he were dead.

Once he could stop grimacing from the pain, Gus opened his eyes to the same darkness that had surrounded him before the fall. He was on his front and began to gently roll onto his side. He stretched out with his hand to steady himself and reached into nothingness. Holding his breath, he moved his arm around until it hit something solid.

He became conscious that he was on the precipice of a far deeper fall than he had just taken. Cautiously, he used his other hand to examine the ground on the opposite side and realized there were a couple of feet of solid footing. Inch by inch, scooting on his belly to his right until he had support on both sides, he turned himself into a sitting position. A rock ledge jutting out from the embankment had obviously broken the fall.

He felt a biting pain in his side and his shoulder was burning. Luckily, his night vision was beginning to return. Looking for a way to get to the top of the hill and climb the face of the cliff, he pulled on outgrowths to test their strength before using them to propel himself upward.

Gus ran out of things to grab onto when he was five feet from the top. He couldn't go up and he couldn't go down. Up to this minute he had been successful in ignoring the nagging pains in his side and shoulder. Now the short pause, caused by the inability to find a step, brought them to his attention in a powerful way.

Gus was afraid to look down. He felt his strength being sapped as he hung next to the cliff. In desperation, he let go of one hand and reached for his Bowie knife. He dangled from the side of the mountain, his shoulder now throbbing with pain. He reached as high as he could and slammed the knife with all his strength into the side of the hillside, hoping its long blade would hold in the soft earth. Agonizingly, he pulled himself up and frantically patted with his free hand for a handhold or outgrowth. He felt the knife giving way.

"Captain, how long has you known Major Hopkins?" the grizzled old sergeant asked.

"Not long, just since I reported in three months ago," the Captain responded. "Why do you ask, Sergeant Hartnett?"

"Well, sir, I've been with him since he come to the territory and something ain't right."

"What do you mean?" asked the Captain.

"He give me an order to quietly pass to the men. I think it's illegal. In fact I think it might get some folks sent to jail or worse."

"Explain yourself, Sergeant," said the Captain. "Are you talking about the security wagons?"

Sergeant Hartnett stared into the Captain's eyes and didn't say anything at first. Then he spat out a wad of tobacco and began to talk.

Miraculously, Gus found a small outcropping that offered just enough of a hold to pull to the next level. Once he had a secure grip, it allowed him to dig the Bowie knife into the top of the drop-off. With a grunt, he heaved himself over the crest and lay on his back in the wet dirt, gasping from exhaustion and fear as rain washed the mud from his face.

When he could garner the energy, he stood and looked around. His horse was gone. He was surprised until he remembered he had his cousin's horse. *Obviously not as well trained as mine*, he thought. He surprised himself that he could still muster a sense of humor.

He began to tread down the trail. The aching in his side and shoulder were growing worse but he continued to slug through the now-pounding rain. He approached a fork in the trail and was unsure of which path to take. The darkness and his weariness were making it hard to recognize landmarks that he had learned years ago. In frustration he took the left fork and walked determinedly for fifteen minutes. He stopped abruptly.

Standing before him looking confused, was his cousin's horse.

"Easy, boy," Gus said in a slow, soft voice as he began inching toward the runaway mount trying not to frighten him. The bay gave a small grunt and stepped back.

To hell with this, Gus thought and made a mad dash for the animal, leaping for his loosely hanging reins. Landing on the trail with them firmly in his hands as the horse tried to pull away, he gripped hard. He wasn't about to be parted from the thin strips of leather that held his transportation.

Working his way up the leads and pulling himself onto the horse, groaning with pain as he did so, Gus and the horse resumed their movement toward what he hoped was home.

"My Dearest Sarah," Stand Watie wrote. "I have but a moment but wanted to write to tell you that I am well although very tired. We are not getting much rest but are busy prosecuting the war every day to good outcome. I hope all is well with you and that this finds the rest of the family in good health. We anticipate a large engagement soon and I am hopeful I will be able to report a success for our cause.

"I look forward to the day I can come home and we can be together as always and can embrace you with my true affections.

"I am, most faithfully, Stand Watie"

General Watie laid down his pen and wondered how long he could fool the people closest to him. He suspected General Robert E. Lee was wondering the same thing.

It had stopped pouring several hours ago and apparently, by the look of the ground, hadn't rained in this area at all. The clouds had drifted away and the moon was creating eerie shadows that danced in the forest. As he cleared the treeline he saw it in the distance. The home in which his small family lived with his in-laws was bathed in moonlight. It was only a few hundred yards away. He started to gallop and then, with a groan, curbed his horse. The bouncing gait caused shooting pains to course through his side and shoulder. He contented himself to lumber to the two-story white house.

Gus dismounted and tied up the horse. He quietly climbed the steps to the porch and knocked gently on the door. Promptly, he could hear movement inside. A flickering light from a candle entered the room in the hand of his aged father-in-law. The other hand grasped a pistol.

The man held up the candle and looked out the window and, upon recognizing him, hurriedly opened the door. "Gus! Son, are you alright?" the man asked with hushed concern.

"I'm all right, Thomas," he said as he quietly walked into the house.

Without further words, Thomas Wilson Bigby handed the candle to Gus and pointed upstairs.

"Thanks, Thomas. I'll see you in the morning." Gus smiled and climbed the stairs to the room in which his wife and child slept.

He carefully opened the bedroom door and walked softly to the child's bed. He knelt slowly and gently touched the boy's face remaining motionless and staying by the bed for several long moments, love silently pouring from him. He examined the boy's petite, childish features—so many of them calling back to his ancestors. His smooth skin and oval face, a hallmark of the Rider family, was suffused in moonlight from the window. He was filled with gratitude for the blessing of this little boy.

Rising, Gus quietly moved to his wife's bed. He sat lightly on the unoccupied side and leaned over to look at her sleeping face. She laid silently, peacefully, a portrait of muliebrity.

She's so frail, he thought. *I don't remember her being this fragile.*

Mary Ann slowly opened her eyes, a little at first and then they blinked wide. "Oh, Gus," she whispered, her brown eyes swiftly filling with tears.

His strong arms were instantly about her, holding her tight. Silently, he stroked her dark hair and, leaning back so he could see her face, sweetly kissed her lips and then her cheeks. He lovingly caressed her beautiful, thin face and ever so carefully wiped away the salty tears that streamed from her enchanting eyes.

When she started to speak he placed his callused finger gently on her lips and shook his head with a small smile. He stood, took off his wet clothes and slipped into the bed, oblivious to broken ribs and a dislocated shoulder, to fall asleep in the arms of the woman he loved above all others.

"No, sir, it ain't about the security wagons. It's more than that. Last night, the major called me in and said he wanted to add a little spice to the next few years for the troopers," said Sergeant Hartnett.

"And?" said the Captain.

Hartnett paused as if deciding if he should proceed. "He wanted me to pass on to the troopers that they'd get five dollars for every scalp they collected from the Rebs."

The Captain's brow furrowed and his eyes narrowed. "You must be crazy. Major Hopkins knows that's against every Army regulation. He'd be court martialed. They'd break him. He'd never get away with it," the Captain said in disbelief.

"We got some savages riding with us. He plans to blame it on them," Sergeant Hartnett said.

"My God, that makes us no better than them. Have you told anyone else? Any of the troops?" the Captain asked.

"Naw, sir."

"Don't. Let me see what I can do. I can't let this happen," said the Captain. "No matter what I have to do."

"Now sir, the Major might do some things that is kinda daft, you know. But he ain't never asked us to break the law before," Sergeant Hartnett said almost apologetically.

The Captain just shook his head.

"Papa!" the little boy screamed with joy as he leapt on top of his long-absent father.

Wincing with the pang of his ribs but quickly hiding his pain, Gus embraced his son and showered him with kisses and tickles.

"Have you been a good soldier?" he asked. "Helping your mother and grandmother?"

"And granddaddy, too!" T.L. answered.

"Then you get more kisses," Gus exclaimed and the two laughed and played for what seemed like only a moment.

He looked to her side of the bed to see that Mary Ann had already crept out. He smelled the frying of bacon—an aroma he hadn't enjoyed in a few months.

"I smell something good! What do you say we go down and see what it is?" Gus said.

"It's breakfast, Daddy," the little boy said as if to shame him for not knowing.

Gus laughed and pulled on his trousers. He took his son in his arms and went barefoot downstairs. The family was waiting at a breakfast table arrayed with food already prepared. Food was scarce all across the territory but somehow they had managed to put together a feast for him.

He sat next to Mary Ann after kissing his mother-in-law and shaking Thomas Bigby's hand. After a quick but poignant blessing the family began to eat with everyone voicing approval at the tastiness of the meal.

"When do you have to leave?" Mary Ann asked as she reached over and put her hand in his. He wasn't surprised she knew he would be leaving again.

"In a few hours. I just got a pass to deliver a message," he said softy. Noting her pained expression he quickly added, "I'm lucky. Most of the others haven't been home in seven months."

He couldn't keep his eyes from his wife and son. Mary Ann had put on a bright calico dress and had her hair pulled back tightly. Even though she was gaunt she looked clean and fresh.

He had missed them so much and just the sight of them was like an elixir to him. He wouldn't allow himself to dwell on Mary Ann's delicate appearance. Seeing her in any way was a blessing to him.

After a meal like Gus hadn't had in months, Mary Ann insisted he put on some of Thomas' overalls while she washed his filthy clothes.

"These rags may fall apart when we wash them. It's a shame the Army can't even provide decent uniforms," she said as she went to start the washing.

"I know. Most of the men are in rags. Maybe that will change if we can win a few battles."

Gus played with T.L. on the floor and then set off into the front yard and pushed him in the swing, reveling in his bright eyes and happy laughs—sounds long absent except in his memories. Mary Ann joined them and the three walked toward a bluff overlooking Evansville Creek. They sat and talked while T.L. played. Gus noticed her fingers, always long and thin, now looked as if they could be crushed with a simple handshake.

"Honey, are you well?" he asked after a pause. "I worry that I should've sent you and T.L. with your folks south to Texas like a lot of others have done with their families." The concern was heavy in his voice.

"Of course, I'm well. I'm not the one fighting a war. I don't even think we're in any real danger here. We've only had Yankee troops by once and they didn't even stop," she shushed. "Anyway, at the first sign of riders we run into the cornfield and hide."

"Tell me what you've been up to. Your letters come so late and intermittently, they sometimes don't even catch up with me," Gus said.

"Well, let me fill you in on the exciting happenings at the Rider-Bigby place. Hold on to your hat," she joked. For nearly an hour she recounted the little occurrences that had occupied the lives of herself, T.L. and her parents. He loved her laughter and the way her eyes danced when she told the stories of the cow getting out or of T.L. being chased by a raccoon.

They sat and talked—enjoyed just being with each other— and watched the sun pass overhead and begin to recede into the west.

"It's time," he said tenderly. He saw her bite her thin lip. They got up and ambled hand in hand back to the house with T.L. on his father's shoulders.

Halfway back, Mary Ann asked, "Gus, do you think the South can win? We keep hearing things that the war is going badly in the east and south."

Gus was silent. "I don't know how it will turn out, honey. The Cherokee Nation is so divided. But, we've chosen our side and we're committed to this path. I hope when this is over, we can be united again," he said. Neither said anything else.

His mother-in-law had his clothes washed and the hot autumn sun had quickly dried them. He dressed and spent what little time was left with Mary Ann saying goodbye. She had noticed his injuries and wouldn't let him dress until she had placed a bandage around his rib cage and rubbed some herbal ointment on his shoulder.

He turned to leave, knowing that by agreement, she would stay upstairs because she could not bear to see him go. He carried T.L. to the porch and bent down to talk to him face-to-face. He was struck by the innocence in the child's face as he gazed with wonder into his son's eyes. There was no war in them, no fear, just love for his little family.

"Son, take care of your mother. And help your grandma and grandpa. I'll be home soon. I don't want to leave, son, but I must for our country's sake. Someday, you'll understand."

"I know. I love you, papa," the little one said.

"I love you, my son," he said, fighting back tears.

The little boy threw his diminutive arms around his father. After a moment Gus went down the steps of the porch to the horse Thomas Bigby was holding for him.

"Let's walk a ways before you get on," Thomas said. They sauntered down the trail, mount in tow.

After they were out of earshot, Thomas blurted out, "Gus, Mary Ann is sick. She didn't want you to know but I think it's your right."

Gus almost expected the news but didn't want to hear it. "How sick is she?" he asked without looking at Thomas. Neither man interrupted his pace. There was a silence and when Thomas spoke, his deep, always strong, voice cracked. This was the child he brought across the Trail of Tears at six-years-old from his native Tennessee and the bond between them was strong.

"Very sick. She continues to lose weight, and gets mighty ill at night. Half the time she's gasping for breath. We've taken her to the doctor at Tahlequah but he doesn't know what to do," Thomas lamented, his speech quivering with fear and frustration.

Gus didn't know what to say. Suddenly, his world was crashing down on him.

"Don't they know what's wrong?" Gus asked.

There was a pause. "No. No, they don't.

"You mustn't tell her I told you," Thomas said instantly as if talking to himself. "I don't want her angry with me. We'll watch over her and do everything that can be done. I just wanted you to know."

"Thank you, Thomas. I'm so tired of this war. Surely it will be over soon. Please take care of her. I'll be back as quickly as I can," Gus said.

He felt so helpless. He couldn't even stay with his wife who might be dying for all he knew. He climbed on the horse and without looking back, rode as fast as he could before Thomas could see the tears coursing from his eyes.

He stared at the ceiling of the tent unable to close his eyes to sleep. No matter how hard General Watie tried he couldn't shake the worry that seemed to encompass him. First Sergeant Rider's report was pretty much what they expected. Lots of soldiers carrying supplies — they'd seen that before and they'd engaged similar forces before. And even though they had been mainly unsuccessful in those skirmishes, it had to do more with weather and geography than anything else.

But this was different. There was an added danger here that he couldn't put his finger on.

The truth was that if they weren't successful in this battle it was questionable whether he could keep the battalion together. The men were hungry and exhausted. They hadn't been paid in months and everyone with a family was hearing of the hardships their families were enduring. Without a victory soon he didn't know how long the battalion could last.

Gus rode at a moderate pace not wanting to tire his animal but in a hurry to get back to his men. It was almost as if he were energized to try and end the war all by himself so he could return home for good.

He made it through the mountains without incident and then began to approach the treeline that opened onto a meadow. He heard voices ahead. He dismounted and slowly walked his horse toward the sounds.

Three men were scattered around a campfire. They were rough looking characters. Their clothes were dirty and tattered and they hadn't shaved in weeks. Gus knew that the territory was essentially lawless and outlaws roamed freely. The men wore no uniforms, which was a danger sign. In this area, every law-abiding man fit enough to fight was in uniform.

Still, he couldn't bypass the camp because it lay directly across the trail. One had to be careful when entering another man's camp. Gus slipped the Bowie knife up his sleeve and checked his Colt revolver. It was loaded. He moved slowly into view.

"Howdy," he said, loud enough to draw attention to himself.

The three men jerked around and he noticed their first move was to put their hands on their side arms. They did not respond to his greeting.

He walked to ten or fifteen feet from the closest one and said, "How are you boys doing? Anybody by this way?"

"Just you," said the youngest one, showing rotted teeth when he grinned. "Where you be off to, mister?" he asked as he slowly stood, all the while eyeing Gus' horse.

"On my way west to hook up with my unit," Gus answered.

"Are you hungry? We was just having a little breakfast," said the man.

"Thank you kindly, but I've already had something to eat," Gus answered.

"Mighty nice looking horse. How about selling it to us?" the man asked.

Another danger sign. Who would sell their only means of transportation?

"Nope, I'm afraid he isn't for sale."

Suddenly, Gus noticed something. One of the men was missing. Just a second ago there were three, now there were only two. He turned quickly to see the third man trying to slip up behind him with revolver drawn.

He looked back and rotten teeth had already pulled his gun. Gus jerked his own weapon and without a moment's hesitation fired, sending the kid to the ground. He barely had time to turn and fire at the man coming up from the rear. His first shot missed and the man kept coming and was firing back.

Gus dropped to his stomach and took careful aim from the prone position, even though the other man was now running and firing as fast as he could. Taking his time as if he were stalking a lion, Gus fired two bullets, both landing in a tight group on the man's forehead. The man fell like a sack of salt.

Just as he thought he had met the immediate threat, the oldest of the three outlaws planted his knee between Gus' shoulder blades. The breath was quickly forced out of him draining all of his energy. The outlaw roughly stuck the barrel of his weapon in the back of Gus' head.

"You son-of-a-bitch! You've killed my brothers," he screamed. "Drop that gun."

Gus had no choice but to let his fingers relax from around the pistol. The man quickly reached down and tossed it away from Gus. He cautiously removed his knee from Gus' back and stood up, all the time keeping Gus covered.

"Stay down!" he ordered. "You're going to pay for murdering my brothers. You should have just given us the damn horse and we might have let you live. But now, you're going to wish we'd just killed you fast. The war will be over by the time you die. I'm going to spread it out for a long time."

Gus knew where this was going since he had been told to stay down. One of the favorite means of torture by his warriors was to stake a man down, slit open his back, arms and legs and then leave him for the insects and animals to devour alive. It took time and was an excruciating way to die. This fool seemed to have all the time in the world.

Gus felt the man tying rawhide strips around his ankles. He moved in front of Gus and threw down another strip.

"Here, tie this around your wrist."

Gus knew his legs were now immobilized and pretty quickly his arms would be, too. His options were vanishing. He took the strip and fiddled with it tying it into a loose circle.

The outlaw bent down to check it and said, "Tighter, boy, you think I'm a foo ... " He never finished the word fool.

"How dare you!" Major Hopkins barked, his face red as fire. "What insolence you have to accuse me of such a malfeasance of office.

"Scalps? Nonsense!" said Hopkins, his hand shaking.

"Are you questioning me, Captain? You know such actions are against Army regulations. Are you implying I would issue an unlawful order?" Major Hopkins asked his ire clearly on the verge of being out of control.

The Captain began to wonder if he had made a mistake thinking this could be addressed in a mature manner between two officers.

"No sir, I was just trying to clear up a rumor so I could set it straight," he said.

"Get out! The next time you make such unfounded accusations, I'll have you court-martialed. Get out!" Hopkins repeated.

Precisely when the man was closest to him, Gus reached into his sleeve and, in a flash, withdrew his Bowie knife and slashed at the man's throat in one smooth stroke. The man dropped his weapons and grabbed at his neck, now spurting blood.

Gus cut his bindings, stood, picked up his weapon and shot the man in the head.

Jaw clinched, Gus walked around the campsite looking at what was left behind by the outlaws. Their saddlebags didn't tell much of a story. He began to check the pockets of the dead men.

Each of them had about $100 in cash on them. That was an unusually large amount for anyone to have in this territory. But the most telling indictment was the kind of cash it was. It was federal money, not Confederate currency. It was obvious these men had been in the employ of the Union and Gus was pretty sure it was for information. They were spies as well as thieves and outlaws. He was glad they were dead.

CHAPTER THREE

Gus was tired when his horse closed in on the edge of the tree line. Cautious as always, he dismounted and made his way through the trees to get a view of what lay ahead. He was concerned when he spotted a Union patrol of about twenty cavalry approaching from the south. They appeared to be skirting the treeline looking for a trail that would lead them into the forest. He knew they could easily swerve into the foliage at any minute and begin a patrol swath that could go deep into the woods.

He ran back to his horse and led him deeper into the wooded area so he couldn't be seen from the treeline outskirts. The trail they were searching for could end up being the one he was on.

The Yankee column closed in on Gus' path. Suddenly, a rider came galloping across the open field. He approached the patrol commander and after having a few words, the troop turned and hurriedly reversed its direction.

That patrol was in a hurry to get somewhere after hearing what that rider had to say. I wonder what he told them, Gus thought. This was not the first patrol Gus had to dodge on his way back to camp. The patrols were everywhere. They were made up of whites, Choctaws and Negroes. He even recognized some of the renegade Cherokees in one of them. That meant that many diverse units were involved in the operation and attested to its importance.

He rode for another hour and then spotted his battalion. He trotted into the encampment and went directly to General Watie's tent.

Major Henry Hopkins had to admit it. He hated these junior officers. Especially the ones who came from wealthy families and were products of West Point like the Captain.

No one had sponsored Henry Hopkins. No one had paved the way for him. He had to claw his way up the ladder, taking dead-end assignments in god-forsaken posts. Being criticized by officers half his skill and experience because he took an occasional drink.

He knew none of his detractors thought he would ever make colonel but he was on the verge of something big and nobody would be able to deny that. His security wagons were going to revolutionize fighting in the backwoods. And it was all his creation.

And now that damn upstart Captain wanted to ruin it all. "That will not happen," he heard himself say. *It didn't seem to matter to the arrogant, young Captain that the Rebel savages they were facing had been taking the scalps of white women and children since the 1600s. He knew the Captain couldn't wait to tell the first senior officer he could find about the rumor. But he knew exactly how to prevent such an occurrence.*

Out of habit, Major Hopkins looked around to ensure no one was watching and took a quick swig from the small flask he kept in his desk drawer.

"Sir," Gus said as he stuck his head into the tent. "Have you had any reports from the scouts?"

"Come in, First Sergeant," Watie said. He was obviously anxious. "What news do you have?" Watie said motioning Gus into the tent.

"I saw at least four patrols and haying parties on my way back. That's a lot, but more important is they're from all different units," Gus said.

"They're not just white. That means every unit they've got is looking after this wagon train."

Usually implacable, Watie was clearly concerned as he heard the report. "Does that give you reason to alter your initial assessment of the force's size?" Watie asked.

Gus was silent. He raised his eyes and then, thoughtfully, said, "General, there's something going on. This is more than just another supply train. First of all, it's huge. Secondly, by committing so many units, they appear to be expecting us. They may have even more men than I saw. If we're expected and the enemy has a greater force than we believe, it could spell disaster for us."

Watie lowered his voice. "I see, First Sergeant. Thank you for your report. That will be all."

Gus saluted and exited the tent. He walked through the camp with a strange feeling that many of the comrades he saw were going to be dead before this battle was over. He might be among them.

Gus found his cousin and returned his horse, trading him for his own.

"Did he do okay for you, Gus?" asked Mitchell Harlan.

"He sure did, Mitchell. I'm obliged to you. He's kind of dirty. We ran into a lot of rain on this trip. A lot of mud. I'll clean him up if you'll give me an hour or so," Gus replied.

"No, I'll take care of it. I know you got to be tired. What's it like out there, Gus. What do you see?"

"There's a lot of commotion. Yankee patrols all over this area. Something big is going to happen."

"Maybe we can get this thing over soon," Mitchell said.

"Maybe so, cousin. Maybe so."

Gus led his horse to the tent he shared with a couple of other sergeants. He tied the mount up and walked to the chuck wagon for some food. After eating what seemed to be some kind of stew, he made his way back to the tent looking forward to having a conversation with a few of his troops. He sat by the campfire and then leaned back. Before he knew it he was fast asleep not to waken until the order to move out was given.

CHAPTER FOUR

Horse Creek on the Military Road

The courier rode hard into the camp, jumping off of his horse as it showered him with foamy sweat and stirred up a wave of dust from the dry ground. He strode directly into General Watie's tent. Streams of sweat tumbled down his face. Heat waves seemed to emanate from his body as he stood, waiting for permission to speak. He handed the message from Col. Gano to Watie. It was succinct.

"Am in position south of Cabin Creek. Our adversary is moving toward our location. Await your forces. Your obedient servant, Gano." According to the messenger, Gano was held up in a deep hollow until Watie got in position. He ran the risk, Watie knew, of being discovered if Watie didn't move quickly.

Watie crumpled the paper in his stubby, strong hand. Within minutes he had assembled his officers and given the order to form the troops and move them to Gano's position.

Quickly, the soldiers began to load their bedrolls, saddle their horses and were on the move. Over five hundred Confederate troops closed in on the area, attempting to keep their movements masked by staying off the dry trails and riding and marching through brush and fields. It made the going tougher but there were no dust clouds that might give them away.

Arriving at Gano's position by midnight, Watie directed the troops to link up with Gano's forces and assume ambush positions behind the crest that overlooked the creek. The Union supply train had stopped and bivouacked about fifteen miles north earlier in the day as Gano had reported and was camped for the night. There wasn't much time to prepare.

Shortly after midnight they settled into positions that would allow clean fields of fire as the Union troops crossed Cabin Creek. Locations were chosen that would allow for massing of troops for a charge.

Watie immediately began to collaborate with his Texas counterpart.

As sunrise neared, the Union wagon train was coming within sight of Cabin Creek.

"Sir, the scouts report no sign of the Confederates. They've reconnoitered both sides and don't see any trace of them," said the Captain as he sidled his mount next to Major Hopkins.

"How far ahead did the scouts reconnoiter?

"I had them thirty yards in front of the column, sir," the Captain answered.

"That's hardly far enough ahead to give us adequate information, Captain," Hopkins chided. "But there is no time now for a more extensive search. We are already behind schedule. Now we are in jeopardy of not being across the creek by sunrise.

"Very well. Position the security wagons first. Then we will pass through them and cross the creek," Hopkins replied. "And Captain, I think it would do well for you to lead the scouts on this. At the head of the column."

The Captain's mouth fell open. To order an officer of his rank to perform a task that was so dangerous that it was always designated to a lower enlisted soldier was no more than a thinly veiled death sentence.

The Captain stared at Hopkins, saluted and then rode back and motioned for the two special wagons to follow him. A group of loaders and sharpshooters pulled their horses out of the column and fell in behind as well.

"Who's going to be coming?" nervously asked James Bigby, another of Gus' relatives. The regiment was loaded with Gus' nephews, uncles and cousins.

"The Yankees, including the coloreds and the Pins," he answered using the slang for the renegade *Pin* Cherokees. "There will be a passel of them. But they've got a lot of supplies. Clothes and ammunition, food. You name it."

The glance Gus got from his cousin—a combination of desperation and relief—said more than any verbal reply could. *They were risking their lives for the necessities of life--something far less abstract than the concept of states' rights.*

CHAPTER FIVE

Gus slumped and cautiously stepped through the heavy bush. Wet with dew, the branches wiped across his face and nettles tugged at his shirt. It was four a.m. and the Confederate troops had been hurriedly arrayed in a skirmish line, infantry in front, cavalry in back, in a draw on the reverse slope of a knoll about 120 yards from the creek's bank. It gave them complete cover and concealment from the enemy. They were hidden below a rise and ready to launch a deadly charge on the Yankees.

As he came upon the various mounted men he was careful to let his presence be known with a low voice. Both the horses and men were jumpy and surprising them could either earn you a knife in the stomach before they realized you were a friend or cause the horses to spook and give away the element of surprise.

"Pssst. Rider coming in," he whispered moments before slipping up beside the mounted men poised with their rifles resting across their laps but staring toward the unknowing Union troops. "What does it look like?"

"I don't think the Yankees believe we'll attack after the last time," Private Ellis Starr said. It sounded more like a wish than a statement. He looked at Gus for confirmation of his suspicion.

"No matter what the Yankees believe, we're going to attack all right, boys. We'll have full stomachs after we capture all they've got. They have clothes, food, guns and ammunition in those wagons. Get ready. Once they clear that rise we'll attack. It'll leave them spread out across the creek. We'll cut them up like a snake that can't turn around. Be still. It's going to happen shortly," Gus said.

The three youthful men were silent for several minutes. They gazed out at a surreal picture. The clearing that would become a killing ground in just a few minutes was eerily peaceful and bathed in rays of murky moonlight. A light fog materialized from the gently flowing water in the creek.

"Look at that moon, Sergeant Rider," said one of the soldiers. "It looks red. It's a Bloodmoon."

"What's a Bloodmoon?" asked one of the others uneasily.

Gus looked up through the trees. The moon was obscured as clouds passed in front of it. As one crawled clear, it revealed a full disc with a halo of reflected light around it. It seemed so close that one could touch it. Its color was a distinct crimson.

"When a Bloodmoon comes, it means someone is going to die. And surely that is the case in the next few hours," Gus said seriously. He paused for effect and then looked at each one of the young soldiers. "Make sure it isn't you."

In a few minutes, the sun would rise and send a blast of light over the horizon. If the Yankees were foolish enough to time their crossing at that moment, they would be blinded just as they crested the bluff that led to the creek.

Gus crouched low and guardedly dashed down the line of horsemen. Just as he got within sight of the end of the line, he heard the creaking of wagon wheels. The screeches were followed by the splashing of water as the mules and Yankee outriders entered the creek. The tension was palpable. His heart began to beat faster. Even though the night was cool, sweat poured down his face.

Gus looked around at the men. They were nervous; no, scared was a better word. But they would do their duty. They always had. He caught General Watie's gaze. The General signaled him to investigate the noise to their front. Gus low-crawled to the crest of the slope and peered like a thief over the top. The noises of the Union supply train grew louder as they approached the Confederate position.

The din changed to a different tempo, one he recognized as the muffled shouts of the mule herders and teamsters trying to induce the mules to pull their load up the steep incline of the shore. Even in the dark, he could see the wagon train was stretched for miles across the creek and beyond the distant water's edge.

Oddly enough, there were two wagons parked sideways midway across the creek. He couldn't see the frantic activity or the numerous men surrounding the wagons or the fact that their wheels seem to sink much deeper into the creek bed than the other wagons.

The backs of Union soldiers began to emerge at the pinnacle of the rise as they tugged and pulled the mules forward. They were being lead by an officer on horseback who struggled up the rise. Within moments they were in full view and, regaining their footing, began to move forward. At that very moment, the sun revealed itself and bathed the northern soldiers in blinding light.

Gus signaled to General Watie that they were closing. Watie immediately gave the signal for the canoneers to prepare to fire from their camouflaged positions. By now the nervous stamping of the Confederate horses was indistinguishable from the chaos occurring sixty yards to their front.

Suddenly, Watie's field guns violently unleashed their shards of lead upon the surprised Yankees. Bark from the trees began splitting and flying through the air from the impact of shrapnel. Union soldiers fell in waves and body parts began to litter the ground. The young Yankee officer wearing the rank of a captain leading the group was quickly riddled with bullets and fell from his horse. Billows of white smoke began to obscure the battlefield.

Instinctively, Gus quickly slid back down the rise to the soldiers who were poised to attack. He landed and sprinted to a location where he could help control the battalion as they moved. Staying in defilade, he felt safe from the enemy bullets that would begin flying in just a few moments in response to the Confederate artillery.

Running to get his horse, he heard the branches above snapping as the fusillade of return fire found its way into the Confederate positions. At exactly that moment the rest of the battalion erupted with blood-curdling screams and unleashed a fierce attack into the panicked Yankees desperately trying to organize a defense. Hail after hail of gunfire filled the air.

Suddenly, a body crumpled and rolled down the incline knocking Gus' feet out from under him. Gus regained his footing and turned the man over. He recognized the young soldier as one of the three he was talking to before the battle began.

The kid was bloody but he wasn't dead. Gus threw him over his shoulder and ran to the rear. He sat the soldier down as gently as he could and leaned him against a tree. His front was soaked with blood from a wound in the side.

Taking a rag from around his neck Gus stuffed it into the man's shirt. He placed the man's bloody hand over the wound. The man half opened his glazed-over eyes.

"Hold this down tight," Gus ordered.

The man put a weak hand on the rag.

"No, you've got to press down even if it hurts. If you can get the bleeding to stop, you might make it," he told the soldier. "Good luck, son."

Yankee bullets began to kick up bits of dirt around them. Gus threw his body over the wounded soldier to shield him. He felt a hot pain in his left arm but paid little attention to it.

The incoming rounds subsided but Gus could not feel any movement under him. He looked and the young soldier stared ahead in a transfixed gaze. He was dead. The bullet had passed through the fleshy part of Gus' arm into the young soldier.

Gus wasted no time in running back toward the front lines. He tied a bandage around his arm as he ran. The tempo of the gunfire had increased and the angry war cries that had opened the attack were vanishing.

Abruptly, there was a loud slam as a Yankee mini-ball sliced across Gus' forehead, causing him to crumble and roll like a toy soldier into the draw. Gus looked up through glassy eyes and then slumped. His head smacked the dirt of the draw. He couldn't see anything but thick blue and black lines that rotated like a spinning barber's pole. Reeling from the bullet's impact on his skull, a wave of vertigo overwhelmed him. Within moments all was black.

CHAPTER SIX

Eastern Oklahoma
One Hundred Forty-Three Years Later—September 2007

Phillip Michaels and his son Austin watched the lush Oklahoma land-scape flash by as they sped east on Interstate 40. Phillip was five-foot-nine with a quickly receding hairline. His handsome face was punctuated with an infectious smile that caused him, in spite of his thinning brown hair, to look younger than his 35 years.

"How much longer, Pops?" little Austin asked excitedly as he squirmed under the restraint of the seat belt.

"It's not too much farther, son. We turn off up here on Highway 59 and head north toward Stilwell. Maybe a half-hour," Phillip said smiling. He knew that answer didn't thrill the six-year-old. *A long car ride and a boring ceremony wasn't a favorite activity for a youngster*, he thought, *but it was time to introduce his only heir to his birthright. And more importantly it was a chance to have a few hours alone together.*

The whole thing had started a month ago when Phillip received a call from a perfect stranger. "Hello, Mr. Michaels? My name is Tess Barnett with the Trail of Tears Association. Your name was given to me as a Cherokee descendant."

"Yes, I am, although I'm afraid I don't know much about that part of the family," he confessed.

"Well, maybe this is a chance for you to learn," the voice said warmly. "We have documented that your long ago grandmother was a survivor of the

Trail of Tears in 1835. We're going to honor her by placing a brass plaque on her tombstone this weekend at Oak Grove Cemetery in Stilwell."

Phillip was becoming interested.

"We have a short biography of her. It is traditional for a descendant to read the biography prior to the bestowing of the plaque. Would you like to perform that tribute?" she asked.

Phillips mind flashed back to his childhood. His mother had often told him the stories of his Cherokee ancestors but they were now foggy in his memory and he hardly remembered any of the names and places in her tales. He had pledged to someday learn more about those people and times, but like so many things, they had been put on the back burner as he raced to build an architectural practice. He had spent three years in the service and felt like he started out behind in business because of it. He was playing "Catch-Up" and didn't think he had much time to waste.

Maybe this was the opportunity to find out a little about his Cherokee lineage and to fulfill the promise he had made to his mother so long ago, he thought. He surprised himself by saying, "Let me see if I can clear my schedule."

The oldest of the three walked to the massive antique oak bar and poured a glass of single malt scotch into a crystal glass.

"Scotch or bourbon?" he asked his guests.

"Scotch," the woman said.

"I'll pass. I've got to drive," said the other man.

He dispensed the scotch and shuffled with two glasses to the coffee table around which they were all seated. He smiled as he handed the drink to the blond woman named Susan.

The trio had grown up together. They had always been close friends. He had settled in western Oklahoma, married and become highly successful in business and ranching. The couple sitting across from him had moved to Oklahoma City but the trio had always kept in touch and he had never lost interest in his friend's political career. He had not only provided a great deal of the funds for the campaigns but had served loyally as his most important advisor. Franklin was by far Gay's largest contributor and oldest friend.

"Your numbers look good now and barring some profoundly unpopular action on your part, should grow. As long as you stay away from controversial decisions," Franklin said.

"Well, I can't guarantee that. I am the Attorney General. I can't tailor my actions to win votes. I may be a politician but I'm not a demagogue," said Nelson Gay.

"Nor would anyone ask you to do that, Nelson. You need to recognize the realities of this situation. Let's just say, hypothetically, that you finish this term as A.G. flawlessly. You do your job and do it well. Then, next year, Hank Brady decides not to run again. That Senate seat is up for grabs. I heard today that he'd been offered a seven-figure package with the Heritage Foundation. Put that with his Senate retirement after twenty years and he'll be sitting pretty," Franklin said.

"Why would he have to take it now? The feds aren't term limited. He could do that anytime," Gay asked.

"Wrong. If we have a change of administration, his stock would drop fast. He's a darling with this President. A new one would have his own guys." Franklin continued, "The Heritage Foundation would start looking for someone who could give them access to the White House. No, he needs to do it now or never."

"There would be a lot of people trying for that seat. Why do you think Nelson would be competitive?" Susan asked. She and Nelson had married right out of high school and she was an astute political weathervane.

"Susan, did you look at who attended Nelson's last fund-raiser? It was as ecumenical a group as you'll find in Oklahoma politics. Democrats, Republicans, liberals, conservatives. They were all there.

"He is, at this moment, acceptable to all political segments. However, the longer he stays as Attorney General that approval will begin to shrink. You can't stay in office forever without pissing off somebody. Every decision you make as A.G. has winners and losers. Right now he's got maximum winners.

"Your question is simple. The answer is difficult. Do you want to remain in a safe office? Or do you want to strive for greater things? For you to lose the Attorney General's office you'd have to get caught in bed with a man and he'd have to say you were no good," Franklin grinned.

Susan frowned.

"Sorry, dear. Just a small attempt at humor."

"Very small," she replied.

"Seriously, you can stay as A.G. for a lot of years. But it will be a terminal office for you. If you want to remain alive politically, you've got to move up. And now is the best time for you." Franklin sat and looked Nelson in the eyes.

"I'll have to think about it," Nelson Gay said.

"Don't think too long. We've got to start the ball rolling right now, this minute. We have to be ready to announce as soon as the word is official that Brady is quitting. And we need to start the rumor mill working that you're the front-runner who's considering the race."

"I'll let you know. Bless your heart; you're always looking out for me."

"Come on honey, we've got to get home," he said and the two rose and walked to the door. Saying their goodbyes, they got into their car.

Michaels' Cadillac turned off the interstate and traveled north on the tree-lined, two-lane blacktop road. It wasn't long before he and Austin began passing pastures dotted with sleek horses grazing. Austin became animated.

"Daddy, look! There are horses everywhere. Can we stop and pet them?"

Phillip glanced at his watch. They were scheduled to be in Stilwell by two o'clock to participate in the ceremony. Phillip liked to be everyplace early. Marine Corps training, he suspected. Stopping here would mean they would cut it close. But this trip wasn't going to have too many fun parts for a little boy. Just at that moment as they climbed a gentle hill and entered Adair County, a deep, blossoming valley, confronted them.

Overwhelmed by the sight, he asked rhetorically, "Why not?" to Austin's thrilled cheers.

They pulled over onto the shoulder of the road, waves of dust engulfing the car as the tires stirred up loose gravel. Phillip turned on his hazard lights and the two made their way across a dry ditch to the picturesque white fence that surrounded the meadow. Austin quickly scrambled to the top fence rail. Phillip helped him balance to watch the horses nibble the rich grass.

Phillip had to admit it was a beautiful sight. A rolling pasture carpeted with green. Shiny coated animals lounging in the autumn sun. A gentle breeze bringing the sweet smell of grass and animals to the pair. They watched as a mare nuzzled her colt. The hard-driving architect was glad he had stopped.

He rarely allowed himself this kind of respite. He pointed out the mares from the stallions and told Austin about the kind of horses they appeared to be.

He again conjured up a memory of his mother, the person who introduced him to the Cherokee Nation. He remembered the stories of her horse, "Troubles", and a photograph of her as a sophisticated sixteen-year-old astride the animal decked out in jodhpurs and riding boots.

The photograph had been taken on a visit home from boarding school and he hadn't realized what a beautiful woman she was until he had enhanced the image with his computer some seventy years later.

"Riding is an important part of your Cherokee heritage," she had said. He had always been promised a horse of his own but somehow, it never came.

The image faded as he realized time was passing. Snapping back, he announced it was time to leave.

"Aw, Daddy. I want to stay," Austin pleaded.

Phillip grinned. "Nope. We've got to go. We'll come back again someday. In the meantime, you can ride this old horse!" he said and maneuvered so the freckle-faced boy could mount his father's back.

"Okay!" Austin screamed and jumped on, wrapping his arms tightly around his father's neck. They started walking back to the car, Phillip giving his rider an occasional whinny and buck. The two had reached the ditch when Austin said quizzically, "Daddy, what's that?"

Phillip, so used to being questioned by this freckled-face, inquisitive child, almost ignored the inquiry. Thinking better of it he said, "What is what, son?" and looked over his shoulder at the boy. Austin's eyes were glued to something to their right. Phillip followed his gaze to the object partially covered in the grass.

He put Austin down and cautiously approached the thing.

"Daddy! How did it get here?" the child said and ran up to his father's side. Phillip grabbed the boy's arm and held him back as he looked down at the object.

The tall man sat alone on a metal chair in the middle of the room. It was a windowless, concrete block walled compartment. If he hadn't been so scared he might have mused at how much it looked like the inside of a rental storage unit. The fact that it was nestled deep inside an abandoned warehouse was a guarantee that what went on inside would not be heard by anyone not meant to hear it.

"So what's this all about? If he wants to talk to me it's easy to do. You don't have to make such a big deal out of it. I'm not sitting here forever," the man said craning his neck to look around. He was, afterall, the Sheriff of Adair County.

"You'll sit there as long as we want you to, Ross, or I swear I'll put a bullet in your head," one of the men standing in the shadows said.

Ross wouldn't have tolerated insolence like that except these thugs had taken his own weapon from him when he entered the warehouse.

Ross tried to listen. Through the open door he thought he could hear the almost imperceptible sound of footsteps coming from a long distance, echoing off of the concrete floor. *Yeah, those were footsteps all right. Now they were getting louder and closer.*

Suddenly the light from the open door was blocked by the silhouette of a short but heavy man. He stopped for just a moment and then walked slowly toward Ross, slamming the metal door behind him. Ross twisted in his chair to see him.

"Harley, what the hell is this all about?" he asked the approaching figure, trying to mask his fear with a feigned sense of outrage. He received no answer.

Harley walked in front of him and looked down. There were no preliminaries.

"I was told you were too stupid to pull off an operation like this. Maybe they were right," said Harley, a hulking, balding man as Ross sat glued to the chair.

Harley was only five seven but was powerfully built and although clean-shaven, had a dark shadow framing a round face that harbored narrow eyes. His swarthy complexion made it obvious he was not a Cherokee. His "associates" remained hidden in the shadows but were ready to intervene if Ross showed the first sign of movement without permission and Ross knew it.

"I promise you I can handle it. I just picked the wrong guy. I would have found out sooner or later," Ross pleaded, his mock outrage completely vanished.

"What we care about is that you find out sooner. We look at it very seriously when $5,000 goes missing. We think it's stupid to let that happen," Harley said, spitting out the word "stupid" as if it were a peach pit.

His Tommy Bahama shirt had gotten twisted around his middle as he leaned over Ross and he stood up to straighten it.

"Look, we got the money back and that son-of-a bitch will never take another dime from anyone. He'll be lucky if he can walk without a limp. It will be a lesson to everyone. What harm is done? We got the money back," implored Ross. The mustiness of the confined space coupled with the captive's profuse sweating gave the room a spoiled odor. He watched Harley as the gangster walked slowly around him.

Without warning, Harley slapped the back of Ross' head hard. It stung when his heavy gold ring made contact with his skull. Harley came around quickly and grabbed Ross by the shirt collar. His men moved a few steps closer.

"Do you know the word credibility, asshole? Are you too stupid to have that word in your vocabulary? Once you lose credibility with us you cease to exist," he said, "literally."

"Understand one thing. We let you to run the drugs and the whores and play like a big man for only one reason. You're the sheriff and that's convenient for us. And don't forget. You're the sheriff because we got you elected. And we can get you un-elected. Do you understand?" Harley said lowering his voice menacingly.

At this point Harley was leaning into Ross' face and the other thugs had closed in more. It was getting hard to breathe, the air was so laden with tension.

Harley slipped out a stiletto knife and flipped it open and continued the obloquy. "Do you know what your Cherokee ancestors used to do to their prisoners? They used to flay them alive. Strip the skin right off the body like they were skinning a deer," he said as he traced the knife blade down the sheriff's arm. "Fuck up again and that's what's going to happen to you. Got it, stupid?"

Adair County's sheriff nodded. He had always thought he was as mean a bastard as anyone in the state but at this particular moment it was all he could do to keep from urinating in his pants out of fear.

"You stay here," Phillip said firmly as he knelt over the limp body of a man. He carefully turned the guy over. The fellow was injured, his hair matted with blood, but Phillip couldn't tell if he was dead or alive. He touched the neck and felt a slight pulse.

"This man is hurt badly," he said and reached for his cell phone. Dialing it only produced a high-pitched noise indicating they were out of their service area and had no roaming capability. That part of Oklahoma was notorious for weak cell phone coverage.

"Great. Why the hell do you carry them if they won't work when you need them? We can't leave him here," Phillip said to no one as he looked around for help. He walked to the highway hoping to spot a car. Sure enough, he could see the faint image of an automobile coming down the highway. He began waving frantically only to watch the car slow and then turn off on some unseen side road.

Phillip stood on the hot asphalt, frustrated that all of a sudden he was on what seemed like an abandoned highway. Just before he was about to give up, a semi-trailer appeared in the distance in the other lane. Again, he began waving his arms in a plea for help, hoping he would be seen in time for someone to stop.

The truck grew larger as it approached. The boxlike shape seemed to slow down and then apparently someone thought better of it. Black smoke spewed from the truck's exhaust stacks as the indiscernible driver downshifted and accelerated. Phillip barely managed to jump out of the way as the eighteen-wheeler flew past him. He covered his face as he was peppered with tiny grains of sizzling sand raised by the huge vehicle.

He stared open-mouthed after the fleeing truck. *How could someone just keep going when a person was in need of help?* Now he knew he had to take the injured man with him. Without understanding what was wrong with him, he worried that moving him might make it worse, but he had no choice. As much as he wanted to, he couldn't leave him here in the grass.

Going back to the prone figure he, once again, felt the man's neck. His eyes opened but he didn't speak.

"Are you alright? Can you tell me what happened to you?" Phillip asked. There was no answer. "We're going to get you to the car."

Phillip gently pulled the man to his feet and put his hand around him, pulling his arm over his shoulder. Phillip was five foot nine and this fellow was considerably taller. He was not far from being limp and it made it ungainly and difficult to move him.

"Austin, go open the car door," he said as he puffed for breath. He reached in his pocket with one hand, grabbed his keys and handed them to the youngster. Austin ran across the ditch and dutifully opened all the doors on the passenger's side of the car.

Phillip, a muscular and lean man, negotiated the gully with the injured man and struggled up the side. It almost seemed as if the mute patient were trying to help him. Sweating, he reached the car and helped the man into the back seat indicating to him that he lay down. With some difficulty, the man stretched out on the seat as much as he could. He was tall and had to fold himself into the seat in a fetal position. Phillip tried to belt him in but the safety belts weren't made or designed for a prone passenger. Quickly, Phillip motioned Austin into the car, fastened his seatbelt, and then ran to the driver's side.

Sitting behind the wheel for a moment catching his breath and wiping the sweat from his forehead, Phillip glanced back at the man before pulling onto the highway. He wasn't old and yet his face was worn and weathered. He was wearing rough-looking work clothing. He looked like an Indian, typical of this area where the heart of the Cherokee Nation resided, but had some distinctly Caucasian features. He was obviously disoriented and seemed dazed and confused. He had lapsed into unconsciousness and that gave Phillip even greater concern.

They quickly drove ahead, looking for the small town of Stilwell. Within minutes they were greeted by a sign that welcomed them to the hamlet and proudly proclaimed it the "Strawberry Capital of the World." They drove in and asked the first person they found for directions to the hospital and were informed it was just a few blocks away on Locust Street. Fortunately, that was not far and the local hospital unexpectedly greeted them on the right. Phillip swerved into the entrance and followed the signs to the Emergency Room at the back of the building, being careful not to stop too abruptly and throw the injured man to the floor. Stopping, he jumped out of the car and ran to the passenger side and opened the back door. He urgently motioned the nurse standing at the door to come outside.

Watching her face turn from curiosity to concern as he explained about the man, he stood by the car as she summoned the orderlies and they systematically unloaded the stranger onto a gurney and wheeled him inside. Phillip signed some papers giving his name and his cell phone number.

"I don't have an address here. We're just visiting and haven't even checked into a hotel yet," he explained to the nurse.

"Let me get settled and I'll come back and complete the paperwork, okay?" The nurse reluctantly agreed.

Getting back in the car, he paused for a moment to take a deep breath. He felt he had done all that could be expected of him and began to put the car into gear and drive away. Austin said nothing. Phillip sensed a conflict within him. *Why should I spend any more time with this derelict? I have someplace to be*, he thought. And yet he felt a tugging and unexplained loyalty to the man.

Suddenly, illogical as it seemed, Phillip found himself making a hard U-turn in the hospital parking lot and slipping the car into a parking space.

"Gosh, Daddy, I was afraid you were going to leave him," Austin said looking at him with fear in his green eyes. Phillip couldn't explain why he should be saddled with this responsibility for a complete stranger but it was a duty that had been crystal clear to his son. He wondered if he had become too cynical or maybe too selfish over the years.

The two entered the hospital and seated themselves in the waiting room. Phillip hated hospitals. The smells, the sounds all conjured up painful memories. It was in such a place as this that he had lost his mother and it only took a simple prompt to plunge him back into sorrow.

His best friend in college had been killed in a freak car wreck and he had also spent some agonizing hours in a stark waiting room just like the one he was in, feeling emasculated and helpless as the doctor walked out to deliver the bad news. Phillip hated hospitals and the fact that he was here because of someone he didn't know amazed him.

Rhonda Goodenough was an angel of mercy. At least in her own mind. Rhonda had completed her certification as a Licensed Practical Nurse many years before the requirements had become stringent and was overpoweringly committed to ministering to the afflicted. The fact that she lived by herself with over twenty cats, each named "Jimmy," in a dilapidated two-story residence and had not gone upstairs in ten years did not seem strange to her at all.

The huge house sat like an ugly blister on a street of well maintained, beautifully restored turn of the century homes. It gave the neighbors daily convulsions that the blight on the neighborhood continued to deteriorate and there was nothing they could do about it. It also did not seem unusual to Rhonda that her only reading material was a tattered Bible or her only contact with the outside world was her work at the hospital.

Rhonda was deeply disturbed by the merciless way the medical establishment failed to provide for many of the patients, often times prolonging their agony long after the Lord wanted them to come home. She had become a nurse so she could lessen the pain of those who came to her for help.

She had nursed her own mother for so many years when none of her siblings would even come see her. Day after day she would meet her mother's needs. The dreaded disease Alzheimer's had affected her dear mother so dramatically she couldn't even express her appreciation. To the contrary, her mother would often berate her for being overweight and for never marrying. Once she even screamed, "Why couldn't I have a real daughter?"

Those times were painful for Rhonda even though she knew her mother didn't really mean the hurtful things she said. She cared for her mother until it was time for her to go home to the Lord.

One day, while talking to her cats and reading her Bible, she had decided she would serve the Lord by carrying out His wishes, in spite of the short-sighted decisions being made by the doctors and the hospital administrators.

It began a year and a half ago when Rhonda "helped" an elderly patient go home to the Lord, just as her mother had done. It was a simple procedure, really. She would draw small amounts of insulin from the hospital pharmacy, ostensibly for different diabetic patients but save the doses rather than administer them. The amounts were so small no one took notice.

Then, when the time came, she would inject the saved up volume of the drug into the selected patient using a tiny needle, which left an infinitesimal hole that was difficult to detect. Breathing disorders would quickly follow and the patient would expire rapidly, leaving no trace of foul play. It always appeared as a natural consequence to a natural condition. No one had yet made the connection between the deaths and Rhonda's work schedule.

Gus lay flat on the cold table and tried to focus on the man looking down at him whose image was partially obscured by the bright light glinting over his shoulder. Something bizarre had happened and Gus was scared. In one moment he had been in the heat of a battle with the Yankees and the next he had been in a quiet pasture. The man who had helped him into an extraordinary wagon was familiar but the surroundings he now found himself in were strange and frightening.

He had heard the people hovering around him use the term "hospital" but it was unlike any he had ever seen. Everything was clean and bright and there were machines that whirred and whined. There was a sharp smell he had never experienced before and people spoke in soft tones. The man they called the doctor continued to ask him questions. Gus was afraid to answer except with a grunt. He didn't know these people—didn't know where he was and didn't want to give away too much information until he was sure he was safe.

He looked at the bottle of water that hung above him and the tubes draped like vines coming out of it, all leading to his arm. He wanted to escape but his clothes had been removed and a flimsy gown without a back was the only clothing he had. He lay still, partially because he was truly weak and partially because he had no idea what to do, and tried to understand his situation.

He could hear conversation outside of the room and, eventually, the men and women in the baggy white and green uniforms came in and began pushing his aluminum table out of the door. They rolled him to another room and placed him in a comfortable bed.

"Would you like to watch television?" the nurse asked cheerfully.

Gus answered with a nod and wondered what a television was.

The woman looked up at a glass fronted box hanging from the ceiling and pushed on a small black box. Immediately, images appeared and were talking and moving. Gus tried to conceal his amazement and fear. She smiled and said, "Try to get some rest," as she left the room.

Gus overcame his fright and watched the screen. There would be scenes of all sorts and then each hour, people would sit in front of him and begin talking. Maybe the "television" would tell him where he was and why things that bordered on the demonic were happening around him.

For four hours Gus paid close attention. By the time he had concentrated on eight newscasts and numerous announcements for products he had never heard of, he had pieced together a picture that was almost beyond his comprehension. He was in the Cherokee Nation but it wasn't the one he had left. And the date, according to the newscasts, was one hundred-and-forty-three years in the future. Was he dead? Was this just a dream? He had thought of all of those options and was still not sure which was correct.

Just as Gus would drop off to sleep one of the women in green or the doctor would wake him up and shine a light in his eyes. At first he thought it was torture but then their gentle voices and manner convinced him that it was only an examination. Someone had stopped the "television" and in the short spaces between the visits he would sink into a deep trance, devoid of dreams.

CHAPTER SEVEN

"Hello—Mr. Michaels?" the young doctor said as he entered the waiting room while looking at his admissions form. Phillip stood and extended his hand to the physician.

"Is the patient a relative?" he asked after they shook hands.

Oddly, Phillip started to say "yes" and then caught himself. "No. We just found him outside of town. We live in Oklahoma City. We're just trying to help."

"That's very commendable of you," the doctor said looking him in the eyes with newfound respect. "What brings you to Stilwell?"

"There was a ceremony here today that we were supposed to take part in," Phillip said.

"Survivors of the Trail of Tears?" the doctor asked with raised eyebrows. He was referring to the infamous forced removal the government inflicted on many of the major Indian tribes, moving them from their ancestral lands on the east coast to the unsettled territory of what would become Oklahoma.

"That's right," Phillip said in amazement. "You know about the ceremony? We thought it was just a small affair."

"We hold those ancestors in pretty high regard around here. They were the foundation of this community," the doctor said.

"My great-great grandmother came over when she was only six," Phillip said. "They're going to put a brass plaque on her tombstone."

"Well, then, you're practically a citizen of Stilwell. Going out of your way for a stranger is also very admirable so you certainly deserve to know his condition," the doctor said.

The three sat down and the physician addressed Austin with a smile, his demeanor softening. "I'll bet this has all been pretty exciting for you, hasn't it?"

"It sure has. Who is he?" Austin asked, looking back and forth from the doctor to his father.

"He couldn't tell us," the doctor answered kindly and then turned to Phillip. "He's had a head trauma—possibly a grazing bullet wound—can't be sure. In any case it's caused a slight concussion and he seems to have lost a lot of his memory. He also had a puncture wound in his arm. Whatever caused the penetration passed through without doing much damage. Our examination shows he's suffering from malnutrition, as well. That's unusual around here. There are plenty of agencies that work hard to make sure no one goes hungry." The doctor was a Native American and it was Phillip's guess he was a hometown boy.

"So, what's your prognosis? Is there anything we can do?" Phillip stunned himself by asking.

"I think he'll be okay. We'll keep him tonight for observation and get some fluids and food into him. Take care of his puncture wound. His memory will probably return with time. If you're going to be in town for any length of time you may be the closest thing he has to family. You might check on him. We'll probably dismiss him tomorrow evening and he's going to need a friend. Otherwise, he'll just end up in some shelter."

Austin turned toward his dad, not fully comprehending the doctor's comments but with a pleading look in his eyes.

In an uncharacteristic move, Phillip said, "We'll take care of him until he gets on his feet. We can stay in town that long."

Why did I do that? Phillip asked himself.

They left the hospital and walked to the car. "Thank you for helping that man, Daddy," Austin said. "Will Mama be mad?"

"I don't think so, son. We'll be home in a few days," Phillip smiled. *What a caring, compassionate child I have. I could stand to be a lot more like him*, he thought.

The two drove around Stilwell and found a small motel just inside the city limits. They registered and got the only adjoining rooms. Once inside, Austin ran from room-to-room testing the bounciness of each bed, thoroughly excited to be in a new place. The mustiness of the rarely rented unit or the repaired holes in the doors did little to dampen his enthusiasm.

Phillip called home and explained to Carri, his wife of ten years, the situation. She was, as they say, the best thing that ever happened to him and he knew it.

Carri had come from a sometimes wealthy, sometimes not-so-wealthy family. Consequently, she had gained the ability to enjoy wealth but not require it. Her solid values and easygoing nature were a stabilizing influence for Phillip who had a tendency to focus on an objective to the exclusion of all else. The arrival of their only child six years ago had given Phillip the life he never expected to have.

"I think that's wonderful, honey. Your mother would be proud of you," she said sweetly referring to his parent who had taught him the principles of caring for one's fellow man.

"Yeah, yeah," he said trying to brush off the compliment. *Damn, I'm surrounded by all of these do-gooders. They're going to turn me into one myself.* Phillip's time in the Marine Corps, his stint as a college athlete and his willingness to take risks and look danger in the face had defined his life. He prided himself on his "take no prisoners" attitude in business and his personal life. He had no intention of softening now. Let Carri be the sensitive one.

He hung up the phone and looked at Austin. One thing was for sure, though. Austin was loving the adventure and oddly enough so was he.

Phillip went into the bathroom and returned with two oblong orange caplets. He had been diagnosed with Type II diabetes several years ago and was trying to control it with medication.

"Congratulations, Phillip. Your mother's diabetes has caught up with you. Didn't you tell me she contracted it in her forties?" the internist had said.

"Fat, forty and family. Those are the key factors in late onset diabetes. If you're overweight, over forty and have a family history of it, you're likely to get it. In fact, my friend, now that you're entering middle age, you can look forward to your body visiting all of the family genetic foibles you've inherited. Let's see," he said as he scanned Phillip's health record. "Great. Heart attacks, cancer—your family history has it all. We're going to have to watch you closely."

"So when are you middle-aged?" Phillip asked, looking for a straw.

"When you're willing to admit it." The doctor chuckled.

"Thank you so much," Phillip answered sarcastically.

It irritated Phillip that after always being a robust, healthy person he was being told that health problems were facing him through no fault of his own. Nevertheless, he tried to follow the doctor's orders and normally did all right if he took his medication and didn't miss meals. There had been a couple of times work had kept him from eating lunch and that had almost triggered a disaster.

The last time he skipped his noon meal he had begun to feel shaky at three in the afternoon. Within an hour, he was having difficulty making a decision and began to feel disoriented. He decided to check his blood sugar and pulled out his testing kit. In seconds he was told his blood sugar was a low 64. He knew enough to realize that diabetics started to pass out when sugar levels fell into the 40s and began to worry what he could do to stop the slide.

His head was spinning and he felt nauseous. He half-staggered into a co-worker's office who was also a diabetic. The colleague saw Phillip's chalky pallor and immediately recognized the symptoms. He seated him before he could fall. He quickly opened his own test kit and punctured Phillip's finger, placing the drop of blood on a small strip. Inserting the strip in the reader, he confirmed Phillip's sugar level was down to forty-seven. It had plummeted seventeen points in a matter of minutes.

His associate went to his desk and pulled out a bottle of large, round orange tablets.

"Take these and chew them up. Don't swallow. Chew," he told Phillip urgently as he handed him two of the discs.

"What are they?" Phillip slurred.

"They're glucose pills. Straight sugar. They'll raise your blood sugar fast."

Phillip chewed the pills and sat with his eyes glazed. Slowly, his heart quit pounding and his breathing slowed. He felt drained but he was okay. For now. For the first time he appreciated the penalty he would pay for a lapse in maintaining his blood sugar level.

Susan Gay was quiet on the way home. They arrived at their small house, tended to their nightly chores and then slipped into the king-size bed together.

"Well, what do you think?" he asked after the light had been extinguished and they were both hidden in darkness.

"I didn't think you were going to ask me. You never have before," she said playfully.

Nelson Gay chuckled. "Well, maybe not before, but we're looking at the last part of our lives together. We're in our mid-fifties. Whatever step we take will lead us into that last half of the course. The back nine," he joked.

"Oh, I don't know, Nelson," she sighed, turning over to face him. "This life has been such a whirlwind. Don't misunderstand me. I've loved it and it's given the children an experience and perspective they would have never had otherwise. It was a great world for them to grow up in. But now they've got their own lives and as you say, do we want to do it from 55 to 70?"

"Will you think about it? We don't have to decide now but you know Franklin as well as I do. If I don't make a decision, he'll make it for me. I don't want to wait too long. You know how I am about unsettled things."

"After thirty years, I think I do know how you are," she said affectionately.

Everyone has a boss, Harley thought as he dialed the secure private number to his. It was a way of justifying the fact that his boss was extremely demanding, not very understanding and incredibly unforgiving.

Harley was one of the shadowy czars of drugs, prostitution and illicit gambling in Oklahoma. There were others, each presiding over a certain geographical area and each guarding their turf with violence if necessary. Often bragging that he was part of the "Oklahoma Mafia" he and his fellow crime bosses exploited the desperation that exists in every economically depressed area the world over.

In this case, his fiefdom was a sliver of eastern Oklahoma. He had risen to his position of power, in part, because he was a sociopath who could take a life as easily as he could shake someone's hand. But, as he correctly reminded himself, he, too, had a superior in the organization. The phone answered after two rings.

"Yes?" the heavy voice on the other end responded.

"It's me," Harley said. "We're on with Maldonado. He's agreed to the shipment. It's going to be huge. We'll have enough product to really last us."

There was a pause. "Not necessarily. As I have told you before, I want the street price reduced to the point that our competition will be driven out of the market. Every time they lower their prices to meet ours, we go down some more," Harley's unseen boss said coldly with a tinge of irritation in his voice.

Harley noticed that the man never called him by his name or any name, for that matter. He just started talking.

"We received enough of a discount on that shipment that we can easily undercut those small operations and enough of a supply that we can go on indefinitely. Now your job is to make sure everything stays quiet and nothing happens that would draw attention to that area of the state. No cockfighting. No Indian uprisings with them fighting among themselves and getting their names in the paper. That's why we have that fellow Ross in place. I want people looking somewhere else for the next few months. Do you understand?"

"Yes, sir," Harley answered.

"Good," came the reply and the line went dead.

There was a new one in, Rhonda noted as she scanned Stilwell General Hospital's admissions chart. *This poor soul had no memory, no family, no job, and no future. He needed desperately to be sent home so the Lord could protect and love him*, she thought.

She noted the patient's room number and looked at the schedule to confirm the afternoon shift change that would result in a predictable flurry of confusion. She waited until the nurses were all about to replace each other and then went to the small hospital's employee break room. She walked casually over to the refrigerator the hospital staff used to preserve their lunches and removed a brown paper bag with her name on it. But instead of food, it contained the latest quantity of insulin she had amassed.

"Eating early aren't you, Rhonda?" asked the Head Nurse who was having a cup of coffee. It startled Rhonda. She was so focused on her task she hadn't even noticed the woman was in the room.

The Head Nurse was tall and slender and looked like a runner. She had a short, almost butch-looking haircut and absolutely no sense of humor. Her whiny, high-pitched voice reminded Rhonda of her eighth grade science teacher, who coincidentally, also didn't like her. She knew it was unlikely the Head Nurse was inquiring because she wanted to make sure Rhonda was receiving adequate nutrition.

Rhonda just smiled and didn't answer. That woman was always asking her questions, always watching her. Rhonda suspected that the Head Nurse didn't feel she was qualified for her job. *Those R.N.s think that Registered Nurses are the only ones who know anything*, she thought.

She took her paper bag and left the break room and went to the room that housed the new patient, "John Doe." It never occurred to her that someone might think it odd that she took her lunch out of the area designated for its consumption. The patient was sleeping. She looked at him for a moment and said a silent prayer. Then, she turned off the television, which had been left on, and went into the bathroom and prepared an injection.

She returned and uncovered the man's arm looking for a hidden hard-to-see place that would hide the insertion point of the needle. It was a long, sinewy arm and if she didn't find the right spot, she might have trouble getting the needle in.

Phillip and Austin had enjoyed a day of sightseeing and touring Stilwell. An old town for Oklahoma, it hosted many interesting sites and the two enjoyed visiting with the locals about its century-plus history. They drove to a small restaurant for supper not far from the hospital on Division Street, which appeared to be the town's main avenue. The café had large glass windows plastered with posters promoting local events, looking out on the street. A heavy glass and aluminum door with a strong closing mechanism forced arriving diners to give it a hearty push when entering. Inside were an amazing number of booths and tables—probably thirty were crammed into the room. The place could obviously accommodate a hundred people and was almost to capacity. The walls were decorated with Indian memorabilia and pictures of countless tribal activities, prints and artifacts. The two slipped into a booth just as it became empty. Austin was enthralled with the items on the wall and immediately cascaded his father with questions.

"Daddy, why are there so many Indians here?" he asked.

Phillip quickly looked around and then lowered his voice as a signal to Austin to do the same. "There are mainly Cherokees around here. They were forced to come here a long time ago because the government wanted the land they had on the east coast," he said. Anticipating the next question, he quickly preempted it by continuing. "It certainly wasn't right for the government to take something that didn't belong to them but it's a mistake that was made many years past when the country was growing up."

"Does everyone make mistakes?"

Phillip smiled. "Yes, everyone does. You try not to but sometimes you can't help it. Sometimes you're not smart enough to see it's a mistake until it's too late. Sometimes you make a mistake even when you know it's wrong."

"Have you made a mistake?" Austin probed, not looking directly at him but listening intently for the answer.

Phillip laughed. "Oh, boy have I!" Suddenly, the father realized he had stumbled into one of those rare opportunities to smoothly introduce a lesson that the boy would likely carry with him all his life. After a short pause he lowered his voice and said, "All you can do when you make a mistake, son, is try to correct it and go on and not make the same mistake again." They sat in silence and Phillip could feel the idea sinking into his son.

After a greasy, high carb but sumptuous meal, they scooted out of the vinyl-covered booth and made their way to the cash register manned by the robust lady in horn-rimmed glasses. They settled the bill and left a generous tip at the table then departed the restaurant and drove to Stilwell General Hospital.

This patient's skin is like leather. He must have had a hard life. He'll be happy in Heaven, Rhonda thought.

She located the spot for the injection. Just under the man's arm. She raised his arm slightly so she could get an angle on the needle. *No need to swab it*, she thought. *There won't be time for infection.* She had maneuvered herself to the side so she would have a little bit of leverage. Just as the needle grew close to the skin she heard approaching voices outside the door. She quickly slipped the syringe into her smock pocket and began to fluff Gus' pillow.

The door opened with the on-duty nurse coming in with a tray. "What are you doing here? You're not assigned to this patient," the nurse asked.

"Oh, just trying to help. He looked a little uncomfortable, so I thought I'd adjust his pillow," Rhonda muttered.

"You're not supposed to be here unless you're assigned to him. You better leave," the nurse responded.

Rhonda, never looking the other nurse in the eye, shrugged, turned and left the room.

Parking in front of the brown brick hospital, they climbed the stairs to the second floor and were spotted by the young physician they had met the day before. He immediately strode over to them, stethoscope wrapped around his neck and hanging down his white coat. "Hello, Mr. Michaels. Hi, Austin," he welcomed.

"Hello, Doctor," Phillip replied. "How's our patient doing?"

"Quite well, actually. He's ready to be dismissed. Can I assume from your presence you're here to pick him up?" the doctor asked.

"We'll help him for a few days. We've got a couple of motel rooms at the edge of town. But after that, we'll have to place him with a charity if he hasn't recovered enough to be on his own," Phillip said, surprised at the sharp edge of his tone.

The doctor stared directly in his eyes and then an understanding smile broke and he said, "I know it's an imposition for you but it's a fine thing you're doing nevertheless. And I know he'll appreciate it at some point when he's stronger."

Phillip tried to hide his embarrassment at being so abrupt and said, "It's nothing really. Well, we better get going if he's ready. By the way, you still don't know his name?"

"No. We're carrying him as a John Doe. Maybe he can tell you," the doctor answered. "He'll be here in just a few minutes. Have a seat and they'll bring him out."

They shook hands and then the doctor knelt so he was eye-to-eye with the brown-haired Austin. "Your father is a good man, Austin. He's showing kindness and compassion for someone less fortunate than he. Watch him carefully and learn well," the doctor said and, smiling a tender smile, took Austin's hand and gently shook it.

The young physician rose, turned and strode down the pristine corridor, never looking back.

Phillip watched him in embarrassed silence. He had just been paid a compliment that he didn't deserve.

Rhonda waited in the laundry room. She cracked the door so she could see and watched as the nurse left the room and returned to the nurses' station.

That patient was scheduled for release today. He'd be sent back into the same hell he came from unless she could accomplish her task and be quick about it.

She slipped across the hall and into the room again. This time she went directly to Gus and, already knowing where the spot was, removed the syringe and started to administer the insulin. Just at that moment, Gus opened his eyes and turned over in bed quickly, pulling away from her and knocking the tray on the bedside table to the floor.

The resulting crash was loud and Rhonda knew it would bring others. She deftly slipped the syringe into her pocket and knelt to begin clearing up the mess on the floor.

The door opened and the on duty nurse came in.

"I thought I told you not to come in here if you're not assigned," she told Rhonda.

"I was just checking his water to make sure he had enough and then this spilled," Rhonda said apologetically.

"Well, I've got to report this," the nurse said.

Rhonda left the room and as she was leaving she was passed in the doorway by other RNs who looked at her as if she were an intruder.

Gus's room filled with nurses who assured him everything was fine and to relax. They cleaned his space and were attentive to the point of being bothersome. They cheerfully informed him he could leave and provided the clothes he had worn in the day before, now clean and laundered. Once dressed, they placed him a strange chair with wheels and began to roll him down the hall. It seemed to Gus that they were eager to see him go.

Not quite clear on what had just happened, Gus was astute enough to know that he could have been in danger without knowing it and once again reinforced the fact that he could trust no one.

Phillip and Austin waited for thirty minutes for the man to be delivered to them. Phillip read the local newspaper provided in the small waiting room while Austin won over the nurses on duty with his engaging disposition and never-ending questions.

The man was brought out in a wheelchair and stoically looked straight ahead as if he were unaware of what was occurring.

"Please sign here, Mr. Michaels. This releases the hospital," said the nurse as she handed him a form on a clipboard and pointed to the signature line.

"Still no idea of who he is or where he's from?" Phillip almost pleaded.

The nurse looked sympathetic. "No, I'm afraid not. Maybe in a few days," she said.

Meanwhile, Austin had sidled up to the man, his hand on the armrest of the wheelchair. He said nothing to the stranger, just gazed at him as if trying to remember an old friend.

Phillip signed the release, looked at the two and said, "Well, let's head to the car," and began to push the bandaged man to the entrance.

Not far from Phillip in the reception room, a woman was paying careful attention to the threesome's activities. With a dramatic streak of white in an otherwise jet-black head of hair that culminated in a long, single ponytail, she stared intently at the trio. She followed them to the door and watched, taking special note of their car.

After helping the man into the back seat, Phillip and Austin sat in the front and began the trip to the motel.

"I don't know if you can hear me but if you can, my name is Phillip Michaels and this is my son Austin. We're going to look after you for a couple of days," Phillip said over his shoulder as he drove. Austin was enthralled with the passenger and twisted in his seat to stare at him.

They pulled into the parking lot of the motel and in front of their units. Phillip helped the man out while Austin dutifully opened the rooms. The man carefully shuffled into the room and Phillip guided him to a chair.

"Everything you'll need is here," said Phillip, pointing to the closet and opening a chest of drawers.

"Yeah, even toothpaste!" Austin said as he ran from the bathroom with a tube of Crest.

The man sat motionless.

"Well, we're right next door and we'll close this but leave it unlocked. Just lie down and relax and maybe we can take a drive in a little while," Phillip said. He slowly, partially closed the door.

"Let's take a little nap ourselves, Daddy," Austin said and climbed into the lumpy bed with Phillip. Within moments, Phillip dozed off but Austin was wide-awake. He lay there until he was sure his father was asleep and then slid out of the bed and quietly tiptoed to the semi-closed door of the man's room. He slowly pushed it open and peered inside. The man was lying on the bed staring at the ceiling, his hands behind his head.

"Are you an Indian?" Austin asked as he slipped into the room. The man looked at him but didn't speak. The silence didn't deter Austin. He went to the bedside and began to shower the man with questions. Sometimes, Austin would look at him with his round brown eyes wide-open when he talked. Other times his eyes would scan the room, never missing anything but simultaneously chattering.

The man's eyes slowly began to close. Austin didn't seem to notice. By now he was shuffling around the room inspecting everything—the furniture, the lamps, the bathroom. He was totally unaware that the man had drifted off to sleep. He ambled idly around the room and ended up back at the bed still chatting incessantly. He sat by the bed and never paused even though the man was in a deep slumber.

Gus had trouble breathing. The smoke of the battlefield engulfed him. He could not see. He could not breathe. He could not find his bearings. He moved on all fours forward trying to feel his way. Suddenly, his hand was wet. He looked down and he had placed it on a fallen comrade's chest that had received a gunshot wound turning his torso into a mass of goo.

He jerked his hand out and frantically wiped it on his trousers. He continued to crawl toward the sounds that seemed to pierce the cacophony of noises. He reached a clearing. It was like an oasis in a sea of smoke. He crouched like a cat ready to spring. He spun around, turning toward the pandemonium that seemed to swirl about the cavity.

Suddenly without warning a Yankee officer came bounding into the circle. His eyes were wild; he lunged at Gus with a long, gleaming horse saber. Gus dodged and grabbed the man's head in the crook of his arm and gave a tremendous twist. He could hear the bones snap and the death gurgle as the man slipped to the ground.

He had not caught his breath when another soldier angrily entered the circle. It was a Creek warrior half-dressed in Union blue and half in his native buckskin. Gus tensed and prepared for the attack. But the attack did not come. Instead, the warrior began to emit a raucous, hateful laugh. Gus didn't understand.

The Creek began to bring something from behind his back. He brought the horrid sight into full view holding it in his outstretched hand, laughing.

Gus gasped and recoiled and then in a blind rage attacked the enemy that flaunted his wife's disembodied head. He grabbed at him and the image disappeared as quickly as it had appeared. Gus closed his eyes and a primordial scream leapt from the very core of his body.

The shriek that had just come from the man jolted Austin so badly he began to cry and ran into his father's room. The scream was loud enough that it immediately woke Phillip. He was off the bed in a flash and to the door just as Austin came flying though it. He grabbed the child and held him close.

"What happened?" he asked excitedly, moving away from the door to the adjoining room. When the child could not answer, Phillip held him until his shaking stopped and then put him on the bed. He went to the door to the adjacent room and looked in, not sure what he would find.

The man was sitting up in bed, his mouth open and he was breathing heavily. Beads of sweat dotted his brow and his fists were clinched revealing strong and muscular arms.

Phillip didn't say a word. *How could I have been so brainless? This was not a good idea*, he thought. *I don't know anything about this person and I've let him have access to my son. My God, what was I thinking?*

He gently shut the door and locked it. *In the morning, that son-of-a bitch goes to a shelter. First thing in the morning.*

The library of the expansive home was a warm and welcoming place. It was spacious and bedecked with trophies. Not the African kind of trophy but the political kind. Photographs of the host with well-known elected officials, special pens that were used to sign important legislation all elegantly framed befitting the significance of their purpose.

The host jovially took drink orders from the antique bar and passed around the libations in the ornate glasses to his distinguished guests.

"Let's all have a seat over here and get down to business, shall we ladies and gentlemen?" he said. "I appreciate each of you being here so much. As I mentioned to you on the phone, Nelson is giving a great deal of thought to his political future. As I'm sure you've heard, there may be a vacant U.S. Senate seat next year and I'm trying to convince Nelson he is just the man to run for it."

"That is, if none of you are considering it," Nelson said to waves of laughter.

"Why the hell would you not run for it?" said the state senator from Adair County. "I can stir up plenty of support for you up my way. There are a lot of union families up there and they would love to have a conservative—ooh, it's hard for me to even say the word—that would support the AFL-CIO." The room erupted in laughter.

"That's kind of you, Senator," Nelson said.

More pledges of support came from the others in the room. "Nelson, I can't support you publicly. It would kill me with the party but I'll do every-thing I can privately. There are a lot of Republicans who would support you, just not in public," said the female member of the House of Representatives from Oklahoma City.

"You all make it hard to say no," Nelson said.

"But there is one thing," said the host. "For the next year, you've got to do your best to keep from getting into controversial situations that could be used against you. If you find yourself being shoehorned into a bad deal, see if you can delay it and let the next AG deal with it."

Nelson was silent.

"It's a dichotomy," the host said. "People want you to enforce the law but when you do it in their hometown, you're intruding. Just keep your decisions and investigations on a statewide scale and we'll be fine. Do you all agree?"

The group all indicated their concurrence. "Don't be messing in local politics and we'll deliver plenty of votes," the senator from Adair County said.

CHAPTER EIGHT

"You'll need to put your clothes in this bag," Phillip said matter-of-factly to Gus. Not surprisingly, Gus did not react. He sat on the bed, hands together with fingers intertwined between his legs and his strong eyes simply staring back. Phillip, slightly irritated, strode over and stuffed the few articles of clothes that he had bought the man into the plastic cleaning bag in the closet and then walked into the bathroom and began gathering toiletries.

Gus quickly deduced Phillip's intention. It didn't surprise him. He didn't understand why a complete stranger had done so much for him. His eyes followed Phillip's movements. He thought he would say something then decided against it. He still didn't quite comprehend why he was here and who these people were. He would continue to listen and learn before he said a word. He'd stayed alive so far by paying attention and keeping his mouth shut until he fully understood his situation.

Phillip finished collecting the few personal items and then glanced directly at Gus and said, "I'll be back in a minute and then we'll have to leave." He told Austin to grab his small bag and he took the larger pieces of luggage. He loaded the trunk and put Austin in the front seat and buckled him in.

"I'm going to get our friend," he said with a little sneer. He had not explained his plans to Austin. He didn't want an argument. He had come to his senses belatedly but not too late. He could still get the menace far away from him and his son.

"Come with me," Phillip said and motioned with his hand for Gus to follow. Gus rose and Phillip was amazed how the man had recovered. He was standing tall and straight and moved like someone with a surplus of energy. One would have never known he had been anything but healthy.

The two men got into the car and began the short drive into Stilwell. Phillip could see Gus in the rearview mirror gazing intently out of the window. They arrived in downtown Stilwell and cruised down the main drag until Phillip saw what he wanted. Unable to find a parking space in front of the storefront labeled *Stilwell Union Mission* he slowed and took an angled parking space in the next block.

"Where are we going, Daddy?" Austin asked nervously.

Phillip paused for a second and then with a small sigh, turned to face the child. "Son, we have to find a place for our friend. We can't stay here and he needs someone to look after him," he said gently.

"But Daddy," Austin started. Phillip stopped him with a raised palm like a policemen signaling a car to stop.

"No argument, son. It has to be this way for everybody's good."

Austin immediately twisted in his seat to look at Gus who sat with a small smile.

Phillip got out and went to open the door. He offered his hand but Gus ignored it and swung his legs out of the car and got out. He opened Austin's door and then walked back to retrieve the small bundle of clothes from the trunk.

Phillip strode out in front of the two, signaling them to follow. Obeying, the unlikely trio marched down the sidewalk on Division Street in Stilwell, Oklahoma.

After a quick nip of his cheap bourbon, twenty-six-year-old James Ledbetter climbed into his 1987 Ford F-150 pickup truck. He had to jerk hard on the door to get it open. It had been damaged in a fracas last Saturday night when James, severely under the influence of whiskey as he usually was, slid into a tree after leaving The Rebel Club, a side-of-the-road honky-tonk.

The truck bore other battle scars of James' proclivity to drink and drive. Because of his spotty employment record he rarely had the funds to repair the damage. Many of the dents and scrapes had begun to rust through.

The sorry appearance of the truck didn't bother James. Perennially in a haze of alcohol and drugs, he tended to focus instead on the injustices done to him by an unfair society and "those Goddamn red bastards"—his moniker for the Cherokees—who seemed to be everywhere in Stilwell and in control of every major business. Today was no different for him.

James Ledbetter hoisted his massive 300-pound body into the cab. His evil smile sported few teeth and those were stained by a lack of care and constant use of chewing tobacco and cigarettes. Unshaven, his shoulder-length hair was matted and shiny from days of being unwashed. But as unappealing as his physical persona was, James Ledbetter was a force with which to be reckoned. At 6'4" he had forearms that looked like small tree trunks and while his gut hung over a belt that was pushed far below his waist, he was still known for his incredible strength and violent temper.

Ledbetter uttered a soft curse as the engine turned over and grudgingly began to sputter to life. He put the vehicle in gear and began to drive to his mobile home that was parked off in the woods on the west side of Stilwell. After slipping from the road onto the gravel shoulder, he managed to get the truck back into his lane and continued on to the highway. Turning left, he headed into Stilwell with tires squealing on the artery that eventually led to Stilwell's Division Street.

"All right, I'll take care of it," the 42-year-old civil servant said into the phone.

"When will you be sending that check? Would you like to pay over the phone? It's very easy and we can simply debit your bank account ..."

He slammed the phone down. *Damn bill collectors. They're more aggressive than ever. They didn't used to call you in the morning. If I had to rely on my piss-ant paycheck, I wouldn't have a chance*, he thought.

He finished dressing and brushed the few strands of hair he had left into a comb-over and then applied a generous cloud of hairspray. He didn't realize that pasting his hair down in this way caused the entire pate to rise when confronted by the Oklahoma wind. It looked as if he were literally blowing his top.

After locking his house he drove his five-year-old car to his office at the Oklahoma Department of Public Safety. He wheeled into the parking lot and hurried inside clocking in at exactly 7:59 a.m.

Taking his position in the cubicle, he donned his headset and prepared for a day of dispatching assets of the Oklahoma State Bureau of Investigation, the OSBI.

"Good morning, Director," he said as the Director of the OSBI walked by.

"Well, good morning. On duty, on time, I see, as usual," Director Amos David responded rhetorically with a smile as he walked by.

The civil servant sat quietly and waited for the first call. Within moments his screen was showing incoming traffic. *It was a halfway boring job*, he thought, *but the little extra tasks he performed made it worthwhile and profitable.*

"Hey, Daddy, look," Austin shouted.

Phillip and Gus both turned to see the child had stopped and was glued to a store window, hands trying to shade his eyes to see inside. Phillip motioned to Gus and they walked back to the window that had captured the boy's attention.

"What's all of that in there?" Austin asked.

Phillip squinted to see but the window was so dirty it was hard to make out the interior. He craned his neck to read the sign above the door, which read *Cherokee Artifacts and Spiritualism.*

"I think it's just a gift shop, son. Let's go. We have to take our friend to his new place," Phillip said, weariness emerging from his voice. This was not a pleasant task and he didn't want to string it out any longer than necessary. The whole trip had been a disaster and he was ready to head back to Oklahoma City.

"Daddy, please, let me go inside. I think it has all kinds of stuff. Please, Daddy." After a pause, Austin quickly blurted out, "There might be something in there we want to take to Mama."

This kid has got to go into sales, Phillip thought in amazement and then, in defeat, nodded his permission. The three entered the shop and were swallowed up in a strong fragrance of incense. Deep in the background was music that had a mystical flavor. One had to strain to hear it and yet its presence was unmistakable.

They wound their way down the pathway that led through stacks of old furniture, memorabilia and long forgotten books and papers, stopping briefly to peruse some of the items. Then they saw her.

Anna Whitebear stood before them statue-still. At 5'4" she was not tall and yet her flowing tie-dyed dress created an imposing stature. Her bright blue eyes were piercing and when Phillip first caught sight of her he wondered if they were colored contact lens. In her late twenties she had a maturity and confidence in her eyes that one would have expected to find in an older person. She was, without a doubt, a striking Indian woman.

Her face was expressionless. The three shoppers stopped in their tracks. Suddenly, her stony countenance broke into a smile that canted to one side.

O-si-yo, she said.

Gus seemed to perk up and Phillip and Austin looked at each other quizzically.

Anna smiled. "Good morning, for those of you who don't speak Cherokee. I'm Anna Whitebear and welcome to our humble store. Are you from out of town?"

"Well, yes, in a way," Phillip said. "We're from Oklahoma City and he's from around here." It was the only way Phillip knew to identify the stranger with them.

Anna's eyes shot to Gus and there seemed to be an instant communication. "Feel free to browse and if there are any questions I can answer, please let me know," she said and turned back to the shelf she appeared to be stocking.

Phillip found himself thinking what an intriguing looking woman she was as he admired her long single ponytail and the dramatic streak of prematurely gray hair. He had not expected to find a woman with such a sophisticated air in a small town.

"Thanks," Phillip said and he and Austin continued to meander through the store. Austin had a field day. He could not get the questions out fast enough.

"What's this?" he said running to a table and finding an old typewriter.

Phillip wasn't sure where to begin. The child had no frame of reference to make an explanation helpful. "It's called a typewriter. They had them before computers. They were used to uh, print letters and things," he struggled.

Austin was quickly off to another table, nothing holding his attention for long. He found a stack of books and decided he wanted to look at the one on the bottom. Before Phillip could get to him the entire mountain collapsed. The child turned to his father with a look of horror.

"It's okay, son. Remember what I said about mistakes. We all make 'em," Phillip said with a small smile as he quickly reached down to help restack the volumes. In a moment he had reconstructed the mound carefully trying to match the separated covers with their correct texts. He glanced down at Austin to see him holding one of the fallen books and staring at it intently.

"And this, Daddy? What's this?" he asked as he held up a weathered book. The pages would have fallen out and crumbled but a faded and tattered ribbon held them.

Phillip took the book and tried to read the cover. Even after he wiped the dust away and looked closely, it was hard to read the title. "It looks like it says *The Earth Speaks*, whatever that means." He opened the book and while the cover was in English, the inside text was in Cherokee "It might be poems," he said.

"Oh, I think Mama would like that, Daddy. You know how she likes poems. She likes my poems, I know," Austin said.

Phillip looked at his watch. They had been in the store for forty-five minutes and needed to get about their business.

"Okay, son, but we've got to leave. Grab the book and let's pay and go," he said.

The two made their way back to the cash register where Anna Whitebear was waiting for them.

"What is this book about?" Phillip asked as he slid the old book across to her.

She took the book and held it reverently for a moment, a small smile creeping over her face. "I didn't realize we still had this. I haven't seen it in years. This is a book that describes many of the sacred rituals of the Cherokee Tribe. It talks about how the spirits of our ancestors choose special members of the nation who can travel with God through time and space and how their spirit can guide their loved ones." She looked up at Phillip.

"How much is it?" he asked.

"I'm afraid it isn't for sale," she said. She saw Austin's face fall and then stared at Gus who had just stepped up beside them. "But I want you to have it as a gift."

"Oh, no, we must pay for it," Phillip said.

"These are cherished words of my people. They cannot be bought or sold. Only given," she responded, smiling, and began to walk the three to the door.

Phillip was taken aback and stuttered his thanks. He sounded like a school-boy who had been given a gift of great value rather than the sophisticated professional who was considered articulate and smooth. "Learn from the message," she said as she held open the door. Austin and Phillip slipped out and as Gus passed by her she grasped his arm and pulled him down to her.

"I know," she said quickly and then guided him outside closing the door behind him.

The trio resumed their trek down the sidewalk of the little town. The shelter seemed to be much farther than Phillip had thought. He stopped and moved to the street curb to try to see the shelter.

"Look, Daddy! I found a puppy," Austin yelled.

Phillip glanced back to see Austin pulling on some poor stray that had the misfortune to come close enough to be captured by the six-year-old.

"Yeah, that's nice, son," he said as he craned to see farther down the street.

"Oh, shit," said James Ledbetter as his truck rolled through a red light to the honks of motorists who had to slam on their brakes to avoid a collision.

He knew he was traveling too fast but *what the hell*, he thought. He viewed Stilwell through a veil of intoxication, even though it wasn't yet noon. He downshifted to pick up some speed and get away from the intersection in case any cops were around.

"Dumb-assed redskins," he mumbled as he jerked a hard left and continued to tear down the main street of the hamlet.

Looking back, Phillip yelled, "Austin! Leave the dog alone. He may have fleas." And began to walk hurriedly back to the little boy.

At that time the animal apparently had become claustrophobic and bolted from Austin's grasp. He darted between two parked cars and dashed into the street.

"Come back!" Austin yelled and ran after him.

Phillip's heart froze. "Don't run into the street!" he screamed. Before he could even finish his sentence Austin was in the middle of Division Street.

Phillip heard it before he saw it. He looked up the street to see a battered pickup barreling toward the spot where his small son was racing.

He began to run but his legs seemed to be frozen. Each step took eons and his body wouldn't obey his brain's orders. He couldn't get there in time. Suddenly, he heard a strong voice call out his son's name and looked to see Gus sprinting toward the street. He had never seen anyone move so fast.

Gus reached Austin seconds before Ledbetter's truck was to make impact and swooped him up like a hawk diving and grabbing a mouse on the run. The momentum took both of them crashing to the concrete out of the truck's path on the opposite side of the street. The truck belatedly began to squeal its brakes and skid to a stop.

Phillip ran to the two and grabbed Austin into his arms. "Are you okay?" he breathlessly asked Gus and he tried to help him up. Gus was bleeding from the fall but had apparently shielded Austin from any harm. Gus nodded and stood on shaky feet.

"Goddamn idiot," came a nasty voice from behind the crowd that had now gathered. James Ledbetter pushed his way forward. "What the fuck is wrong with you and that stupid kid? I could have killed you. Dumb shits!"

"Hold it buddy," Phillip said loudly, putting Austin down and moving quickly in front of Ledbetter. He was shaking with fear and anger. "You were driving too fast. You're the one who needs to be answering the questions."

Phillip never saw the roundhouse punch that landed on the side of his head. He went sprawling backward to Austin's scream. Ledbetter took a step toward him to administer a few well-placed kicks to the crumpled body.

It wasn't the first time Phillip had been sucker-punched but it was the most excruciating. The years since his last fistfight had slowed his reactions and doubled his sensitivity to pain. His head was pulsating and his vision was blurred. There was numbness over part of his face. Nevertheless, the adrenalin rush quickly accelerated his movements and thinking. He rolled twice trying to get away from Ledbetter's boots as he swung his leg and missed.

Phillip jumped to his feet and dodged a right cross from the brute. He punched as hard as he could in Ledbetter's kidney area but it simply turned the man around. He could smell the body odor and alcohol coming from his attacker.

Ledbetter moved menacingly with his arms spread wide as if he were guarding a man in basketball.

Philip remembered the instructions from his college football coach when planning an attack against a 300 tackle on the opposing team. "Well, it's obvious we're not going to go through him," the coach had said.

Phillip tried to follow that advice and move to his left but Ledbetter was too quick and grabbed him by his shirt, jerking him backwards and off of his feet.

Phillip fell on his back and saw James Ledbetter raise his boot to stomp him. He closed his eyes and moved his arms in front of his face waiting for the blow. But it never came.

He opened his eyes in time to see Gus step forward and place a heavy hand on Ledbetter's shoulder causing him to turn quickly. A mask of loathing covered James Ledbetter's face when he realized Gus had touched him. He saw another Indian casualty who had it coming. But before Ledbetter could regain his balance, in one lightning movement, Gus gripped his windpipe with such ferocity his victim could only stand wide-eyed gasping for breath.

Ledbetter tried to resist but the clutch instantly drained him of strength. Gus held him tightly until his lips turned blue and then, instead of twisting his fist and collapsing the man's windpipe as he had done so many times before, let him drop to the ground like a large sack of sand.

It was clear to the onlookers that this stranger had the ability and experience to finish the job. But for some reason he had chosen to spare the man.

There was a murmur as the crowd looked up to see the Adair County Sheriff's car pulling up with siren blaring and lights frenetically flashing. Sheriff Ross was here.

CHAPTER NINE

Phillip slumped on the street curb. The rough textured concrete rubbed at his trousers and the heat quickly rose through the fabric making him feel as if he had sat on a griddle. It hurt but it hurt more to move. Purple and swollen, his left eye was shut and his head throbbed like a mule had kicked him. Austin was parked by his side, trembling. Gus stood close by saying nothing but taking everything in.

A tall wide-shouldered sheriff strutted toward Phillip. A muscular man who looked to be his senior deputy accompanied him. His nametag identified him as Deputy Cole. The closer they got, the more imposing they became. They had been talking to witnesses and had just finished instructing the medical technicians on the transporting of an unconscious James Ledbetter to the hospital.

"You got some ID, mister?" the sinewy sheriff barked at Phillip.

Phillip looked incredulously at his alligator boots and worked his gaze up to his face. He struggled to his feet. "Yeah, here," he said as he pulled out his wallet and passed the slim but muscular man his driver's license. The sheriff looked at it, then at Phillip, then back at the card. He slowly handed the license to Deputy Cole who perused it carefully. After a moment he handed the license back to Phillip as he scrutinized Gus and Austin.

"So what brings you over from Oklahoma City to cause trouble in Stilwell?" the sheriff scoffed, turning his raised eyebrows back to Phillip. It was clear he was not joking.

"Just visiting," Phillip replied, then added when he read the man's nametag, "Sheriff Ross."

"Just visiting who?" the sheriff badgered, his eyes narrowing as he spat out the words.

"We're here for that ceremony at Oak Grove Cemetery yesterday. We didn't make it, though. Something came up," Phillip said with a twinge of sarcasm.

"Uh huh. What about you, boy? You got some ID?" he turned and asked Gus.

Quickly, Phillip interjected, "He's with me. He's, uh, a relative. He's been ill and we just got him out of the hospital. You can check it out. He's got amnesia."

The sheriff's eyes narrowed, seated in sockets ringed by dark circles that made them look as if they were beads floating in two pools of crude oil.

"The folks I talked to say he acted like anything but a sick man. How do you explain that?" he asked.

"It was an emergency. He was protecting me. Sometimes, even sick men can do incredible things in an emergency," Phillip answered.

Sheriff Ross looked away as if he were contemplating Phillip's answer. Slowly, he unbuttoned his shirt pocket and removed a toothpick. He placed it in his mouth and then turned back to look at Phillip. "You got family here?" he asked.

"No, at least not that I know of," Phillip said.

"But you said you came here for a ceremony. That's your family, ain't it?"

"Well, yes, I guess so. From a long time ago," Phillip said.

"I ain't asking you again. Who's your family here in Stilwell?"

Phillip was a little puzzled. "Well, I guess it would be Rider."

Gus' head jerked up.

The sheriff said something under his breath that sounded like "lousy treaty bastards" but it meant nothing to Phillip.

"I think you folks better head back to Oklahoma City real soon. There ain't going to be any ceremonies around here for a while. And take your mute with you," he said and nodded toward Gus. "You've caused enough trouble in my county."

As bad as he hurt, Phillip's face turned red. "Look, here, sheriff. We haven't done anything wrong. That idiot you put in the ambulance nearly ran over my son and then assaulted me. In fact, I want to press charges against him," Phillip said, his voice rising with every word. *I'll be damned if some hick sheriff is going to try to strong-arm me,* he thought.

The looming tower of a sheriff moved menacingly close to him. Phillip didn't back down even though Ross' hot breath hit him right in the face. He was so close Phillip could see the nick in his face from shaving with a dull razor and the large pores in his hawk nose.

The sheriff's voice was low and dangerous, "Listen to me, Mr. City Slicker. He may just say you assaulted him. We all know James Ledbetter around here and we don't know you. Get my drift? If I see you again in Stilwell, we might just have to do a little interrogation with you. You know, to clear up the facts? Those interrogations can take hours and hours. So if you want to prefer charges against ol' James Ledbetter, then just come on down. I'll have a few questions for you as well," Sheriff Ross said.

The sheriff paused to let his words sink in and then stepped back, never taking his eyes from Phillip.

"Sheriff, we better head back to the department. They may need us for the report," said Deputy Cole who had come up behind the sheriff.

Sheriff Ross did not respond but turned and walked to his squad car.

Deputy Cole moved close to Phillip. "Listen to me, you dumb shit. You're in way over your head. You don't mess with Sheriff Ross if you want to stay healthy. This isn't Oklahoma City. You best get your ass out of here," he said, jabbing a sharp forefinger in Phillip's shoulder, causing him to twinge in pain.

The deputy walked to the sheriff's cruiser, paused, shot Phillip a look and then got in as Sheriff Ross pulled a "U" turn on Division Street, squealing his tires as they accelerated away.

Nothing was said as Phillip, Gus and Austin drove back to the motel. They stopped by a drug store and bought some over-the-counter medications for swelling and pain. By now all were hungry so Phillip stopped by a Sonic Drive-In and picked up some hamburgers. Austin gobbled his down. Gus, at first examined the food skeptically but was so hungry he disregarded its unfamiliar look and smell and ate his as well. By the time they made it to their rooms it was mid-afternoon.

Phillip carried an exhausted Austin to the bed. The little boy was already asleep and had his book from the store clutched tightly in his hand. He had held onto the prize throughout the ordeal.

Phillip gently pried the aged pages from his small fingers and took it as he walked into Gus' room, gently shutting the door behind him. He laid the book on the television. Gus sat on the bed staring at nothing. He was obviously in a different place.

Phillip lowered himself into a chair and for a moment was quiet. Then he said softly, "You saved my son's life and probably mine as well. All I can say is thank you. I know now that you can speak and I know you realize what's going on.

"I won't ask you to explain. You don't owe me that. I owe you. But I want to help you. So tell me only what you like and let me try to repay the astonishing debt that I incurred this afternoon. Please."

Gus looked up. Phillip hadn't noticed the character that exuded from his thin face. He realized he'd never really looked at the man. His piercing blue eyes reflected a great deal of strength but were clouded with sorrow as well. His shoulders were broad and his hands were wide with long fingers. Phillip had missed it before but Austin had not. Somehow Austin had seen what was inside the stranger.

"I will explain soon," Gus said. "And you owe me nothing. Your son is a fine child and I will care for him as my own while I am here."

What power this man's voice has! There's clearly more to him than what shows, Phillip thought.

"All right. You have already shown a father's concern. I don't understand what is happening but I'll do all I can for you. But we'd better hurry. I have a feeling that sheriff is going to be watching us closely and that could mean trouble. I don't know why he's out to get us," Phillip said.

"You don't know much about the Cherokee, do you?" Gus asked.

Embarrassed, Phillip shook his head. "No, that's why I'm here. To try to learn. When we got the call that the ceremony was going to occur, well, I just thought it might be the right time to start learning so Austin could be a part of it."

"The sheriff's name was Ross. The Ross faction opposed the removal of the nation from the ancestral lands in Georgia and Tennessee. There were many murders and killings as a result of the anger the removal caused," Gus explained.

"I knew they were forced to come here but I didn't know about the other. When did that happen?"

"It started in 1835," Gus answered quietly.

"That was over 170 years ago! And what's it got to do with me?" Phillip asked.

"He obviously thinks you're a descendent of the other side—the Watie side that signed the treaty that allowed the removal. They called them the Treaty Party. And, you're an outsider," Gus said.

"Oh, great. I've got a guy mad at me for something that happened 172 years ago. Great," Phillip lamented. "What a town."

"Hatred burns for many years in the Cherokee soul. It's sad because so much time is lost that could be used for building," Gus said.

Phillip stood. "Look, friend, we don't have much time either. We've got the sheriff after us and I can't stay here forever. Whatever you need to get you where you want to be, we'll have to come up with soon. I have a little money I can give you if that will help but it won't last you too long. I can send you some more when I get back to Oklahoma City."

"Time. Time is what I need. Your money will not help. Just help me buy some time," Gus said looking at Phillip.

Phillip took a deep breath. "I can give you a day, maybe two. Then I've got to go back to Oklahoma City. I'll even take you with me if you want but that's all I can do," Phillip said. He looked out the window and then turned and asked, "I think I'll pass on dinner tonight. How about you?"

Gus nodded. Phillip turned to leave and then stopped. "Can you at least tell me your name?"

And once again, Charles Austin Augustus Rider was faced with the dilemma of having to trust someone when he had learned long ago to trust no one.

He looked at Phillip and pursed his lips. "Gus," he said and then noting Phillip's hesitation as he waited for the last name, uttered, "Just Gus."

"That will be enough. But Gus, why did you scream last night?" Phillip asked.

"A dream. I had a bad dream. I'm sorry it frightened Austin," Gus answered.

"It's alright. We were both just a little jumpy. Try to get some rest," Phillip said and stepped out of the room.

Gus tried but couldn't sleep. The wounds he suffered were still not completely healed and the exertion and excitement of the day had caused him more pain than he expected. His head ached rhythmically and no matter how he turned in the bed, his lower back alternated between dull and sharp pains.

After what seemed like an eternity, he twisted his body so that he literally rolled out of bed, putting the least amount of stress on his spine with his feet hitting the floor. He sat on the bedside for a moment, turned on the light, then walked over to the television and noticed Austin's book that Phillip had inadvertently left.

He picked the volume up and began to scan it. The opening words intrigued him and by the time he got through the first chapter he was totally engrossed. By six a.m. he had finished it. He re-read the most important parts and then knew what he had to do.

He dressed and paced the floor. He heard Phillip and Austin stirring and was standing in the center of the room when Phillip tapped on his door and opened it.

"Hey, you're all ready. I guess you're as hungry as we are. Ready to go for some breakfast?" Phillip asked.

"I must go to the shop we visited yesterday," Gus said.

"Well, okay, but don't you want some breakfast first? You haven't had anything to eat in a while either," Phillip asked.

He had no idea how many times Gus had gone without food all day and how the nagging pangs of hunger were a familiar companion.

"No, I will go to the shop while you have breakfast," Gus said and moved toward the door.

"Okay, Gus, it's your show," Phillip said.

At that moment a refreshed and excited Austin pushed his way through the door into Gus' room. "Your name is Gus? What's your last name?"

"That's enough, Austin," Phillip said firmly. "Gus is enough for us right now. And I think you'd better ask if you should call him Mr. Gus."

Confused, Austin looked at Gus.

A smile crept over Gus' face as he watched the little boy's quandary. "You can call me Gus. It's what my friends call me. But I'll tell you a secret. My real name is Austin, just like yours."

"Hey!" Austin squealed with joy. "We're twins!" Suddenly they all broke out in laughter and the tension dissolved.

"Okay, guys, let's get about our mission. Austin and Dad to breakfast. Gus to the shop. And all of us hiding from the sheriff," Phillip said good-naturedly as they headed for the car.

Although his demeanor was light-hearted, it hid the apprehension he felt about Sheriff Ross. He knew he was a dangerous man and the longer they stayed in Stilwell, the more they were at risk. Deputy Cole had been right. This was not Oklahoma City. This was Ross' backyard.

Phillip wasn't sure it was the right thing to do but he decided to call in a favor. He slipped away from the two while they bantered and picked up the phone and dialed a number in Oklahoma City.

CHAPTER TEN

Anna Whitebear was having a fitful sleep. She was dreaming in spurts and then awakening with no idea what the dream was about.

She looked at her clock and sighed when she saw the red numbers indicate 2:30 am. She fluffed her pillow and tried one more time to get some rest. This time she gratefully drifted off to sleep. As slumber enfolded her, she once again began to dream and see indistinct images. Suddenly, out of an ethereal mist, her most important persona appeared, that of her grandfather. He seemed to zing out of nowhere.

"Granddad, what are you doing here? You died five years ago," she said to the wrinkled but distinguished figure who began to speak to her. His kind face was framed with a white goatee mustache.

"Visitations" were not unusual for Anna. Blessed with psychic abilities since birth, she had gotten used to messages being transmitted in dreams and they were often sent by long passed relatives. Premonitions, precognitions and various and sundry psychic insights were common for her. For this reason she always kept a notepad and pencil on her bedside table to jot down her impressions. Those messages could quickly pale once she awakened.

"Child, you must be cautious. There are those who would harm you. Do not let yourself be vulnerable. Help the warrior and watch for the sky. The sky will protect you."

"What do you mean, *i-du-du*?" she asked, using the Cherokee word for grandfather. "What do you mean about the sky?" but no answer was forthcoming and the image faded away in spite of Anna's best efforts to prolong it.

Anna sat up in bed. "Why do they always do this to me? Why can't they just say what they mean instead of making me solve a riddle?" she lamented. She quickly scribbled the essence of the dream on the pad.

"What the hell is the sky? Jeeze!" she said and settled back in the bed, this time quickly falling asleep.

The stack of books and photographs she had methodically placed on her desk the night before in the cluttered, small cubicle that served as an office were waiting when she arrived. Anna immediately began to pore through them. Before long she was joined by Donna Still.

"Do you think it's in there?" asked Donna, her childhood friend who spent at least part of every day with her and had decided to begin this day in her company.

"If it isn't here it's someplace else but I know damned well who that was. I've seen a picture of him someplace and it was the same man," Anna replied never taking her eyes from her task.

"Anna, look at us!" Donna persisted. "We all come from the same group of ancestors. Our names are intermingled and certainly the families are inter-married. Just because someone looks like an old picture doesn't mean he's a hundred years old. It just means that one person looks like someone who came before. It's only normal that we all share similar physical characteristics."

"Oh, yeah? How many Cherokees have red hair like you?" Anna asked never looking up.

"Well, more than you think, if they've got Irish ancestors as well," Donna smiled. "And besides, Anna, there are so few fullbloods left, most of us are a mixture of Cherokee and European ancestors. Your blue eyes are not exactly a Cherokee trait."

"It's more than just physical characteristics, DeeDee," she said, using her friend's nickname, "The day I saw him when we were at the hospital visiting your aunt, I knew he was not from this time. There was something about him. I don't know. I just felt it. You know how I am about things like that. Then when he came in here with that man and his son, I was sure. I don't come from a long line of medicine men for nothing. And I'm going to find his picture," she said as she began lining up old pictures.

"Did you hear about what he did to James Ledbetter yesterday? They say he put that brute in his place," Donna said.

"Hear about it? It happened right down the street! I could hardly miss it," Anna answered.

"But now Sheriff Ross is out to get him. He told a bunch of them at The Rebel Club last night that he was going to have a real up-close-and-personal conversation the next time he saw him," Donna said, all the while twisting a lock of her short auburn hair.

"How we ever got a criminal as a Sheriff is a puzzle to me. The man blatantly associates with scum and people of questionable character," Anna said as she reached in a drawer and pulled out a nickel-plated .38 caliber revolver and held it up in her pristinely manicured hands for Donna to see.

Donna's eyes got bigger at the sign of the large, shiny Smith & Wesson with Anna's slim fingers grasping it.

"The last time he came in here and tried to make evil-handed advances to me, I pulled this gun on him. I told him in no uncertain terms he'd better not ever come in here again unless he was on official business. He hasn't been back. I refuse to be intimidated by the fool but that doesn't exactly put me on his favored list."

"Anna, be careful of him. He's dangerous. Everyone knows that," Donna said with urgency in her voice. "It's not as if you have someone to take care of you."

Anna Whitebear loved Donna but for the duration of their lifelong friendship had put up with her frightened mind-set. "DeeDee," she scolded, "I don't need anyone to take care of me. I was able to take care of myself before Mickey and I were married and that hasn't changed just because he died."

"Okay, okay. I just worry about you," Donna said as she stood and picked up her purse. "I've got a lot to do today. I have to get the girls' school supplies before they come back from camp plus I have to do my grocery shopping. Want to come over tonight for supper? We're having fried chicken."

Anna smiled. "No thanks, kiddo. I'm going to find that picture today if it takes all day and night."

Donna left the store, smiling as she heard the small bell over the door tinkle as she exited. It always reminded her of the bell in the revered 1946 movie *It's a Wonderful Life* that signaled an angel had gotten his wings.

Anna Whitebear wondered if she really was in danger from Sheriff Ross. She'd only been a widow for two years and still wasn't quite sure how her role was to be played.

Her late husband, Mickey Whitebear, had been a good and strong man. They had gone to college together but were never romantically involved. Just friends. Then, after graduation and a year or two of Anna working in Oklahoma City and Mickey in Tulsa, they had migrated back to their hometown of Stilwell.

Mickey was an engineer for the state and never pretended to understand the spiritual world that engulfed Anna. Soft-spoken and gentle, he and Anna's paths eventually crossed and the old friendship was quickly renewed. But this time it was different. She admired his quiet strength and appreciated his willingness to allow her to pursue an area that he thought, she was sure, was mumbo-jumbo. He, on the other hand, was amazed at her ability to maneuver in a world for which he had no comprehension or understanding.

Anna often wondered if perhaps it was because Stilwell was such a small town and it was impossible to not be thrown together or if she and Mickey were honestly meant for each other.

It didn't matter because their union was a happy and mutually supportive one. Even though Mickey wanted children badly they were not forthcoming and so they enjoyed each other's company and dreams. It was Mickey who encouraged Anna to purchase the store when it came up for sale after the owner's death. He happily agreed to put a second mortgage on their home to provide the needed funds.

Overall, Anna had been happy until two years ago when Mickey was sideswiped and killed by an 18-wheeler while surveying a road. He was bent over his transit, totally unaware of the truck's driver who had violated company rules and was on a 24-hour straight driving binge. The man dozed off just long enough for the semi to wander three feet off the road and right into Mickey. Mickey never knew what hit him.

In the ensuing days of grief Anna was surrounded by family and friends, as well as Mickey's colleagues from the state. All were intent on protecting her and began by keeping the lawyers from the trucking company, eager to limit the company's liability, away from her. Although they would later, through her attorney, settle the wrongful death claim out of court, they also in the process made Anna a wealthy woman.

During the days that passed after Mickey's death Anna kept a frightening secret, never sharing it with anyone, not even Donna Still. In one of the many visions that Anna had experienced over the years, Anna had seen the accident that killed Mickey. It happened years before in a college dream. At the time, she just didn't know the identity of the victim.

The civil servant surveyed the monitors that surrounded his cubicle, each one telling a different story of locations and unit positions as well as numbers of incoming calls.

Today could be lucrative. He had gotten a call from one of his "clients" requesting information. Whenever that happened he received a bonus in addition to the monthly under the table retainer that they paid to keep him ready to work at a moment's notice. This time it was from eastern Oklahoma, which always had something going on that required information only he could provide. He didn't ask why they needed it or what they would do with it. He had his own ideas, however. Everyone knew what went on in that part of the state and that was enough.

Still, he couldn't procure the information sitting at this console. He would need some time and privacy.

He buzzed his supervisor. "Craig, I don't know what's happened to me. All of a sudden I feel sick as shit," he said over the headset.

"What's wrong?" asked his boss.

"I don't know. I think I have a fever. I feel sick at my stomach. Man, I need to go home. I'll come back if I start feeling okay. I may have to go to the doctor if it doesn't stop soon."

"Well, okay, I'll try to get someone to cover for you," sighed the supervisor.

"I appreciate it, Craig. I'm sorry. I don't know what's happening to me. Maybe the flu," the civil servant whined.

He disconnected his headset and, holding his head, left the communications room.

He walked into the parking lot and stopped before getting into his car. He slowly walked around the worn looking vehicle viewing it critically. *Yep, it was time to get a new ride*, he decided. *He could use the new bonus money he was going to earn today. It also sounded like things were starting to happen in Stilwell and that meant more special projects and more dishonest bonuses.*

The idea of using his additional illicit income to reduce his debt to the credit card companies or his other creditors never came to mind. It had always been that way.

"Instant gratification," his ex-wife had said. "That's what you have to have. Everything right now."

Well, to hell with her. He could have it right now. And he knew just exactly how he was going to get it.

There are some good things and some bad things about small towns, Phillip thought as he drove on the back road to the restaurant where they had eaten before. The good thing was that it didn't take a genius to find everything. The bad news was that it didn't take a genius—like the sheriff—to find you.

He spotted Division Street and realized that Stilwell's primary thoroughfare was only a few blocks long. He quickly recognized all the places he had already visited, the cafe, the strange little curio shop and the site of the attack by James Ledbetter. He followed the street to the closest intersection, turned down the side street and pulled to the curb. Although it was early in the morning, the temperature had already begun to rise.

He turned to Austin and Gus and said, "Okay, guys, this way we won't advertise our presence. What do you say we go to that same restaurant, Austin?"

"Yeah!" Austin replied as they climbed out of the car.

The man and his son held back and watched as Gus carefully stepped out of the car. *He's like, well, an Indian scout,* Phillip thought as Gus moved.

"Gus. We'll be at the café three doors down when you're through. Or, we'll come get you in there," Phillip whispered, pointing to the curio shop. Gus nodded and then faded around the corner.

Father and son then began a circuitous route that would lead them to the café without revealing themselves to any inquisitive onlookers on Division Street.

CHAPTER ELEVEN

Gus peered around the corner before committing himself to stepping onto the sidewalk that would take him to Anna Whitebear's. The cracked concrete walk was deserted and there was a two-foot shadow bank created by the angle of the sun and the top of the buildings that would help hide his movements to the store some thirty feet away.

Spotting a sheriff's car on the side street down from the store he strained to see inside through its heavily tinted windows. It was either casing something or just parked. At this point he didn't care.

He moved quickly but cautiously toward the door and, finding it unlocked, slipped into the store. He grimaced at the doorbell's small tinkle that unexpectedly announced his arrival. Nevertheless, he stepped silently through the stacks toward Anna's office, immediately noting the staleness that enveloped the surroundings.

"What do you know about an old boy named Phillip Michaels? Supposed to be from the city. Tag number XXC-344," asked Sheriff Ross as he sat uncomfortably in his squad car and pressed the receiver of his cell phone closer to his ear. Ross' ear had a small nick in it as if a dog had bitten him and the pressure of the phone's receiver began to cause it to throb.

"Just a second," came the response and was followed by the sound of the tapping of fingers moving quickly across a keyboard. Moments passed and then the voice broke through again. "Architect. Lives at 3455 Castle Rock. Nice neighborhood. Has two high-dollar cars registered—probably has some bucks and is probably a Republican. Wait a minute, that name's familiar. Hold on." Again the line went silent but this time remained that way.

Within moments Ross realized he had lost his signal. Several aborted attempts to reconnect made him decide to wait and call back when the signal to Oklahoma City was stronger.

Anna looked up when she heard the familiar jingle of the doorbell. Seeing Gus, her heart almost stopped. She had been thinking about him all morning. She got up from the desk and, while trying to maintain her composure, walked into the path that led to her office. She did not speak.

As Gus approached she couldn't help notice how he carefully scrutinized the store, looking for other people.

"There's no one else here," she heard herself saying.

Gus looked at her and spoke. "You said *I know* when I was here before. What did you mean?"

Anna was flustered by his directness but kept her poise. "I know that you're not from this area. I know everyone in Stilwell and I've never seen you before—and yet you are very familiar. I also sense that you are from far away and yet very near."

"Who are you?" Gus asked, his eyes narrowing. The Cherokee Tribe was a matriarchal society so Gus was fully familiar with females who spoke their minds and were not afraid to assert themselves but he could sense this woman was exceptionally strong.

"The greater question is who are you? But I'd wager you're not ready to let that out. So, I'll go first," she said. "I'm Anna Whitebear. Daughter of Melba and Tom Demaris. Roll number 54003." Gus showed no reaction to her recitation of a roll number. It was as if it meant nothing to him. The Dawes Roles, registering the Cherokee, had not been recorded until 1898.

"Well, that obviously doesn't ring a bell. How about this? Granddaughter of William Pace and Mittie Demaris and great granddaughter of, uh," Anna paused as she probed her memory for the names of her long-ago ancestors.

"Margaret Deeson and Samuel Adair," Gus softly finished the thought for her.

Anna's eyes widened. "How did you know that? How do you know who my ancestors are?" she shot back in utter disbelief.

Gus didn't respond at first and then dodged the question, "I know much of Cherokee history. But now I need your help, not your questions."

Anna was bursting with things she wanted to ask but something told her they could wait. She would be advised when the lean and mysterious stranger was ready to tell her.

"All right. How can I help you?" she asked.

"First, the book that you gave to little Austin, the child that was in here with me yesterday. Have you read it?" he asked.

"Of course. A great aunt of mine wrote it. Why?" Anna responded.

"Do you understand the ceremonies that are written?"

"Some of them," Anna replied.

"This one," Gus said as he pulled the tattered book from his pocket and opened it in front of her to a marked page.

Anna lifted the glasses that hung from the chain around her neck and placed them on her nose at the same time giving Gus a wary look. "Traveling Through the Ages" was the title of the page. It chronicled the various alleged journeys of tribal elders from one era to another. It was clearly the stuff of legend and perhaps mythology but spoke of the "Ritual of the Flying Spirit." It was this ceremony that the patriarchs had supposedly used to accomplish time travel.

"I want to know how this is done," Gus said firmly.

After a moment of thought Anna said, "Come back here where you can sit down and we can talk." She locked the front door and then led him back into the office cubicle

"All right. You want to know about the *Flying Spirit*. I want to know the answer to this riddle." Anna began to spread out old photographs on her desk. "These are all photographs—tintypes actually—of some of the early members of our community. Starrs, Hannahs, Adairs, Vanns—they're all here."

Gus said nothing as he looked intently at the faces of men he was shoulder-to-shoulder with in battle just days ago.

"And this one is particularly interesting," she said as she slid a weathered tintype in front of him.

Gus looked down and his head began to swim. The figure staring back was he just a few days and 143 years ago. Picking it up gently, he focused on the photograph, transfixed by the faded picture.

He slowly raised his eyes to meet Anna's.

"I'm the only one who knows and I'm the only one who can help you. But you must tell me what's going on. I know something has happened but I don't know exactly what," she said.

Lips pursed, Gus managed a soft, "How did you know?"

"I'm not sure. I guess it's this damned psychic ability that my family keeps passing on to its descendants. I seem to be this generation's favored recipient. I'm a psychic or a medicine doctor, as our tribe calls them. Your blue eyes also set me off. As you can see I have them too and they're pretty rare in this community. But it doesn't matter. I know you're in a place you don't understand and you're being sucked into things that are beyond your ability to deal with," Anna said. "You need help and apparently I'm the only one who can give it to you."

"Very well, I'll tell you the whole story as best I can understand it. I don't seem to have much choice," Gus said reluctantly.

The café was a packed sanctuary of locals indulging in massive doses of cholesterol. The spicy aroma of frying bacon and eggs mixed with the constant acrid output of the dedicated smokers wafted around them as Phillip and Austin purposefully made their way to the back, near the kitchen. Even in the midst of the cacophony of clattering dishes, yelled orders to the kitchen and dozens of conversations, heads turned as they wove their way through the crowded array of tables. *We may have been strangers two days ago but we're a news item now*, Phillip thought. *Another reason for wanting to keep an eye on the front door and achieve a certain amount of concealment.*

The duo had only just ordered when they saw the Praying Mantis-like shape of Sheriff Ross force his way into the café. The front had several people waiting in a small space that created a chokepoint into the restaurant. The commotion caused by the tall man pushing his way though the crowd caused a few people to look up and then quickly return their gazes to their food.

Phillip immediately saw him but the sheriff had not yet spotted them. He watched the towering figure carefully scan the assembly knowing it wouldn't be long before they were discovered. He was convinced the sheriff would make good on his promise to take them in for a grueling interrogation. He slipped some bills on the table and whispered to Austin. "Come on, son, the bad guy is here. Let's skeedadle," he said, his heart beginning to pound. Phillip had decided to try to put this situation in a light vein to not scare Austin and it seemed to be working because the child hopped out of his chair with a big smile.

The two headed directly for the back door only twenty feet away. When they were within reach of the door, Phillip heard a gruff, "Hey!" He didn't need to look back. He knew who it was and what he wanted. The architect hit the door knocking it wide open and, grabbing up Austin in his arms, quickly exited the restaurant. As the door slammed shut he found himself in a narrow alley.

He started down the trash-laden, constricted passageway first at a fast walk and then breaking into a trot. The pungent odor of the open trash containers hit his nostrils as he passed them. He knew Ross would be behind him in seconds and now the sheriff had an actual charge against him. Evading a police officer or something.

Where the hell did I park the car flashed though his mind. *Good thought, idiot. What are you going to do? Have a high-speed chase with Austin in the car? Not the best option.* Panic began to overwhelm him as a concern started to surface that he had never considered. He was running out of steam. Carrying Austin was an added factor that was contributing to his fatigue. Then he saw it.

The back door marked Cherokee Artifacts and Spiritualism.

Gus began to unravel the bizarre happenings that had resulted in his presence in Anna Whitebear's store 143 years in the future. As he talked, Anna remained spellbound, never letting her eyes leave him.

"You may think I'm crazy but that doesn't matter. I have to get back to my place, my time," he said.

"I don't think you're crazy but then a lot of people think I'm crazy so maybe we're just kindred spirits," she responded with a kind smile. "Let me have a moment. I seem to remember seeing something in the book about this." Anna began to read through the chapter *Traveling Through the Ages.*

"Um. Here it is. It says that there are times when the Great Spirit will call on us to leave our home—that must mean our time—and provide aid to the Cherokee people in another home. They use the word home to mean time. When that happens the elders don't ask permission. They just move you. I think I understand that is what has happened to you," Anna said.

"What aid can I provide?" Gus asked. "I know nothing of this age or of this town."

"I don't know. I suppose it will be made clear to you when the time is right. But what I don't understand is your eagerness to go back to an era that was so hard and dangerous. Why would you want to do that?" Anna asked.

"Because I have a family that needs me. And I have relatives and friends that are in the middle of a battle that is mine to fight," he said his eyes darting from side to side. "I don't know why I have been brought here. I have to believe that it was the Great Spirit who made it happen. And if that's the case, then the only way I can see to get back is by believing in what the elders have told us and to follow their ritual."

Anna quickly blurted out, "But you must realize, I have never conducted such a sacrament as you ask. I don't know if they'll really work. For all I know they may be just myths."

Gus looked deep into her eyes. "I don't have a choice," he said for the second time in ten minutes.

Anna thought for a minute and when it was clear he wasn't going to volunteer any more information, asked, "You said you had a family—back there. Tell me about them. Wife and children?"

Yes, one boy."

"What are their names?"

"T.L.— my son is Thomas Lafayette, but we call him T.L. My wife's name is Mary Ann." He seemed to drift off in thought and then his voice lowered. "She's very ill. She needs me. I've got to get back to her."

Sensing his discomfort but overcome with curiosity, Anna continued on. "What battle were you talking about? You said you had friends and relatives that were in a battle. Was it one around here?"

"It doesn't have a name. It's over at Cabin Creek," he said, still speaking in the present tense.

"Cabin Creek?" she asked curiously.

"Yes."

"Was it the one where the Yankees had the big wagon train?"

Gus suddenly looked up and his eyes flashed, "Yes, how did you know?"

"I remember studying it in school. It was a major battle for this area. That's another strange thing. It was fought about 100 miles north of here,"

"What happened?"

"Are you sure you want to know?" she asked.

"Yes, I must know," he said, desperation clear in his voice.

"If I remember correctly, the South lost. That was where General Stand Watie was killed. I think there were a lot of Southern casualties."

Gus looked away for a long moment. She could see his shoulders sag as if a huge weight had been put on them. Gus turned back to Anna. "I need to know everything that happened in the battle. Do you have a book here that will tell me?"

"I think so," Anna replied. She rose and walked to the center of the store and began to pore over volumes that were in stacks on one of the dust-covered tables. "Ah, here it is," she said and raised a small volume entitled *Oklahoma History*.

"This is old. It was published in 1934, but it has an excellent account of the battle," she said.

Gus took the book and quickly turned to the index. It was clear to Anna that even though he was supposedly from nearly two centuries ago, he was well educated.

"Where did you learn to read?" she asked.

Gus looked at her quizzically. "At the Male Seminary," he answered as if he were surprised he had to tell her. The Cherokee Nation had established a school system consisting of Male and Female Seminaries long before Oklahoma's white settlers had arrived.

Gus began to read. The story that unfolded was enthralling. He read about the happenings of which he and his friends had been part just days before. It chronicled the events exactly as they happened. Then Gus realized that the saga progressed beyond the point in time he remembered.

The book detailed the battle in sequence. He read out loud, "Once the Confederate forces unleashed the attack, the Union troops were taken by surprise. Watie's infantry laid down suppressing fire and cavalry overran the lead elements of the wagon train and advanced with loud war cries on the column, which was stretched across the creek and was vulnerable.

"The Confederate plan was to cause havoc with deadly accurate artillery fire and follow up with a slashing Cavalry attack. The strategy was well conceived by Generals Watie and Gano but it did not take into account an unknown factor.

"The Northern Forces had devised a secret weapon, the brainchild of the Union commander. They had constructed wagons that housed multiple, well-protected marksmen. The men were so situated as to allow them to bring a virtual wall of accurate rifle fire on the attacking Confederates.

"The rebel forces, who began with such superiority, were cut down unmercifully by the wagons and, after suffering fifty percent casualties, including the loss of their beloved General Watie, withdrew and were effectively finished as a fighting force for the rest of the war.

"The wagon train continued unmolested delivering tons of supplies to the Union forces that had earlier fought in the Battle of Pea Ridge for control of the Trans Mississippi-West Theater of Operations."

Gus put the book down, staring into space. He had known something was going on. *The numerous patrols he uncovered, the Yankees' willingness to continue the wagon train even after they knew they were being watched. They baited his battalion so they could finish them once and for all with their secret weapon. It was a struggle between two commanders—the Confederate General who only wanted revenge for past defeats and the Union commander whose only desire was to kill rebels. This had nothing to do with why they were fighting. Or did it?*

Suddenly, frenzied pounding came from the store's back door.

"Stay here," she said to Gus and ran to the sound, slamming the office door behind her. She looked out the peephole and saw a panicked, puffing Phillip Michaels with Austin in his arms, frantically looking behind as if someone were after him. She hurriedly swung open the heavy metal door.

Sheriff Ross was lurching through the small café. His ungainly size caused him to upset tables and push people out of the way but still, he could not effectively pursue Phillip and Austin.

By the time he reached the back door and found himself in the alley, the two were out of sight. He hustled, breathing heavily, down the alley looking for a hiding place. His long stride helped him cover ground fast. Rapidly checking all obvious hiding spots, dumpsters, boxes and the like, he was about to head to his car and call in some deputies when he decided to make a quick sweep of the businesses whose backdoors faced the alley. *Maybe those big city bastards broke into one of the shops and the owners don't even know it.*

"That sheriff is after us. Please help us!" Phillip gasped as he burst in the door.

"Quick, come with me, both of you," she said and ran to her small office and opened the door for them to enter. Gus looked at the two with surprise but said nothing. Anna quickly shut the door to the office. "There's only one place to hide in here and that is in the attic. Can you all three squeeze in there?"

"We'll find a way," Phillip said and pulled over a table to stand on.

"I'll go first," Gus said and bounded on the table and smoothly lifted himself up and into the attic and then reached down for Austin.

Phillip handed him up and then, not quite as smoothly as Gus, pulled himself into the small space. Anna scooted the table away and watched as they replaced the wooden access panel in the ceiling.

Ross rounded the corner to Division and began questioning the owner of the first store. He searched the property until he was convinced that the fleeing pair was not hiding within. He moved methodically down the street and quickly found himself standing in front of Anna Whitebear's store.

Wouldn't it be just like that bitch to harbor fugitives to get back at me?

He tried the door but it was locked. He began to knock loudly but there seemed to be no response. He checked the posted hours on the door and was well into the 9-5 window that the shop should have been open.

"Open up! Police, Open up!" he shouted, his deep, bellicose voice almost rattling the window in the door.

He saw movement as Anna came from the back. She had an irritated look on her face.

"What is it, for God's sake?" she asked as she opened the door.

"We have suspects loose downtown. I need to come in and look for them. I'm checking all the businesses whose backdoors face the alley. Mind if I come in?" Ross asked but it really wasn't an interrogative.

"There's no one here but me," Anna responded.

"Oh yeah? How come you're not open? Your sign says you should have been opened 45 minutes ago."

"I was doing some bookwork and just got caught up in it. Is that a crime?" Anna answered sarcastically.

"I better take a look anyway. Unless you've got something to hide," Ross said with a raised eyebrow.

Anna hesitated and then thought better of it. To deny Ross entry would just raise red flags. "Don't be ridiculous. Come in. As you pointed out, I need to be open."

Ross cautiously moved into the store with his hand on his holstered pistol.

"Just what kinds of vicious criminals are supposed to be threatening us poor shopkeepers?" Anna asked. She didn't want to provoke Ross but it was hard for her to speak to him without sarcasm finding its way into her words.

"Just some out-of-town boys. Couple of men and a little boy. You seen anybody like that?"

Suddenly, Anna's sixth sense kicked in. There was a trap being set here. She could feel it.

"Sounds like the three that came in here yesterday," Anna said.

"Yeah, those are the ones. Just testing you. I already heard that they was seen coming in here. So you ain't seen any more of them, huh?" Ross asked.

"Hell, no, Sheriff and you don't need to test me. Just ask your questions and I'll answer them." *Easy, easy, Anna. Don't blow it.*

"I think I'll just look around in the back. Just for your own safety," Sheriff Ross said shooting a glance at Anna.

Trying to hide her anxiety, she followed him toward the rear of the store and, after testing the door and looking around the storage room, Ross seemed to be satisfied.

"What kind of criminals can two men and a little boy be?" she asked.

"It's pretty complicated. They were involved in an assault and are material witnesses," he said trying to evade her question.

He started toward the front. Anna inwardly sighed a sigh of relief that he was leaving when the door to her office caught his eye.

"What's in there?" he asked.

Anna's heart stopped. "Just my office. It's so small, believe me, I'd know if anyone were in there," she said forcing a small laugh.

"Well, let's take a look—just the same."

CHAPTER TWELVE

"Daddy, this place stinks. And it's scary," Austin said to his father as he looked around the tiny attic space they had crammed into above the store's ceiling. Austin was right, Phillip thought. A scant three feet of headroom and only about five square feet of flooring made the spot cramped and claustrophobic. Dusty and hot, it was more like an old coffin than a storage space.

Phillip was seated and bent over while Gus was spread beyond the flooring with his legs bridging a truss. It looked painful but it was the only way all three could fit.

"Austin, you must be very quiet. We don't want the bad guy to find out we're here. It won't be for long but you have to be quiet as a mouse. Right, Gus?" Phillip whispered.

Gus maneuvered his prone figure over to Austin and said softly, "Austin, this is the way a scout in the Army does it. Would you like to be a scout?"

Austin nodded, wide-eyed.

"All right, then. None of us will move or make a sound until the Yankees are gone. And once that happens, I'll make you a real scout. Agreed?" Gus said. The inadvertent use of the word "Yankee" was lost on Austin but not on Phillip.

The sound of conversation below caused all three to hush immediately with Gus holding his hand to his mouth for Austin to see. Austin nodded his understanding.

The trio could hear talking and it seemed to be fading in the direction of the back of the store. After a brief pause, the conversation began to return toward them. As the voices got closer it was clear that the interloper was, indeed, their pursuer.

If he finds us here, we're as good as locked up. This maniac won't waste five minutes before we're in that lousy hole that probably serves as a jail.

No telling where he'll put Austin. I'll bet he gives a whole new meaning to "being held incommunicado," Phillip thought.

The voices came nearer and nearer until it sounded as if the sheriff were just below them.

"So, Anna, you haven't seen anybody today, eh?" Sheriff Ross repeated his question as he walked into Anna's office.

"I've told you, no. I appreciate your concern but as you can see, there's nobody here. Has been nobody here except Donna Still, and unless I can get to work, won't be anybody here," Anna said trying to hide her nervousness.

"What are these?" Ross asked.

Anna's heart stopped as Ross reached down and picked up some of the tintypes on the table that she had arrayed for Gus.

"Just some old tintypes I've been collecting. May make them into a montage. They're a popular framed accessory," she said casually.

"Who are they?"

"Who knows? They're just old tintypes but people like them," she kept up the scam.

Phillip was horrified. The Sheriff was directly below them in the little office cubicle. One tiny movement would surely send dust floating down and alert Ross to their presence. *Anna must be having a heart attack.*

Phillip's eyes turned toward Gus. The Cherokee lay perfectly still. He didn't even appear to be breathing. *Interesting. Lying motionless like that is exactly what a scout would have to be able to do,* Phillip thought.

Oddly enough, observing Gus in such a state took Phillip back to his past Marine training and his metabolism actually started to slow. He began to remember the days when ambush exercises consisted of hours of never moving while you waited on the enemy to enter the kill zone.

Phillip began to relax even further. His body settled down and was establishing a rhythm and essentially beginning to feel comfortable. Until he looked over at Austin. The kid was about to sneeze.

The civil servant got into his car and drove home. Once he entered, he went to the spare bedroom. It didn't have a bed, rather it was lined with computer monitors exactly like the ones in his workspace at the office. In fact, he had created an exact replica of his office cubicle. If anything, it actually had more equipment. He could monitor not only OSBI but Oklahoma Highway Patrol traffic as well.

He sat down and began to type commands into the keyboard. Within seconds the screens came alive with data. It wasn't just one type of information; scads of records were being displayed. Driver's licenses, auto registrations, telephone call records, names and occupations were all flowing onto their appropriate screens.

"Uh huh," the civil servant said as he rubbed his chubby chin and examined the different sources. The system he had created to tap into the communication lines of state government was working well.

His client had asked for information about a specific individual, a Phillip Michaels. That was easy enough. He would have that in just a few moments.

The civil servant began to query the system. If his client kept requesting information like this, something must be going on. If he could go beyond the request and provide even more secret intelligence and reveal it at the proper time, it could be worth a bundle.

Finding the first bit of information was easy, a simple search into the database of license tags. It gave him all the info he needed. He had performed that task earlier. And then, he had an idea. He would test the new addition he had recently made to his system. The expensive and highly technical piece of electronic gear allowed him to scan thousands of telephone conversations made between state government agencies in the last few days. He would put in certain keywords and the systems would search the recordings and alert him when any of them were used. It took a little bit of time but if he could find something that applied to the key people in this unfolding situation, then he could pick up a nice chunk of change.

He ran a keyword search for "Ross," "Michaels," "Stilwell" and "Sheriff" and sat back as the computer lights began to flash. In about thirty minutes the search stopped and presented him with short list of reference points that, in turn, directed him to bookmarks in the recordings.

He listened to the first forty conversations and was disappointed to find that they were not related at all to his client or eastern Oklahoma. Then on the forty-fifth conversation, he hit the jackpot. He uncovered a conversation between the Attorney General's office and the head of the OSBI. It contained details of a plan for which his client would pay thousands.

"I may be onto something," he would say to his client. "I think I might be able to find out if this Michaels called anyone in state government. But it will cost. I'll have to grease some palms."

He knew he could bait them and get two or three times what they normally paid. And he could dribble out the information a little at a time and get even more bonuses. He could literally make a fortune off of this one assignment. They had tipped their hand. They wanted the information badly.

Nelson Gay was confused as to what to do. *He was the Attorney General of the state and he could damn well do whatever he wanted when it came to law enforcement, so why was he so hesitant*, he wondered.

The situation was simple. He'd received the call from Phillip Michaels that something was going on in Stilwell and somehow Phillip, he didn't quite understand why, was involved in it and apparently at risk. All he had to do was to call the District Attorney in Adair County and have him look into it. What was holding him back?

"Ronnie, please ask Jack Oates to come to my office," he said over the intercom to his secretary.

Gay was no stranger to eastern Oklahoma. Although he was from the opposite part of the state he was well aware of the area, having tried many cases there when he was in private law practice. He also had no illusions when it came to the brand of justice performed in the old Indian Territory. It was still a rough frontier compared to other parts of the Sooner State.

"It's the only place in Oklahoma where you can have a man murdered for $500 and put it on a credit card," one of his law school cronies had teased another member of the class from Stilwell. Maybe it wasn't that bad but it was bad, nevertheless.

"Did you want to see me, Nelson?" Jack Oates asked as he stood at the doorway.

"Yes, come in Jack," Gay said as he reached behind his desk and pushed the button on his credenza that automatically shut the normally open door behind Oates.

The handsome young Native American Assistant Attorney General took his seat in front of the A.G.'s desk.

Without delay, Gay summarized the call he had received from Phillip Michaels. Oates nodded as he listened but didn't offer any opinion. Even though he had definite feelings about what he was hearing, he carefully waited until his superior had finished.

"So, here's the dilemma. You've lived in that area all your life. Should we contact the local D.A. and have him investigate?" Gay asked.

"I guess my question should be, why would we not? Do you know something I don't know?" Oates replied.

Gay looked around the room. He seemed to be searching for his next word.

"I'm not saying the D.A. covering that area is crooked. I'm just, for some reason, uncomfortable about bringing him in to investigate corruption in an elected office. You know how everyone around there is related. Especially, since the same people who elected him are probably the ones who elected the Sheriff. What's his name? Ah, yes, Ross, " he said after consulting his notes.

"Honestly, given what we both know about the vicinity, I think we might be better off, and your friend might be safer, if we found another way to check it out," Oates said. "The Oklahoma Mafia operates up there so that makes everyone a little suspect."

"You're probably right. That's your task. Get back to me after lunch with some recommendations," Gay said.

Oates rose and walked out. He was a Democrat as was virtually everyone in northeastern Oklahoma but today he didn't feel very partisan.

What's he doing in there? Donna Still thought as she watched Sheriff Ross enter Anna Whitebear's store. She left the small grocery and began to walk toward her friend's shop. The closer she got, the more anxious she became and the faster she began to walk. Nothing good could come from having Sheriff Ross in Anna's place.

When she arrived at the door she was practically running. She burst in without looking and immediately screamed as loud as she could, "Anna, are you here?" She heard no reply and began to frantically run through the store, stumbling slightly and overturning a table of lamps that went tumbling to the floor in a cascade of shattering glass and breaking light bulbs.

Anna and Sheriff Ross had just begun to respond to her scream while, simultaneously, there was sound of a small sneeze that was drowned out by the din of chaos resulting from the falling table. Both raced toward the sound of the collision.

"DeeDee, are you alright?" Anna asked as she helped the shaken woman from the floor.

"Yes, yes, I'm okay," Donna said as she looked quickly to Anna and then at Ross.

"Are you okay?" she asked quickly looking directly into Anna's eyes, searching for a secret signal that Ross was hurting her.

Anna knew exactly what was happening. "No, everything's fine," she said with a reassuring smile. "Sheriff Ross was looking for some fugitives but is now sure they're not here. Would you like him to help you to your car?" Anna asked.

"Surely, you're through here, aren't you Sheriff?" she asked with raised eyebrows.

Frustrated, Ross could see no other way out and said, "Yeah, I'll help you to the car. I guess it's okay here." He helped Donna pick up her groceries and they both left the store, Ross trying to help the woman while at the same time clearly reluctant to touch her. It almost seemed as if Donna were enjoying his discomfort as she waited for him to open the door. Ross stumbled a little trying to get the door, clearly not familiar with this level of chivalry.

Anna locked the door behind them and quickly made her way back to the office.

"It's alright to come down now," she said and pushed the small table beneath the undersized door that opened into the attic allowing the men to use it to stand on.

Gus slid though the opening first and then took Austin as Phillip handed him down. Phillip was right behind them and they all hustled into the refuge of the office.

"Daddy, I'm sorry I sneezed. I couldn't help it," Austin said.

"It's alright son," Phillip replied.

"But I won't get to be a scout now will I, Gus?"

Gus replied, "Maybe a scout in training. When you're ready, I'll make you a full scout."

Clearly disappointed, Austin persisted, "How will I know when I'm ready?"

"I'll tell you," Gus said firmly. This time there was no softness in his voice but a hard edge that silenced the child and made both Phillip and Anna look at the man with a slight apprehension.

Never forget who this man is, Phillip thought. *Beneath that sometimes gentle exterior is a man of incredible power ...and, for whatever reason, hatred.*

CHAPTER THIRTEEN

"So you think that'll do it? It's going to anger some people, you know that?" the Attorney General asked.

Jack Oates, young but a pantheon of self-confidence, quickly responded, "Of course, but if you don't want to take a chance on it coming back to haunt you, it's your only way. If this thing goes bad and the press finds out you knew and just turned it over to the suspects themselves, and at this point everyone up there is a suspect, you're going to look like you're in with them."

"But don't you think the District Attorney up there is clean?" Gay asked.

"Sir, I think so but I'm not sure. Are you? Do you want a story in the paper about someone who called you directly and asked for protection from a dishonest sheriff and then you handed it over to someone who may at a later date be implicated? At best you'd look like a fool and at worst you'd look like a crook," Oates said.

"All right, then, go ahead and get the head of the O.S.B.I. over here. I had hoped I wouldn't have to call in the Oklahoma State Bureau of Investigation, but I guess there's no other way. This raises it to a whole different level. Now we're committed to an investigation of an elected official. Hell, it could be another county commissioner scandal," Gay said referring to the infamous purge of dozens of dishonest county commissioners some three decades before.

"You're right, though. Phillip Michaels is too high profile to have something happen to him and not be able to show we did the proper thing. Maybe it'll turn out to be nothing. Why is it I feel another Vietnam coming on?" Gay said as he rubbed his forehead and leaned back in his plush chair.

"What will you do now?" Anna asked as the three brushed themselves free of the dust and insulation that clung to them while in hiding in the attic. She decided they looked like people who had been tarred and feathered.

"I think we'll wait until we're sure that the sheriff has gone for good and then we'll try to make our way back to the motel," Phillip said. "That was a close call. It's clear to me we simply can't stay in Stilwell much longer."

Gus had wandered into the middle of the store and was poring through some books on a table. He heard Phillip's last statement and looked up sharply.

Anticipating Gus' reaction Phillip said, "Well, Gus? I know you say you can't leave but honestly, your options, and ours, are becoming fewer and fewer."

"Not yet. I can't leave yet," Gus answered.

Phillip shook his head slightly in frustration, his jaw tight.

"Austin, do you like picture books?" Anna suddenly asked the child, breaking the tension that was building in the room.

"Oh, yes. Mama and I have some picture books we look at all the time," Austin said, glad to have someone ask him a question about something he knew.

"Good, because I have a wonderful picture book that I'll bet you've never seen. Come on," she said and extended her palm to him. He quickly grasped her hand and cheerfully followed her to a tiny alcove.

After situating him with books and pillows she returned to Phillip. "Gus, please come here."

Gus closed the book he was scanning and walked over to her, volume still in hand.

Before she could speak, Gus said, "Anna, look at this. Tell me about it." He showed her a page in an old Army training manual he had found among the stacks of books.

"I don't know anything about it. It's a machine gun but that's all I can tell you," Anna said.

"How does it work? It says it fires many bullets. Do you know how many?"

Suddenly a voice came from behind Gus causing him to jump. He had been so engrossed in the book he had forgotten that Phillip was still there.

"I can tell you what you want to know, Gus, but don't you think it's time you trusted me with the truth?" Phillip said.

"You know, Gus, I'm not stupid. I've been able to put a lot of pieces in the puzzle. For example, I know you were a scout in the Army. And not the American Army."

Anna put her hand on Gus' arm. He was obviously in a quandary as to the next step to take. "It's only fair that you share with Phillip what you told me before all of this happened. He's in it as deeply as you are and as near as I can tell, it's a result of trying to help you."

Gus had a disturbed look on his face. He was being forced into revealing his secret to too many, too fast. He hesitated.

"She's right, Gus. It's no longer a choice to keep your secret," Phillip said.

Still defiant, Gus stood mute. Looking around, he caught a glimpse of Austin poring over the picture book and suddenly realized it must soon come to an end one way or another lest the child's safety be jeopardized.

"Yes, you're right," he said and began to tell his story once again.

After nearly an hour of sitting quietly and recounting his tale, Gus fell silent. After a moment he said, "I think with Anna's help I can get back to where I belong. But just going back isn't enough. I've got to make a difference. My friends and neighbors, my kinfolk are all in that battle. General Watie will be killed. They're outnumbered and outgunned and don't know it. I've read your book, Anna. They need help and now, otherwise the entire future of this area will be threatened."

"How do you see that, Gus? The South will still lose the war even if the Confederates win the battle," Phillip asked.

"Because many of the people who will lead this area and the Cherokee Nation will be killed. Phillip, you don't yet know enough about us. The nation has been split over the removal and now over the war. We must have strong leaders after the war to try to bind our wounds and make us one nation again. It's all that will ensure our survival. The leadership that is so critical to us will be lost," Gus said.

Phillip looked skeptical. "I don't know how you got here but you can't go back without likely being killed. In fact, you can't stay here without likely being killed. You've gotten yourself, and us, in a hell of a mess."

Anna and Gus looked at him without saying a word. "Okay, so I don't know everything about the Cherokees. But what about this time travel issue? I'm not a physicist but I do know something about the theories of time travel. And from what I understand, in order to move through time you have to be able to move faster than light. If I remember my lectures on Einstein, that's about 300 million meters per second. Tell me how a guy in 1864, when science hadn't figured out how to break fifty miles an hour, could accelerate fast enough to skip ahead in time? Not only that, but how are we supposed to get him back there when we don't have that kind—hell it hasn't been discovered yet— technology?" Phillip sputtered.

Anna seemed to also become frustrated and suddenly interrupted, "Phillip, this is a spiritual exercise. The mystical teachings of the ancient Cherokees are not subject to the modern view of physics. The sacred ceremonies are known but to a few. Make no mistake they are magical. I know you are an educated person and I know that you have come here to learn about your Cherokee ancestors. One of the first things you must learn is faith in their traditions and beliefs."

"So, Anna, do you think Gus can get back where he was at exactly the same time? Just pick up where he left off?" Phillip asked with a tinge of incredulity.

"Maybe," said Anna. Both the men looked at her. She stood with Austin's book open in her hands.

"The book says if you do exactly what it instructs and if, and it's a big if, you do it on the day that corresponds with the day you want to arrive and if there is a Bloodmoon, you can reach your destination at that time," Anna said. "And here's the caveat, if the Great Spirit wills it. According to what Gus has told me, he was in the middle of the Battle of Cabin Creek, which occurred on September 18, 1864. And there was a Bloodmoon that night. I checked out the weather forecast on the Internet and, believe it or not, there is going to be another Bloodmoon on September 18, 2007, tonight. Looks like it's your Bloodmoon, Gus." Anna turned to look at him.

Just as Phillip was about to ask a question, Austin appeared rubbing his eyes.

"Daddy, I fell asleep reading the picture books," he said.

Phillip stood and picked the child up in his arms. "Come on, son, let's get you back to the motel and have a nap." He looked at his watch. It was almost one o'clock and they had yet to have anything to eat.

"I'm going to take him back and feed him then let him rest. But we had better meet later and talk about this," Phillip said.

"I'll stay here," Gus said. "Anna and I have much of the Cherokee to talk about. I'll wait for you here." Phillip, clearly concerned about what he had just heard, hesitated.

"Go on, Phillip. I'll make Gus some lunch and then bring him to the motel. He'll be fine with me now that Ross is convinced he isn't here. Just be careful. He's looking for you too," Anna said.

After cautiously surveying the area, Anna signaled and Phillip and Austin slipped out the shop's back door and made their way to the car which was stashed a couple of blocks away. Retrieving the Cadillac, the two wove their way through the back streets on the way to the motel.

"That's the last goddamn straw. I know those bastards were in that store. I just couldn't find them. I'm tired of them causing trouble in my county, turning my own people against me," Ross said.

He puffed on his cigarette and then slipped off the corner of the desk and began to walk among the small cadre of assembled deputies.

"Well, we're going to take care of them. It's time for some questioning in regard to the fracas that occurred yesterday. In fact, there may be a charge of assault and even complicity to commit assault."

"Sheriff, I thought James Ledbetter attacked them?" said one of the deputies.

"Oh, I think old Ledbetter is having a change of heart. His memory is improving. He just don't know it yet," Ross sneered. "So, I want them picked up — all of them, even the kid. Start looking around town for them. Deputy Cole" — he nodded to his second in command — "check the motels. If you don't find them, then get the license number and description of their car. Find out how long they're registered for. I want them all brought in here within 24 hours. Got it?"

The deputies began to amble out and make their way to their patrol cars mumbling among themselves. Sheriff Ross sat at his desk and watched them depart and then started to wonder how long he would have to hold the out-of-towners so that their Cadillac could be "fixed".

"This little baby will get up and move," said the car salesman. "You'll have to fight off women with a stick."

The civil servant opened the door and sat in the gold Nissan 350Z. The aroma of fine leather surrounded him like a warm blanket. He had never experienced such luxury in a car. He carefully surveyed the array of dials that read power all over them.

The salesman slid into the passenger seat and invited him to take a quick spin. They left the dealership and drove for several miles. Encouraged by the salesman, he tested its acceleration. He was literally pressed into the back of the seat. The exhilaration of having that much horsepower under his command gave him chills.

The real thrill came as he pulled up to a stoplight. At first, he didn't notice them. Then as he looked to the lane on his left he saw two beautiful girls in a silver SUV. They looked as if they could be college students. They were busy talking and then the one in the passenger side turned and smiled. She rolled down her window and motioned for him to do the same. He complied and she said with a picture-perfect smile framed in a beautifully tanned face, "What kind of cologne do you use?"

Taken aback, he stuttered and finally said, "Old Spice" because it was the only cologne he could think of. "Uh, why do you ask? " he yelled back.

"We're doing a survey of guys who drive hot cars," she said happily as they sped off.

The civil servant sat for a moment in awe. He had never been hit on by beautiful women before. And it had to be because of the car. Just the car. *This was cool.*

He returned to the dealership and completed the papers to purchase the `Z'. He hadn't planned on buying something so flamboyant but after the incident with the girls, he decided he deserved it.

"We'll have the car detailed and ready to deliver to you within 24 hours," the car salesman said cheerfully. "What about your old car? Want to trade it in?"

Better keep the old car, too, he thought. *I can drive it to work and no one will ever know I have the 'Z'. No need to raise suspicions. I've worked around cops for so long I think like them,* he chuckled to himself.

"No, I think I'll keep it for a fishing car."

As he rose to leave the salesman said, "Not so fast."

The civil servant froze. *Why would he say that? What does he know?*

Grinning, the salesman produced a red baseball cap with a "Z" on the front. "Now you're official!"

The civil servant was grinning as well as he left the dealership, the proud new owner of a 350Z.

"It says that you must first pray at the resting place of your ancestors. And you must do that the day of the Bloodmoon. Do you have any ancestors buried here?" Anna asked as she held the book of ceremonies open and methodically went through the steps outlined.

Perplexed, Gus said, "No, my grandfather was buried in the Old Nation," the name for the ancestral lands in North Carolina.

"What about your father?" Anna asked.

"My father is still alive," Gus responded quickly.

For a moment neither said a word and then Anna spoke softly, compassionately. "Gus, this is 2007. Your father is not still alive," she said.

Gus looked shocked and then, hurt.

"Of course. Maybe he is buried here."

"Well, Oak Grove Cemetery has been around for nearly 200 years. We could go out there and look around," Anna suggested trying to keep the mood positive.

"Let's go," Gus said strongly. It was clear that in his mind he had been in a place filled with emotion and was ready to leave it behind.

They drove along the highway until they came to the dirt road that led to the little cemetery enclosed by a chain link fence and shaded by massive oak trees. Some looked well over 100 years old. The gentle breeze softly whistled through the trees and gave the plot an unusually hallowed feel.

They entered the gate, latching it behind them. Slowly they walked across the 100 feet to the rows of tombstones, many leaning and some barely legible after a century or more of weathering.

"What name are we looking for?" Anna asked.

"Austin Rider."

They moved cautiously, each taking a separate line and each kneeling down to carefully examine the different headstones. Some markers were simply slivers of stone implanted into the ground. Suddenly, Anna stood and stepped back, her eyes transfixed on one of the markers, "Gus, you need to see this," she said tenuously.

Gus came quickly and bent down to read the tombstone at which Anna was staring. As he did, all color drained from his face as he examined the inscription: *Mary Ann Bigby Rider, 1834-1865.*"

"Oh, no," he whispered as he dropped to his knees. Anna couldn't control herself; she felt such pain for this man that she knelt beside him putting her arms around him, burying her head in his shoulder. She was surprised that she had tears streaming down her face for the death of a woman she had never met and who left this life over a century ago.

"You're not the first person who has been concerned about the goings-on in Stilwell," said Amos David, the Director of the Oklahoma State Bureau of Investigation. "In fact, we've had a man undercover in that community for nearly seven months. I haven't brought it to you because we don't have anything concrete yet. It's an ongoing investigation and so far, it's all circumstantial."

"What seems to be the trouble over there?" asked Attorney General Gay.

"The usual thing. Illegal drugs, loan sharking, self-dealing. It doesn't look like this Ross character is the ringleader. He's not smart enough, but he's definitely involved. Probably supplies the muscle. We think the whole sheriff's department is on the payroll," Director David said. "Plus, this could be a positive link to the Oklahoma Mafia as it's called, and could lead us to the bigwigs that are behind it."

"How much danger is Phillip Michaels actually in?" Gay asked.

"Make no mistake. Those people are ruthless. As far as they're concerned he's some intruder from the city messing with their business. They'll do whatever it takes to get him out of town and if he goes too far, they'll kill him and we'll never find a body," David said.

"He has his little boy with him," Gay said nervously.

David looked directly at the Attorney General, "It won't matter to them. At all."

Gay stared at him intensely for several moments and then said forcefully, "Okay, what can we do to protect Michaels?"

Phillip slowly maneuvered the Cadillac through the back streets of Stilwell, getting lost twice but each time finding his way with the help of his onboard compass back to the direction of the motel.

As things began to look familiar he started to feel some comfort with his location and the way he and Austin were traveling. He made the final turn that brought the motel into sight and was about to let out a cheer as he steered into the driveway when he spotted a figure exiting the office.

At first, Phillip only recognized the uniform. Then, the face became visible and he shuddered. It was Deputy Cole and he could have no other business at the motel than looking for Phillip and Austin.

"Get down, Austin," Phillip said and fought the urge to speed by the motel. Instead he passed the motel normally and noted that the Deputy was undoubtedly walking toward their rooms.

The clock is ticking down. They're actively looking for us now and this car is going to stick out like a sore thumb, he thought. He stayed on the same road knowing he couldn't get lost if he just turned around to go back. After driving for nearly fifteen miles, he pulled into a run-down convenience store. "Stay in the car, son. I'll be right back," he said.

Inside the store Phillip bought a couple of pieces of fried chicken that were under the bright pink lights of a heat lamp along with some barbeque. For himself he picked up a Diet Coke and then a small carton of milk for Austin.

Not exactly the most nutritious meal in the world but it will keep him from getting sick, he thought.

He paid for the items and then walked outside looking to each side for any sheriff cars. He didn't see any but when he got into the car he realized he didn't see something else. Austin was gone.

Frantically, he jerked to look in the back seat to be sure the little boy wasn't hiding and when he saw the empty back seat his heart began to beat rapidly and bile rose in his throat.

He jumped from the car and began calling almost hysterically for his son.

Anna and Gus continued their search of past ancestors.

"The more ancestors that are here make the ground more sacred and the pleas to them more powerful. Their locations will also help us find the best place to conduct the ceremony," Anna said.

After an hour of searching, it appeared they had located all the ancestors. Suddenly, Anna realized that Gus needed his privacy. A man such as this would never show his emotions and he had just come to the realization that many of his loved ones were only memories.

"Gus, I've got to have help on this. I just don't know enough about conducting the ceremonies. There's a woman—I think she's still alive—who lives outside of Stilwell. She's strange as she can be but I think she knows more about Cherokee mythology and spiritualism than anyone else in the Nation. I'm going to go out to her place and see if I can get some help. Will you stay here? I'll be back in a couple of hours. You can continue to search and see if you come across any other relatives," Anna said as she walked to her truck.

Not surprisingly Gus did not answer.

Long after the dust raised by Anna's SUV had settled, Gus still stood by the large oak at the entrance to the cemetery. Neither the oak nor Gus moved.

Then slowly, carefully, as if he were afraid of stepping on a snake, Gus walked to the tombstone he had discovered only hours ago. First, he stood silently before it and then ever so reverently, knelt down.

Gingerly, he reached to touch the name and lightly ran his callused fingers over the weathered name. Mary Ann Bigby Rider. 1834-1865. A thousand years ago. And yet only days ago he touched her sweet face and felt the warmth of her body next to his. He felt his heart pounding and his eyes welling with tears.

How could this happen? Even in the chaos of war he had his family, his land, his cause. Now he was in a strange place with strange people in the grip of hatred. And his precious Mary Ann was but a memory.

"Oh, dear one. My heart aches for you and our little family. I want to be with you, to protect you, to care for you. Can you be so far when I feel you so close to me? Mary Ann, I don't know what to do. I don't know when to be strong. I don't know for whom I should fight. Without you I'm lost. My future has become my past and with it every dream I've ever had," he lamented.

For the second time and without warning he began to cry uncontrollably in deep and excruciating sobs that wracked his body. For nearly thirty minutes he endured the most concentrated grief he had ever felt, a grief that reached across the years, the centuries.

Anna thought she remembered where the old lady, Ester Shinnyfeld, lived. She had been there once before many years ago and the visit was still burned indelibly in her mind. The woman may have very well been in her 90s by now and probably crazy as a loon but she knew her subject matter, crazy or not. Known in the old days as a "divinator", she was the only one who Anna could think of that could help fill in the blanks on the archaic ceremony.

She drove five miles past the outskirts of Stilwell and slowed down carefully looking for the familiar turnoff. It appeared on cue. She recognized it even though it had been paved since she last was on it.

She veered off and drove down the road. It abruptly reverted to gravel. *These poor folks can't even get their whole road paved*, she mused. She continued along and then she saw the unmistakable house. *It's a hovel, not a house*, she thought.

Three old rusting cars, washing machine carcasses and assorted pieces of trash, surrounded the tiny clapboard structure. The lawn, if one could call it that, was overgrown with weeds and had only a path worn to the front door. The tiny porch was leaning as if it were ready to collapse. Positioned proudly on the roof and in stark contrast to the rest of the house was a gleaming aluminum satellite dish.

Anna pulled up and warily made her way to the door, always on the lookout for snakes and guard dogs. When she knocked on the door she could hear the fierce barking of dogs on the inside. She waited patiently, knowing it would take Ester a while to make it to the door.

Finally, a small voice inside yelled out, "Who is it? What do you want?"

"*O-si-yo*, Ester," she said using the traditional Cherokee greeting, hoping it would soften up the old woman. "It's me, Anna Whitebear. William and Mittie Demaris' daughter? Do you remember me?"

There was no answer so Anna tried again.

"Ester, I need to talk to you. I need some help with one of our tribal ceremonies. I have to know how to conduct it. Can you help me?"

Slowly, the door creaked open and two eyes peered out. Anna was not ready for what she saw when it was completely open.

CHAPTER FOURTEEN

"Hello, stupid," came the sarcastic greeting over Sheriff Ross' cell phone. Ross shuddered to hear that voice. If his Caller-I.D. had shown it was Harley instead of registering "Unavailable" he wouldn't have answered.

"I'm starting to hear some bullshit that you're playing your games again with some dude from Oklahoma City. What the hell's going on?"

"Aw, it's some city slicker who thinks he can come down here and beat up one of my boys. I'm just going to teach him a lesson and send him home," Ross said.

"Ross, if you start bringing heat down on us because you're trying to play local tough guy you'll regret it. Do your fucking job and that is to keep things quiet. Keep the whores working and collect the loans we make. And make sure we don't have any spotlights on us. Period." Harley said. "There's a big shipment coming in next week from Mexico. It's the largest one we've ever gotten and I don't want anything going wrong. I don't want anybody looking at Adair County for any reason. Understand?" a pointed pause and then the phone went dead.

Ross stared at the small cell phone. *How the hell does he find out about this stuff,* he wondered.

Standing in front of Anna was a person who did not have one inch of her body that wasn't covered in wrinkles. It was as if the skin had been roasted and tanned. Her face was so wrinkled Anna had trouble making out her features. The woman weighed about 90 pounds and was completely bald.

"Ester? Is that you?" she asked timidly.

"Yes, of course, it's me. Who did you expect? What kind of ceremony?" Ester asked and opened the door for Anna to enter. She had on a crumpled, faded print gunny sack-type dress.

Anna was not excited about going into the house but knew it would be the price of the information. She walked in only to be assaulted by the pungent odor of animal urine. As soon as Ester shut the door the light dropped dramatically. The only illumination then came from the flashing of the scenes on the black-and-white television as it played some soap opera. Beams of light stabbed through the cracks in the walls and ceiling.

Ester tottered to an over-stuffed lounger with the innards working their way out and onto the floor. She sat down and only turned the volume down on the TV leaving the images dancing. She wore a breathing apparatus that fit in her nostrils but the neoprene tubing that normally led to an oxygen bottle simply dangled in the air connected to nothing.

Anna tried not to notice the sets of eyes that watched her. She didn't know what happened to the dog—at least she thought it was a dog—that was barking but she could count at least three more sets of eyeballs trained on her from various spots in the room. The torn and faded wallpaper was obscured in places by the piles of clothing and other items. She saw about 300 plastic butter tubs in one corner that were neatly heaped ready for some unforeseen emergency.

And to think I used to believe stacks of National Geographics in the garage were clutter.

Anna did not want to waste time. "Ester, do you know anything about a ceremony called the Ritual of the Flying Spirit?"

Ester acted as if she didn't hear. She looked around the room as if it were her first time to see it. Then, suddenly, she turned to Anna. "Yes, I know of it. I have only seen it performed twice. It is dangerous," she answered. "The first time I was a little girl. My grandmother performed it for a good friend of hers. The next time I was a grown woman but I did not know the man who was the traveler."

"Does it work?"

"Sometimes."

"Why is it dangerous?

"Because the heart must stop in the traveler. Sometimes it does not start again."

"What do you mean, his heart must stop?" Anna asked in disbelief.

"The traveler must reach a state of One with the Great Spirit. To do this he must reach a level of peace that can only be achieved by total submission of the body, mind and soul," Ester explained. "If the traveler is not pure, then once he reaches that state of submission, he cannot return."

"What must I do, beyond what is written, to perform the ceremony?" Anna asked nervously. She had not expected there would be a chance of physical danger attached to the event.

At that moment a screeching cry was heard and a fat Calico cat landed on Anna's shoulder. Anna sucked in a deep breath and it took all of her composure to keep from screaming and jumping to her feet.

"The happy cat likes you. That's good," Ester said.

"How nice," Anna replied. "But what must I do to make the ceremony successful? I don't want the traveler's heart to stop beating." *This woman is nuttier than a fruitcake but she's the only one who knows anything about this arcane ceremony*, she thought.

"Would you like a cookie?" Ester asked cordially as if she were entertaining at high tea.

The idea flashed in Anna's mind, *if this weren't such a nightmare, it would be funny.*

"Thank you, no. I must get back to town as soon as I learn about the ritual," Anna said.

Ester's tone changed. "Follow the sequence exactly as it is written and make sure you have all the pieces the ceremony calls for, especially the turtle," Ester said matter-of-factly and stood up. "You must leave now."

Suddenly, before Anna could protest, she was surrounded by animals all showing their teeth and advancing on her. Now she knew where the dogs were. But these were not dogs. They were full-grown Red Wolves, each weighing at least 80 pounds. She could swear she heard the hiss of a snake. She began to back toward the door.

"I don't understand about the turtle. What does it do?" she shouted to be heard over the growling wolves and hissing cats. She looked up from her aggressors for a moment and Ester was nowhere to be seen. She found the door quickly, felt the handle and slipped out while trying to block the animals from following her. She was unsuccessful and they pushed the door open and followed her out of the house.

Who was she kidding? They could have her anytime they wanted her. She ran to her truck and was happy when she was behind the locked doors. She paused to catch her breath.

The largest of the three wolves, clearly the Alpha Male, jumped on the hood and began frantically scratching the windshield, tearing the rubber from the wipers, yelping and whining at his inability to get to her.

Anna recoiled and fumbled with the keys. She started the truck but the wolf wouldn't move. It just kept barking and scratching.

I'm scared to think what the other ones are doing.

She finally realized the Alpha Male wasn't going to move and gunned her engine. The truck bucked and the wolf slid off, rolling on the ground and then recovering and running in pursuit. She sped away and watched the crazed animals in her rearview mirror sprinting after her with their mouths foaming.

When the hounds were out of sight she began to play back Ester's words. *The turtle? What turtle? I need to get her together with my grandfather. Neither of them makes any sense.*

"When was the last time they were there?" Sheriff Ross asked Deputy Cole.

"The owner said they left this morning. They were driving a big-ass Cadillac. Green. License plate XXC-344," he answered.

"Yeah, I knew he had an expensive car. I just didn't know what kind. Did you cruise around and look for it?"

"I drove to the usual places. Didn't find anything but they can't hide a car like that around a town of 2,600 people for long," said Deputy Cole.

"Put out an APB for our guys only. And here's what I want you to do if you find them," said Sheriff Ross and leaned close to his senior deputy's ear and whispered instructions about the All Points Bulletin he didn't want anyone else to hear.

Anna pulled up to Oak Grove Cemetery and Gus was waiting for her. He got in and they drove in silence from the little cemetery back to the store. The truck's darkened windows provided a certain amount of concealment from anyone looking for them. *What is he thinking*, Anna wondered as she stole a glance at Gus as they traveled.

They pulled into the alley behind the store and Gus got out and unlocked the back door then turned and tossed the keys to Anna through the truck's open window. After finding a parking space on Division, Anna entered the front door of the store. *Just a precaution in case someone was watching*, she thought.

Once inside she relocked the door and went back to the office to find Gus again reading the old Army Training Manual.

"Anna, what's the next step in the ceremony?" Gus asked.

Finally, she couldn't hold back her true feelings any longer and said, "Gus, I really wish you'd reconsider." She pulled up a chair so she could look Gus in the eyes.

Gus glanced at her quizzically.

"Look at the reality of the situation. You're talking about taking a huge risk. I've found out the ceremony itself is dangerous. Not to mention that traveling back to a time that was in turmoil. And for what?" she asked. "You've read the book on Oklahoma History so you know that the South lost the war. Your cause is lost! You see how there are some in the country who, even now, hate the Confederacy and spend all their time trying to denigrate it. We can't even fly the Confederate flag at the State Capitol."

Gus was staring at her with a furrowed brow. He seemed confused why she was launching off on such a tirade.

"And as tragic as it is, Mary Ann will die almost the same year the war ends," Anna said almost pleading.

Gus winced inside when she used Mary Ann's name as if she knew her.

"Why not stay here? We need you in Stilwell. The Cherokee Nation needs you. And this is still a young state. There's room for leadership," Anna said, her voice becoming more and more strident.

Anna moved even closer to Gus, who never let his eyes leave her, and put her hand on his arm. It was hard as steel and yet had a gentle feel to it. "Look at Austin and Phillip. I know you care about them and little Austin is a Rider descendant—I'll bet he's even named after your father," she said, now softly. "Why not make a contribution in a world that has a future? Not one that is a dying gasp of a lost era?"

Gus turned his eyes down, his face reflecting the deep concern and conflict that he obviously felt in his heart.

Realizing she had unloaded on this man with so much painful information, Anna felt drawn to him. Carefully, slowly, she stroked his cheek with
her hand. His eyes went to the caress and then back into her gaze.

Before Anna knew it, she had leaned close to him and gently touched
her lips to his.

Phillip ran around the parking lot looking under every car, finding nothing. *How could I have been so dim-witted to leave my little boy in the car
by himself,* he asked.

Horrible scenarios raced through his mind. Perhaps he was kidnapped.
What if the sheriff or one of his men took him? What if some no-good saw
the expensive car and grabbed him for a ransom?

By this time Phillip was nearly hysterical. He dashed back into the store.
"Did you see a little boy come in here?" he asked breathlessly. When the
clerk shook his head Phillip burst back outside.

He quickly began searching behind the store. He found nothing and made
his way to the trash area in the back by the trash dumpster, all the time yelling for Austin. He was screaming so frantically, he almost didn't hear the
pleading that was close to him.

"Daddy, where are you?" came a small voice from the massive trash
container.

Phillip scrambled to the top of the metal box. Throwing open the heavy
metal lid, he looked down to see his son peering back with a terrified look
and his blue jeans undone.

"My God, son, what are you doing in there?" he said almost in tears as
he reached down to lift the child out of his dungeon

Sensing his father's fear, the boy began to weep. "I'm sorry, Daddy. I
had to tee-tee. So I climbed up on a box to go in this big trashcan and I fell
and then the top slammed shut. I yelled as loud as I could."

"It's okay Austin. Don't cry. I'm not mad. I was just scared," he said as
he held the boy close to him. "Everything's okay," he said, but now more
than ever, he didn't believe it.

The civil servant remembered a cute little reporter for *The Oklahoman* he had met yesterday at Panera Bread. He had struck up a conversation while they waited in line to order. Now with a new car, his image would be changed. Maybe he would call her and give her a tip. Something that could turn into a big story for her. That could lead to a date and who knew where that would go? Things were definitely looking up.

Phillip turned the car around as soon as he could and dead reckoned his way back to the main street. Just as he had found an alleyway in a residential neighborhood that would serve to hide the car, his heart stopped as he caught a glance two blocks down the lane. It was a sheriff's car and it stopped at the same time Phillip saw it.

Without hesitation, the back-up lights came on and the patrol car did a turning maneuver and was racing down the rough alley, headlights jumping as it hit ruts and potholes.

Phillip didn't need to be told twice. "Austin, jump in the back seat and buckle up your seatbelt tight!" he ordered. Austin complied in seconds and Phillip jerked the car around and put the accelerator to the floor.

The Cadillac's powerful Northstar V-8 roared to life and the front-wheel drive sent power to the large tires pulling the car to 60 miles-per-hour in just seconds. They flew down the narrow streets of Stilwell with Phillip desperately trying to get to the open highway he had just left.

Phillip's unfamiliarity with the streets caused him to hesitate in navigating his way through town and that hesitation was catching up with him. So was the sheriff's car.

Phillip hit the highway with tires squealing. It looked blessedly clear. In his rearview mirror he could see the cruiser, lights and sirens blazing, closing on him. His only chance was to put some distance between the two before they could have other units converge on him. If that happened it was all over. They could add evading an officer along with a dozen other offenses to the trumped up charges they had waiting for him.

His car jumped as he picked up speed on the highway. Although the deputy had gained, the Cadillac was now in its element. The numbers on the digital speedometer were flashing over each other—90,105, 107. Within moments he was pushing 135 miles per hour and the car was performing beautifully, still gaining speed. Even with the engine revving madly toward its redline, the inside of the car was devoid of wind noise and was as quiet as if they were going 35 miles an hour.

The Deputy Sheriff had fallen far behind. His car would have been invisible if not for the frenetically flashing lights which could barely be seen.

"Give me another three minutes and I'll be out of his grasp," Phillip muttered.

This wasn't the first time he had been in a high-speed chase. Once, while in the Marine Corps and stationed in Abu Dhabi in the United Arab Emirates as an attaché, he had observed what appeared to be terrorists planting a bomb near the American Embassy.

Realizing they had been discovered the two men sped away and Phillip gave pursuit in the rental car that had been provided him by the embassy, all the while calling in locations and descriptions to the military security. The chase reached speeds of 100 mile per hour but in the end he was out run by a much more powerful car. The terrorists were caught shortly after and convicted and the bomb was disarmed.

But there was something distinctly different about this situation. His son wasn't in the car in Abu Dhabi.

Suddenly, hot air began streaming out of the air conditioner. No sooner than Phillip had noticed, the Cadillac began to cut out, bucking and becoming hard to handle.

"What's happening, Daddy?" Austin yelled.

At first Phillip didn't know and then it hit him. His excessive speed had damaged the air conditioner compressor and he had breached the limit that caused the factory-installed governor to shut down the engine. The deputy would be on him in a minute with the engine acting up.

"It's okay, son, the car is fine. Hang on. We're going to do a bat-turn," he yelled back. He had to get off the road and fast; he just didn't know where.

At the same time he saw ahead what looked like a Godsend. A gravel road veering off to the side. There was only one way he could make this work. He slammed on the brakes. The 4000-pound car slid nearly a hundred yards with blue smoke rising from the tires. Phillip fought to hold the car straight and, as it came to a grudging stop, the gravel road was immediately to his right. He couldn't believe his good luck.

Phillip whipped the Cadillac onto the gravel side road and hoped he could get to a hiding spot without raising a dust cloud to alert the pursuing deputy. He drove for a half-mile then saw a service road snaking into a cotton field. The stalks were high enough to hide him if no one looked too hard. He drove the car into the field to hide it.

"Austin, stay in the car. I'll be right back," he said as he rolled the windows down and got out.

He ran to the edge of the field just in time to see the sheriff's cruiser fly past, still on the highway searching for him.

Phillip ran back to the car, purposely slowing as he approached the car to try to calm Austin.

"This is really pretty fun, isn't it?" he said, not believing a word of it.

Austin brightened, his face glowing red from the heat. "Yeah, Daddy, are we going to do it again?'

"We might. It's all a game we're playing with the policeman. Sort of like hide and seek, you know?" Phillip said.

When he thought it was safe, he edged the car back on the highway and started toward Stilwell. By now, his shirt was soaked with sweat and his shoes covered with dirt.

Finally, he and Austin maneuvered the car, whose engine was now missing seriously, back to town. Phillip was once again lost as he tried to find his way through the maze of residential streets.

The car seemed to be running on two cylinders. It was missing and the electrical system was flickering sending gobbledy-gook onto the digital screens on the dash.

Anxiously, Phillip was trying to get a sense of direction. For the second time, he found himself on a dead-end street. *If this thing dies on me now, I'm as good as caught.*

He backed out and saw a street named Tahlequah lined with homes. He felt as if it were familiar, although he acknowledged it was probably wishful thinking. As he made the turn, the Cadillac began to shake uncontrollably and jerk, forcing the tires to emit short squeals.

Suddenly the engine simply stopped. The power steering ceased to work and simultaneously, the power brakes failed. Phillip struggled with the steering wheel trying to maneuver the heavy car to the curb. Unable to effectively stop the Cadillac, it bounced against the concrete curb, the scraping of the aluminum rims piercing the silence and finally came to rest half on top of the road's restraint.

"Oh, hell," he said. *What am I going to do now? I don't know anyone here so I don't know who I can trust to call. I don't even know the name of Anna's store. Let's see,* he thought as he racked his brain to visualize the front window. *Cherokee Artifacts and Spiritualism. That's it. Maybe I can get the number from Information.*

Phillip pulled out his cell phone. This time the reception was clear. "Can you give me the number of a business in Stilwell called Cherokee Artifacts and Spiritualism?" He looked around. Fortunately, the street was deserted of people with the exception of one female homeowner deadheading her flowers and a heavy man in Bermuda shorts and black socks mowing his lawn. He found himself unconsciously sucking in his stomach as he viewed the man's substantial gut hanging over the waistband of the shorts.

He could hear the operator querying his database. "Yes, here it is. Have a nice day," the plastic voice said and repeated the number. Phillip didn't want to lose the connection so he quickly dialed the number. The phone rang four times and then gave the telltale sound that signaled a switch to an answering machine.

"Sorry, we can't come to the phone. Leave a number and we'll call you back. Thanks for calling Cherokee Artifacts and Spiritualism," played the machine.

"Damn," Phillip said softly. "Come on, Austin, let's see if we can fix this old car." Happy to get out of the sweltering automobile, Austin unsnapped his belt and hopped out onto the grass. Phillip looked around. He popped the hood and stepped back as waves of heat were released from the engine compartment.

"Whew! I guess we heated this baby up," he said.

Phillip may have sounded glib but he was totally dejected. What he saw under the hood was not like the cars of the late sixties and early seventies that had provided his mechanical education. Instead, it was a solidly packed engine compartment with protective hoods over every part of it. He couldn't even find the spark plugs.

"Aw, no. What am I going to do?" he whispered to himself. *It won't be long before a cop car spots us.*

From behind, a voice said, "Having a little trouble, are you?"

Phillip jerked up from under the hood to find the lawn mowing homeowner standing with his baseball hat in his hand. He was wiping his forehead with his forearm.

"I can't believe it. This thing just stopped. I'm from out of town and I don't even know anyone to call. Is there a Cadillac dealership in town?" Phillip asked.

"Nope. Nearest one is Tulsa. Got a Ford and a Chevy dealership, though. Really only one independent garage and they're closed on Monday," the mower said.

"Why would they close on Monday?" Phillip asked trying to keep the frustration out of his voice.

"Well, they stay open on Saturday so I guess they figure it's their week-end."

"Well, it's probably too complicated for them anyway," Phillip muttered a little derisively.

"Probably so. Any idea what's wrong with it?" the man asked.

"None at all."

"Smells like you been driving it pretty hard. That so?" the man asked.

"Yeah, I guess," Phillip responded.

"These things are pretty complex but let me get a wrench," the man said and walked away.

Fine. I've got a shade tree lawnmower mechanic getting ready to work on my $50,000 car. I might as well leave it for junk.

The man returned and, after a moment of looking around the engine compartment, began to disconnect the battery.

"Go turn the key to the 'on' position and leave it there," he said authoritatively.

Phillip did as he was told.

The man raised up and said, "Now come over here and let's have a nice cold glass of water." He looked at Austin, "Would you like that?"

"Yes! I'm thirsty after we ran away from that policeman," he answered innocently.

Phillip rolled his eyes. "We were playing a game. You know, sort of like cops and robbers," he said lamely.

"Uh huh," grunted the man giving Phillip a side-glance as he led them toward his home.

Afraid of giving offense and sending the man to the telephone to call the police, Phillip took Austin's hand and followed him to the small front porch and sat in the folding chairs positioned there.

As if from nowhere, a pleasant looking woman appeared with a tray containing a pitcher of ice water and several glasses. She smiled at the strangers and set the tray down on a small table, giving the man a quick kiss on the top of his balding head.

"Thank you, sweetheart," he said.

The three drank their water and made small talk about the weather and the Oklahoma University football squad and their national ranking in the polls. Not once did the man ask a question about Austin's remark.

After ten minutes, he said cryptically, "Well, let's see if that did it." The trio returned to the car.

The man said, "Get in and turn the key off." Again, Phillip did as he was told.

The man went under the hood, reconnected the battery cable and said, "Try it now."

Phillip turned the key and the engine roared to life. The dashboard screens told him all systems were "go."

Phillip got out. "That's amazing! What did you do?" he asked.

"It was really nothing. The computer controls everything. We just forced it to reset itself," the man said smiling. "You won't have any air conditioning, though. It sounds like you may have blown the compressor."

"The guy who owns the garage better look out for you. You're big time competition!" Phillip said cheerfully.

"Oh, he doesn't have to worry. I'm the guy who owns the garage." The man grinned.

Phillip's face was red with embarrassment. Once again he had underestimated the people in this small town. "Well, can I at least pay you?" Phillip pleaded.

"Sorry. The garage is closed on Monday." He beamed and walked away waving over his shoulder.

Surely, I can find my way to Anna's little store. The car's running, we've evaded the cops, at least for a while, and this town can't be that big. He carefully meandered his way through the quiet neighborhood streets. He came to an intersection and after carefully weighing his options decided to let Austin in on the decision.

"Okay, son. Which way do we turn? This way or that?" he said pointing his finger from one side to the other.

"Hmmm. Let's go that way," Austin said and aiming his hand to the right.

"Aye, aye, sir," Phillip said to Austin's delight. He turned the corner and suddenly felt strange. Instantly, he was weak and wanted to throw up. *It was a good thing he hadn't eaten so there was nothing to vomit*, he thought. Then it hit him. *Oh, my God. I haven't eaten. In all the excitement my adrenalin must have kept my blood sugar up and now it's fallen.*

His first thought was to measure it but he remembered the test kit was back at the motel. He'd have to listen to what his body was telling him and his body was saying he wasn't far from passing out and slipping into a diabetic coma. *Should he stop the car to prevent having a wreck? No, then Austin would be helpless.*

He reached for his glucose pills but those, too, were back at the motel. Experience told him he didn't have much time. He was profoundly frightened about his situation and that anxiety was no doubt exacerbating his condition. He knew Austin thought something was wrong but was afraid to say anything. *Maybe there was a drug store but where?*

He looked ahead and saw a small roadside store. He pulled the Cadillac in, hitting the concrete parking stop, the car jumping back. Without saying a word he stumbled into the store. There was staleness in the air found in many stores of that type that lack regular cleaning. The disinterested clerk did not acknowledge him.

"You got any glucose tablets?" he said with a thick tongue. It wouldn't be long before he passed out. He estimated his blood sugar in the low 50s.

The clerk looked at him dumbly. "Got what?" she said blankly.

"Glucose——never mind," he said and turned. Before him was a candy rack. He quickly moved to it and grabbed three dusty Hershey chocolate bars. *Maybe it will work*, he thought in panic.

He threw a five-dollar bill on the counter and lunged to the car, getting into the driver's side. He struggled with the new fangled plastic wrapper and finally tore open the candy bar and devoured them. Within minutes his body began to recover with his heart rate calming and his dizziness fading. *That was close. Too close*, he thought. He was unaware that Austin had scrambled into the front seat and had been watching him in awe. "Daddy, how come you didn't save one for me?" Austin asked in amazement. Surprised at Austin's close proximity and even in his state, Phillip couldn't help but smile.

Re-energized, Phillip found his way to Anna's store and parked in the alley.

"We've got problems," he said as she opened the door for him. "The deputy who is Ross' henchman was at the motel when I went by. They've got us under surveillance. It won't be long now until we're surrounded.

"Plus, I just had one chase me. I outran him but I doubt my car will do it again. I may need to hide it," Phillip panted.

"Daddy, I'm still hungry," Austin implored.

"The child hasn't had a thing all day except some cold chicken and some lemonade. Okay, son, hang on for a little while longer. Just like a real scout, okay?" Phillip said.

Austin looked at his father and then at Gus. Gus smiled and nodded and Austin showed a look of fierce determination at the challenge.

Anna leaned close to Phillip and whispered, "Why don't we let him go to my friend Donna Still's? She's my dearest friend and her girls are at camp until next week when school starts. He'll be safe with her until we can get this sorted out."

Phillip was not crazy about sending Austin with someone he didn't know but it seemed like a safer idea for him than staying. He nodded his consent and Anna picked up the phone.

"Son, I'm going to send you to spend the night with Miss Donna. She's real nice and she'll feed you supper and then I'll come get you. Okay?" Phillip said to Austin.

Before Austin could protest, Gus said, "Do this, and be brave, and I'll make you a full scout. Good enough?"

Austin nodded. Within what seemed like only minutes a knock came at the back door and Donna Still appeared, properly briefed and ready to take Austin.

"Let's take some fun books with us, shall we Austin?" she asked.

"Sure, I was reading these but I fell asleep," Austin said and ran to the alcove to retrieve the books he had started earlier in the day. Almost as quickly as she had arrived, Donna spirited Austin away.

Phillip was left with a strange feeling of relief coupled with anxiety. Once again he was reminded time was running out.

"Anna, I need to stash that Cadillac. Everybody is going to be looking for it now," Phillip said as Austin left.

Anna thought for a moment and then said, "It can go in my garage. Come on and follow me.

"Gus, we'll be gone for just a minute."

Gus nodded his assent.

The two left the store and took their small convoy to Anna's house. She stopped in the street and activated the garage door. Phillip got the idea and drove straight in. He locked the car and then ran out and got in the SUV.

"Did I hear you say you were in the Marine Corps?" Anna asked as they drove back to the store.

"Yeah, for three years," he said.

"Why the Marines?"

"Oh, I guess I liked the challenge. It wasn't something just anyone could do," he replied.

"So, you and Gus must have a lot in common?" she wondered.

"Some things. But Gus has fought a far more brutal war than I ever have. The fact that he's survived tells you how tough—and smart he must be."

Anna seemed to ponder that as they pulled into the alley of the store.

"General Gay?" inquired the pleasant voice on the phone.

"Yes, this is Nelson Gay."

"This is Tammy Kern. I'm a reporter for *The Oklahoman*," the young woman said. "I'm inquiring into a situation in Stilwell that involves your office."

Good grief! How could she know that? We just started talking about it this morning.

"You'll have to be more specific," Gay sidestepped. *Was she on a fishing trip?*

"Well, we just heard that your office was conducting an investigation in that area. What can you tell me about it?" she persisted.

"Ms. Kern, as I'm sure you know we do not confirm or deny that any investigation is underway. Likewise, we do not discuss ongoing investigations," he said in friendly manner. "Perhaps I might refer you to our Public Information Officer for background on areas that we can discuss?"

"Okay, I have his number. Thanks," she said and hung up.

We dodged a bullet on that one. A more experienced reporter would have handled it differently. She would have been sitting across from me and wouldn't have taken no for an answer.

But now there was a bigger problem. Gay picked up the phone and hit a speed dial number. Immediately, OSBI Director David answered.

"You're not the only one with someone working undercover," Gay said. "I just got a call from what sounded like a cub reporter at *The Oklahoman* wanting to know about our interest in activities in Stilwell.

"Any idea how she found out three hours after our conversation? It could be someone on this end as well."

"You're kidding me? No, I don't have any idea but I'm going to find out fast," David said. "I'll call you back."

As soon as the receiver hit the cradle it rang again. "Yes?' answered Nelson Gay with an irritated tone.

"Sir," said the receptionist apologetically, "The senator from Stilwell is on the phone. He seems very angry and insists on speaking to you."

Deputy Cole was driving in an ever-expanding circle around Stilwell when he saw Donna Still's Honda pull up to a stop sign. One of the convenient things about living in a small town like Stilwell was you knew everyone, knew their kids and could recognize new people, even children, easily.

He thought he saw a little boy in the back seat. Ordinarily this wouldn't have made a difference but with the outsiders in town that the sheriff was looking for, and the fact that the deputy knew Donna Still only had two girls, maybe this meant something after all.

He followed at a safe distance and watched as Donna pulled into her driveway, got out and unbuckled the little boy then led him by the hand inside.

Instead of picking up his radio, the deputy pulled out his cell phone and punched in a few numbers.

"What are we going to do about Gus, Anna?" Phillip asked. "I don't think we have another 24 hours before the sheriff and his guys nab us. If we're going to try this crazy stunt to get Gus back then we better get after it. If it doesn't work then we'll go to Plan B."

Both Anna and Gus looked at him.

"It will work," Gus said. "There is no Plan B."

Anna sighed. "It very well could work. These ceremonies are tremendously powerful. Don't ask me how. I can't explain it and someone unfamiliar with the traditional Cherokee culture would never understand."

This is incredible. I can't believe I'm acting like I think it can happen, she thought.

"Well, Gus, are you determined to try this?" Phillip asked.

Anna held her breath.

"Yes," Gus said and paused. "I must go."

"This is crazy but let's do something even if it's wrong," said Philip out of frustration. Perhaps if they could get this behind them then Gus would consider other options. As it was, he was adamant that this was the only solution.

"Very well," said Anna resignedly.

Nelson Gay sat and stared at his wall. It was the home of numerous awards and honors all attesting to his contributions to law and order. He could remember the events surrounding each of them.

But now he was faced with one of the greatest decisions of his life. His friend was right. He could stay as AG or he could take a leap and go for the U.S. Senate where he could have a real impact on not just Oklahoma but the entire nation. But within hours of the meeting with those who would form the core of his support he found himself in a situation that might force him to do exactly what he promised them he would not do.

He considered his options. He could back off this investigation since it had been on-going by the OSBI for sometime already, and let it run its course. The threat to Phillip and his son was probably exaggerated. The inquiry would be concluded after his term as AG was finished. He could still claim credit even it he was in the Senate.

If he didn't back off now, the support, that was so crucial to win a senate seat, could be lost. But on the other side of the coin, what if Phillip Michaels and his boy really were in trouble? It was a dilemma he was not happy about facing—one that pitted his future against his present.

"We should start about seven. First, we must go back to Oak Grove Cemetery and Gus can pray there. That's the first step," Anna said and then turned to Gus. "And now that I know a little about you, I can tell you that the cemetery was donated years ago by your family, Gus, so that's sacred ground for you. We can conduct the rest of the ceremony there. We have to be there after midnight, on the 18[th,] under the Bloodmoon."

"There is one more thing," Gus said.

"What?" Anna asked with disbelief in her eyes.

"I think I now understand why I have been sent here. And I think I also understand what I must do, what aid I must provide," he said. There was a poignant pause then Gus said, "I must go back and I must take this with me." He held up the book and the photograph of the M-60 machine gun.

Anna exploded, "What? Are you crazy, Gus? They're illegal unless you're in the Army. I don't know where we'd ever get one. And I don't know how you would work it. And I'm not even sure the ritual will work if you introduce an alien element into it.

"You're asking too much."

"It must be so. Phillip, can you help me? Will you help me?" Gus implored.

Phillip's face was red. "Gus, now your plan is putting everyone at risk! And if this works, you'll be back home and we'll be the ones that can be arrested."

Suddenly, he thought of all that Gus was going to go through. A battle in which he could be killed. Unspeakable hardships regardless of the outcome of the fight and a struggle just to survive when the South was defeated. In a second he found himself ashamed of his self-centeredness and without further delay said, "Yes, I'll do it."

Anna was not ready to acquiesce so easily and had one last attempt to dissuade. "Gus," Anna said in an inquisitive tone, "when you arrived here did you have everything you left with?"

Gus looked perplexed.

"Look, you were a soldier. You were in the middle of a battle. Weren't you carrying a knife or a gun or some kind of weapon?" she asked.

Gus thought for a moment and then answered, "Yes, I had both a pistol and a Bowie knife. Why?"

"And you didn't have them when you arrived here?" Anna said making her point. "I don't think you can transport such things as weapons through time."

"Well, here's another twist," Phillip interjected seeing where Anna was going. "Gus, I assume you want to take the machine gun with you to influence the course of the battle you were in, right?"

"Yes," Gus said, "that's correct."

"Well, you can't change history. Don't you know that? It's already been written. You saw it in the book," Phillip said.

"Phillip, do you not think history has been changed before? The elders have been traversing time for centuries. Each time that happens, something is changed. Maybe small things that we don't notice but they are altered by their mere presence," Gus said.

"But you saw it already written in the book!" Phillip persisted.

"That was a book of this reality. If I'm successful, then the book will be rewritten to reflect the new reality," Gus explained.

"I see what Gus is saying," Anna spoke up, keeping her eyes on Gus. She was beginning to waver. "He's saying that it's part of the Creator's overall plan. That's why he allows the ritual to work. He has given us free will to make our own decisions and to correct our own mistakes. Here is a chance to correct a mistake. I don't know why the outcome of the battle should be otherwise than it was—and we don't have any guarantee that, even after all of this, it won't be exactly as it occurred in the history we know—but we are exercising our free will to attempt to influence happenings."

Phillip gave a long sigh and gently shook his head like someone who had given up arguing and said wearily as if the conversation had not taken place, "This is nuts to even be discussing such a ridiculous idea. The whole thing is insane but we're all so far in now I don't see any other alternative. "Okay,"

Phillip said and appeared to be deep in thought. "The first thing we'll have to do is find out where the nearest arsenal is. Anna, is there a National Guard Armory in Stilwell?"

"Yes, it's down by the high school. I've never been inside, though. I know they have a large area and sometimes use it for grade school basketball games or banquets," Anna said smiling.

"That would be the drill hall. But we're going to need to get into the room that has the weapons," Phillip said. "We're not going to be able to start the ceremony until we can breach the armory and we've got to wait until late before we try."

"How late?" Anna asked.

"At least until ten," Phillip said. "Then we go. We'll enter under the cover of darkness and hopefully, be out within an hour."

"I know why I'm doing this but why are you?" Anna asked Phillip.

"I think it's crazy and I don't think it will work. But this guy saved my child's life yesterday. It's real simple," Phillip said.

"But why you?" he asked.

"I don't know that you'd ever understand but somehow I've known this was coming for a long time," Anna responded.

"Oh, brother," sighed Phillip.

"Have you ever heard of a Cherokee word *gadugi*?

Phillip shook his head *no*.

"It's a concept—one of family and community. It's the essence of Cherokee society. The group bands together for the good of our brothers. That's part of the reason," Anna said trying to explain a complicated idea in just a few words.

Phillip smiled but said nothing.

CHAPTER FIFTEEN

OSBI Director David was driving home when he decided at the last minute to stop by and see his neighbor, Charlie Burnett, the sales manager at the local Nissan dealership. The dealership was always open late and he remembered that today was Charlie's day to close. They had a golf game planned for Sunday and somehow, after the week he was having, David felt he'd be ready for it.

He pulled into the parking lot and walked into the opulent building. He could see Charlie through the glass windows of his office. He was in a meeting but saw David and waved his recognition. David waved back and decided to use that waiting time to admire the new automobiles on the showroom floor.

He began to examine a beautiful new 350Z, the latest Nissan $30,000 sports offering capable of 165 miles an hour. He slowly ambled around the car letting his fingertips lightly follow the contour of the body, marveling at the plush leather interior and the deep, perfect metallic paint. Its angular outline reminded David of a Stealth Bomber, which was obviously the intent of the designers.

Daydreaming how someday he might be able to afford an automobile like this when his kids were out of college, he noticed this particular car had already been sold and had a paper tag, a temporary cardboard license plate.

Those plates usually listed the purchaser. David couldn't help himself. He always wondered who was successful enough to own one of these cars. He leaned over and, out of curiosity, read the name of the buyer.

Suddenly, everything made sense.

Phillip looked at his watch. It was 10 p.m.

"It's time. Anna, will you drive us to the armory? We've got to recon the target," Phillip said. He was surprised at how the old Marine jargon was quickly infecting his speech.

"I'll do it but you're just asking for it, both of you," Anna admonished, her forehead furrowed with concern. "You may be committing a federal crime. If you get caught they'll lock you under the jail!"

Anna had anticipated the need to execute unobserved exits and entrances and had parked her SUV in the alley close to her back door. The three slipped out of the store and the men, as Anna got into the driver's seat, crawled onto the floor of the truck. Even though it had tinted windows that made seeing inside more difficult, especially at night, there was no sense in taking a chance.

She slowly maneuvered the SUV three blocks to the intersection that framed the mixed brown brick building, which served as the National Guard Armory. The night was still and humid. Even though the building was shrouded in darkness there were flashes of light when clouds drifted across momentarily exposing the moon. The moonlight briefly illuminated the walls and the stark sign highlighting the famed 45th Infantry Division insignia planted in the front lawn. It reminded Gus of another night.

"That looks like circa 1950. All of their wiring for an alarm system is likely to be exposed. That might make it easier," Phillip said. "Can you circle the building again?"

"Only once or we'll have every resident around here calling in reporting terrorists," Anna said.

"What are terrorists?" Gus asked.

Phillip and Anna exchanged glances. "You don't want to know, Gus," Phillip said.

Once more they made a careful loop around the armory with Phillip writing frenetically in a small notebook. He noted the windows, barred from the inside and the window air-conditioning units that protruded from the window frames. The tall, barbed wire topped fence surrounded the back portion of the compound.

The three began the return trip to the store. They approached a four-way stop at the corner of Second and Division and, even though it was late at night with not many cars on the road, Anna dutifully stopped. Arriving at the stop on her left at exactly the same time was a black-and-white Sheriff's Department cruiser.

"Oh, Lord. Please make this someone who doesn't know my car," Anna whispered.

The cruiser didn't move. Anna didn't move. Both cars sat, waiting for the other to take the first step. Finally, Anna couldn't stand it and nudged the SUV forward. The deputy did the same and they both stopped a few feet into the intersection. It was a standoff.

"Oh, to hell with it," Anna said and drove across the crossroads watching her rearview mirror to see if the cruiser would turn after her. Instead it remained in place for a few seconds as if its driver were contemplating what to do, then crossed the street and continued on its own route.

"We're going to need some equipment, Anna," Phillip said reviewing his list.

"Whatever I have, you can have. What do you need?" she replied.

"To start with, how about a ladder?"

"I've got one," Anna said.

"And some wire cutters, a pry bar, some Allen wrenches, WD-40 and maybe some bolt cutters," Phillip said.

"Well, I think I have most of that," Anna said as she mentally took inventory of the tools she kept at the store. "Let's go look in the office. Be careful and follow me. Don't knock anything over," she warned as they wound their way in the dark to the office where they could shield any light from the outside.

Anna pulled out a battered metal tool kit and started to lift it on to the counter. Gus quickly grabbed the obviously heavy box and placed it on top of the desk.

Surprised at such a show of gallantry Anna uttered a "Thank you, Gus." Gus did not respond nor acknowledge the comment.

"This tool box has been here for at least fifty years. It was here when I bought the shop and I've just thrown tools that I've bought over the years in it so no telling what you'll find," she said.

Deftly, Phillip began sorting through the box, pulling various items out and laying them out on the desk. He paused to look at one item, a miniature grappling hook, and started to ask Anna where she got it and then just decided to take it.

"This should do it," he said. "Have you got a back pack or knapsack of some kind we can use to carry this stuff in?"

Anna quickly found an army surplus pack and the two men loaded the tools into it.

" I guess that will do it. Now we just need some luck," Phillip said. He could feel the tension building inside of him. He was becoming involved in something that he not only was ill prepared for but also was unsure of its chances of success.

Just before they started to leave Phillip held up his hand. "We need some camouflage. What can we use? Got any make-up, Anna?"

Anna wasn't sure if it was a joke but said, "No, you don't need it when you're a natural beauty." She smiled. "But I think this will work for what you want." She took them to an old fireplace in the back of the store. It hadn't been used in years but still had a film of soot on it.

The two men knelt down and began rubbing the soot on their faces.

"Phillip, I'll bet this is the first time you've ever put on war paint," Gus said.

Not only was it the singular attempt at humor Gus had made but also it was the first time he had called Phillip by name.

Phillip couldn't keep from laughing. "I think you've got us all doing things for the first time," he said. The tension was broken; the men finished their cover-up and moved to the SUV.

Once again, the truck made its way to the "target," this time unloading its cargo silently and quickly in the darkest area surrounding the armory and then promptly exiting.

The two men quietly inched around the corner of the aged building. It appeared to be unoccupied. No lights were on nor were there any civilian cars in the parking lot.

"Most armories have security, someone who watches the place," Phillip whispered.

"Yes, I know what security is. We call them pickets," Gus replied. Even in the dark Phillip felt the flush of embarrassment. Gus knew more about combat than Phillip would ever learn.

"Well, it looks like we lucked out on this one. Let's see if we can find a place we can enter," Phillip said.

The men crept to the back of the building that was obscured by tall oak trees and then Gus pointed to the windows.

"Those cages around the windows are damn near impenetrable. The only way you can get in is to cut them with a welding torch. But if this is one of the few armories that hasn't been updated, then we can get onto the roof and try to go down through it," Phillip said.

"What do you mean?" Gus replied clearly confused.

"The new government rules require buildings that house weapons to have a metal roof so you can't break in. But this is an old armory and may have escaped the requirement. Only way to know is to go up and look. But first, we've got to disarm the alarm system," Phillip said. The two searched until they found the alarm bell located under a roof outcropping.

"This kind has to be disarmed at the power source," he said as he followed the alarm wires as they snaked their way to a power pole. Look, see that metal covering?" he said pointing to a metal jacket that enclosed a powerline running down the pole. "Dead giveaway."

Phillip went over and using his crowbar bent the thin metal covering back to expose the alarm's power cable. "If we're lucky this will be like the Kirby Drug Store system and not their competitor the Stewart Drug Store system."

"What's the difference?" Gus asked.

"The Kirby system just goes dead if it loses power. But the Stewart system notifies a central location that power has been lost so they can dispatch repairmen," Phillip answered.

"Oh," Gus said. "How do you know these things?"

"I'm an architect. A designer of buildings. I work with these systems all the time."

Phillip pulled back the cover even more and, after putting a small flashlight in his mouth and covering his head and the wires with a black cloth to shield the light, he began to work. The summer evening had cooled the air but it was still humid when covered by a cloth. Streams of sweat found their way to Phillip's eyes and he could hardly keep them open as the salt caused streaks of pain. His jaw was beginning to hurt from being extended to accommodate the flashlight. His mouth was filling with drool, a natural reaction to the overextended jaw.

He tried to breathe in and unintentionally sucked in a mouthful of the accumulated saliva and began an involuntary coughing spree. The flashlight was expelled and fell to the ground. Phillip was fiercely trying to overcome the natural reflex to cough.

Gus looked around nervously hoping the noise wouldn't give their activities away. In just a moment Phillip regained control and all was quiet. Gus grabbed the flashlight and handed the tool back to him. Phillip nodded and re-covered his head and resumed his work.

Finally, he had separated the gaggle of wiring and found the two main wires. *Please be a Kirby system, not a Stewart system, he thought. I'll be damned if I can tell which it is by just looking at it.*

"Hey," he whispered to his partner, "get ready to run if this bell goes off."

Phillip reached for the wire cutters, put them on the red wire, took a breath and then squeezed.

"Come on, Austin," Donna Still said as she watched the little boy finish his dinner. "You can sleep in the big bed tonight. It's very comfortable. Then your Dad will come and get you in the morning."

"Where is my Daddy? He doesn't like to be away from me," Austin said.

"Oh, I know that! But he's working with Mrs. Whitebear on a very important project and they may work so long that he thought it would be best if you spent the night here. Then you wouldn't have to stay up late," Donna said. "That was very thoughtful of him, wasn't it?"

"My Daddy is a good daddy," Austin said seriously.

Donna ushered the child in to brush his teeth and then led the boy to the bed, handed him a pair of pajamas she had bought for her nephew and said, "Now, get into these and I'll be back in to say your prayers with you."

Austin complied and within moments she was tucking him under the sheets.

"At night we sleep with the windows open and the attic fan running. You'll have a nice breeze here," she said.

Austin watched as she turned the light out and just before sleep overtook him, he wondered what an attic fan was.

The knock on the door startled the civil servant. He was just getting ready to go to bed. He walked to the front door and looked through the peephole. He was surprised to see some men he recognized from the OSBI.

"What is it?" he asked without opening the door.

"OSBI. Open the door," came the response. This was clearly not a social call.

He quickly looked around to make sure no incriminating material was around and cracked the door.

"What's this all about?" he asked the men.

"Just open the door," the agents said.

"Alright, just let me put on some clothes," he answered shutting the door.

He went to the bedroom and opened the window and then slipped under the bed.

Within moments the doorjamb splintered, as it was forced in. The police raced through the house and ended up in his bedroom. They immediately spotted the open window and the curtains blowing into the room. Without stopping to check, one broadcast into his walkie-talkie.

"He's bailed out the back. Call in the helicopter and have it start combing the neighborhood." They bolted out of the room and outside the front door.

The civil servant carefully emerged from under the bed. He grabbed his billfold and car keys and tried to plot his next move. He needed to get out of the house before they came back to start searching the place. He decided he would boldly walk out as if nothing were wrong, get in his car and drive to the airport and then maybe catch a plane out. Or maybe it would be smarter to abandon the car and catch a bus to Dallas where he could get a new identity.

He looked up and standing in the doorway leaning against the door jam was one of the agents who had broken in.

"Trying to figure out what to do next?" the agent asked casually.

Before the civil servant could answer he was on the floor with his arms being pinned behind him. He felt the cold bite of the handcuffs as they were clamped down.

The agent spoke into his two-way and within moments the little house was swarmed by a small army of specialists taking photographs, checking his computer, drawers, telephones and answering machines.

The civil servant let his face sink two inches to the floor and closed his eyes. He knew what was ahead of him. And most of all, he knew he would never see his beautiful new 350Z and that for him it would always be a chimera.

CHAPTER SIXTEEN

The sharp snap of the wire cutters caused Phillip to inhale quickly. He expected to be greeted within nanoseconds by the earsplitting siren of the alarm. Instead, there were only the gasps of his own labored breathing and the hum of night gnats as they feasted on the rivulets of sweat that trickled down his neck. He still didn't know if the system was sending a signal to a control center alerting them to the lost power. But at this point he had to proceed as if it were safe.

The two men quickly receded into the shadows and surveyed the neighborhood to see if any lights came on. The houses remained dark.

They stepped back out into the open and looked up at the armory's flat roof. It was a good sixteen feet above the ground and Phillip set up the fold-out ladder they had brought from Anna's store.

"It's going to be a stretch. If we stand on the top rung we can reach the top. Then we'll have to pull ourselves over and hoist the ladder up. When we're ready to leave, we'll lower it back down again," Phillip said.

"If everything goes as planned, right?" Gus smiled. It was clear he knew things rarely went as planned. They attached a rope to the top of the ladder to allow them to pull it up after them.

"I'll go first. I'm taller," Gus said and scrambled up the ladder with Phillip holding it steady. He made the move look relatively easy, grabbing the top of the roof's ledge and smoothly lifting himself over, then signaled for Phillip to proceed.

Phillip started up the ladder carefully. Without the extra support provided by someone holding it, the ladder seemed fatally unstable. Phillip's progress slowed.

"What's wrong?" Gus whispered.

"I'm afraid this thing is going to slip out from under me," Phillip said softly.

Gus extended his hand to Phillip but he was not yet high enough to reach it.

Phillip was standing on the next to the last rung of the ladder. Trying to grasp onto the outcroppings of rocks on the building's façade, he pushed himself to the last step. Wavering, he reached for Gus's hand and was relieved when the strong grip confirmed he had made a connection.

"I'm going to pull you up on 'three'. Hang onto the rope so we don't lose the ladder. One, two, three!" Gus said and gave a robust tug. Phillip, at the same time, pulled and could feel himself being lifted. He could also feel something else. The ladder was indeed, slipping out from under him.

Phillip found himself dangling halfway to the roof with the rope to the falling ladder in one hand and Gus's life grip in the other. Gus was struggling to hold on and Phillip's left arm felt as if it were being pulled from its socket. His backpack suddenly seemed tremendously heavy.

"Drop the ladder!" Gus said. "I can't hold you and the ladder."

He complied and the aluminum ladder clattered to the ground. He reached up and grabbed Gus's arm with his other hand. Both were powerful men but it took their combined strength to hold on.

His muscles straining, Gus hauled Philip over the transom and both fell to the roof gasping for air. After catching their breath they both sat up looking at each other with an unspoken question.

Phillip peered over the roof's parapet and took a last glance to make sure no one observed them. He saw the ladder crumpled on the ground then he spotted a car turning the corner, its headlights wiping across the armory. Phillip ducked. He was still breathing heavily. Not used to the exertion or the pressure, the stress was beginning to show. He listened intently to hear if the engine indicated the car was slowing or stopping. Instead, it drove by without reducing speed, oblivious to the armory or its uninvited visitors.

"How the hell are we going to get down when it's time to leave?" Phillip wondered out loud.

"Have faith, Phillip. We'll find a way," Gus said.

"Come on. Let's find a soft place to enter," Phillip replied.

The two crawled on their hands and knees around the roof, testing for a weak spot in the structure.

"Here! Look," Gus said and pushed with his hand, showing an area that sank with the pressure indicating that the structure was rotten.

Quickly and silently the two began to rip the tarred covering exposing the wooden trusses. Taking the saw from the backpack, they launched the tedious job of cutting away the wood to make a hole large enough to allow entry. Finally, they had cleared enough of an opening for a man to fit into.

"Can you see anything?" Gus asked as Phillip leaned into the hole with his flashlight.

"It's just a room. Nothing special. But it's a standard eight-foot ceiling. Lower me down and I'll only have a couple of feet to drop."

Gus lowered Phillip and let him fall the short distance to the floor. Phillip quickly moved a desk under the hole and Gus lowered himself down.

The room had two doors. One was metal and securely locked. The men tried the other. It opened easily and they suddenly found themselves on a balcony overlooking a vast empty hall.

"What is this?" Gus asked in disbelief.

Phillip smiled, remembering his Marine Corps days. "It's the Flying Bridge. They use it to hang flags for ceremonies."

The two stood gazing over the wall of the Flying Bridge. Phillip began to walk down the length of the loggia. When Gus turned toward him, he was gone.

"Phillip! Where are you?" Gus said, alarmed.

A painful groan came from below. Gus looked down and saw a three-foot square opening. Metal rungs led down from it protruding from the wall. On the third one hung a dazed and bleeding Phillip.

Gus scaled the rungs with the agility of a chimpanzee and reached Phillip, untangling him and helping him to the floor below.

"What happened?"

"I'm an idiot," he groaned. "I forgot the Flying Bridge has an open hatch to descend to the floor. Usually it's covered but not this time. That's a ten-foot drop. It could have broken my neck.

"I can't move my left arm," Phillip said finally after catching his breath. "I don't think it's broken but it may be dislocated. I'll just have to make do.

"Come on, let's see what we can find," he said to Gus. They moved slowly across the darkened expanse of the drill hall, feeling their way along the wall. Phillip's hand hit something and he could feel it move. A scratching sound followed. He quickly grabbed at it and just barely stopped the downward fall of what must have been a photograph.

He seized the frame with his good arm and held it tight to the wall, his heavy panting the only sound echoing up and down the hallway. He slowly lowered it until it rested on the floor. Confident it was safely situated, the two continued until they reached what appeared to be a padlocked room with a heavy steel screen across the door. By now, his eyes had adjusted to the dark. Phillip removed the bolt cutters from his pack and guided them as they bit into the lock, breaking it in two.

The air conditioning was off for the night and the temperature had risen to over 100 degrees inside the building. The heat and stagnant air were stifling and already the men's clothes were becoming soaked. Finally, after nearly thirty minutes of cutting, they pushed open the heavy metal door and crept into the solidly locked weapons store that housed rifles, pistols and machine guns. There was a strange odor in the air. Gus was in awe of such a display of armaments but it didn't keep him from methodically moving through the room looking for the ideal weapon.

Suddenly, Gus froze as if he heard something.

"What is it?" Phillip whispered.

"We're not alone," he said and slowly, his movement barely perceptible, turned his head to look into the dark. He and Phillip saw it at the same time. Two glowing marbles in the dark.

Before either could say a word the dots grew exponentially and were accompanied by a rough, guttural noise.

With a primal growl, the 100-pound pit bull leapt for Gus. The man blocked the dog's assault with his arm. It only provided a handle for the animal to lock onto. The canine's weight and the momentum of his attack slammed Gus against the locker. The pit bull was shaking his head ferociously, trying to tear the flesh off the arm. Gus desperately struggled to keep the dog from reaching his neck.

Phillip didn't know what else to do so he reverted to his Marine training. He jerked the small grappling hook from his pack and used it to seize the dog's collar. With all his strength he twisted it tightly to choke the dog. It didn't seem to slow the crazed creature's viciousness. Still, Phillip kept trying to deprive it of oxygen.

Gus was losing the battle with the beast as well. Frothing with rage, the watchdog inched closer to his neck. If it could get close enough to sink its teeth, it would be all over.

"Stop this bastard," Gus yelled.

"I'm trying!" Phillip responded and, mustering all his strength, gave the grappling hook another strong twist.

This time the dog emitted a loud coughing noise. Spittle spewed from its mouth. Without further resistance, it collapsed on the floor. Phillip and Gus backed away from the animal and Phillip shone his flashlight on him. The pit bull wasn't dead but was close to it.

"That will keep him down a few hours," Phillip said. They sat exhausted beside the comatose animal. "Let's go before something else jumps us," Phillip said breathlessly and the two dragged themselves out of the arms store.

Again, the two began feeling their way along the wall. Phillip turned. "How can you see anything in here? I can barely see my hand in front of my face."

"I'm used to it. I work a lot in the dark. Look at this. Use your light," Gus said.

Phillip complied and focused his flashlight on the spot indicated. There it was. An M-60 machine gun. The weapon was probably Vietnam vintage but was still a deadly killing tool.

A chain ran through the trigger guard and secured the M-60 to the rack. Phillip quickly snipped one of the links and allowed the chain to slide free. It instantly broadcast a small but biting sound. The two men froze and stared at each other for an instant. When no alarm was raised, Gus gently lifted the 18-pound machine gun.

Philip looked around and whispered, "You're going to need these."

Walking softly to another locked closet with a griddled wire front and, using his wire cutters again, Phillip removed the padlock. He reached inside and pulled out a green metal box labeled .62 *caliber ball ammunition.*

"You have to have something to shoot," he said tiredly. Gus only nodded and took the box.

"What are you doing?" he asked as he saw Phillip replace the disabled locks they had cut.

"It might buy us a little time. If they come in and see the locks are missing, they'll know immediately they've been robbed. This way it might take a few more hours before they notice the lockers have been tampered with and sound the alarm. By then it may be too late for them to stop us," Phillip said. "That is, if the damn dog isn't dead when they arrive in the morning.

"Now, let's get out of here before our luck runs out. We've already been attacked once and we've only been here a few minutes. Follow me."

Keeping an eye on the sleeping dog they headed out into the corridor securing the door behind them. As soon as they hit the darkened corridor,

Phillip stopped in mid-tracks. A blinking red light stared down at him from the ceiling.

Just as they started to leave the room something caught Phillip's eye. He turned and said, "Oh, hell."

"What is it?"

Phillip pointed to a tiny red light in the corner of the ceiling. "We're being videotaped."

Gus looked at him quizzically and said softly, "What does being videotaped mean?"

"Our photograph is being taken. That's a camera up there," he pointed. "We've got to find the recorder and erase it or we might as well make our reservation for prison."

Phillip began to follow the wiring as it rose into the ceiling. He struggled up on a metal locker and raised the ceiling panels that had been installed in a recent renovation, tracing the cable with his flashlight. He climbed down and said, "It looks like it goes this way," and began to walk to the point the cable disappeared into the wall.

They continued to follow the wiring into another room, with Phillip periodically getting a boost from Gus and searching under the acoustic ceiling tiles. After rummaging around for an hour, the two discovered themselves in front of the administration office that housed the staff who ran the armory.

Phillip tried the metal door. It was securely locked. "Well, I don't know how to pick a lock so our only option is to force it open. I'm afraid the noise will give us away," he said.

"I have an idea," Gus said. "How much room is there between the ceiling and the roof?"

"Not much. Maybe 12 to 18 inches. Why?"

"I can slip through up there," Gus said.

"No, Gus, you're too big for that," Phillip said.

"I've done it before," Gus said with steely eyes.

Phillip thought, *what do I know? No telling what this guy has done.*

"Okay, let's do it," Phillip said.

Quickly, the two men rigged a platform by moving some trophy cases under the door. Gus scampered up on them, careful to put his weight on the frame rather than the glass top, and raised the ceiling panels.

"Let me have your lantern," he said to Phillip who passed up the flashlight.

Gus peered above the panels and illuminated the ceiling. He was grateful to find the wall did not extend to the roof but stopped at about 15 inches short. He pulled himself over the partition, careful to not put any weight on the false ceiling. He was precariously balanced on the wall. If he moved forward, he would fall the ten feet to the floor. If he moved back, he would crash into the glass trophy cases.

He took the flashlight and fleetingly lit up the office. The desks and file cabinets were positioned several feet away. There was nothing to break a fall except a linoleum covered concrete floor. His options seemed clear. He propelled himself over the wall and dove to the floor head first, trying to roll when he hit to avoid breaking his neck.

Donna went into the kitchen and began to prepare the coffee pot for the next morning. She loaded the last of the dishes into her dishwasher and started the wash cycle. It was old and noisy but, nevertheless, dependable. She ran one last wet cloth over the worn Formica countertop, turned out the light then walked down the hall to her bedroom, checking on Austin along the way.

She entered the bedroom to find her husband, Denny, already deep asleep. She undressed, removed her makeup and slipped into a nightgown that had a small tear in the shoulder strap. She had meant to replace it but not until the tear got worse.

Donna sat on the bed and looked at her nightstand that had a new Reader's Digest. Exhausted, she decided she would postpone reading the digest until she had more energy because tonight she was pooped.

She reached up and turned off the bedside lamp and slid between the sheets. Within moments, she was gently snoring and had joined Denny in a heavy slumber.

As the lights faded in Donna's bedroom, a figure crept from the garden to behind a tree. His careful observation had told him where Austin was located and where the woman and her husband were as well.

The man, large to move so quietly, began to inch his way to Austin's bedroom window. He moved closer to the house in complete silence, not even betrayed by the rattling of his knife or the gun that were both secured close to the body.

The intruder stopped to catch his breath and listen. After a moment of hearing only the barking of distant dogs and the motor sounds of cars traveling on nearby streets, he carefully looked though the corner of the screen. He waited for his eyes to adjust and automatically focus beyond the fine mesh of the screen. Inside a lump in the bed slowly began to materialize. He was sure it was Austin. The sound of the rhythmic breathing told him the child was deep asleep.

His hand went to the K-bar knife strapped to his leg. Slowly, he slid it out and gently inserted it into the wire barrier. It was so sharp it sliced easily through the rusted screen and he began inching its way to the top of the frame. Soon, he had the entire side of the screen slashed and began on the final cut across the bottom. He started the incision and then stopped abruptly as if he had heard something.

Austin stirred and then, in a restless sleep, turned over so he was facing the window. Inexplicably, his eyes popped open and he was staring directly at the motionless face peering into his bedroom.

Phillip heard a sickening thud as Gus hit the floor.

"Gus, are you all right?" he whispered. There was no answer. Phillip crawled up on the trophy case and stretched to look over the wall into the next room.

Gus lay on the ground looking like a broken shell. He was completely still and there was a small pool of blood on the concrete floor. The flashlight cast a beam down the floor to nowhere.

"Gus! Are you okay? Can you hear me? Gus!" Phillips whispered as loud as he could. Gus didn't move.

Phillip scampered down and began looking for a way to get to his friend. *The only way I can see to get to him is to knock this damn door down, no matter how much noise it makes. He could be bleeding to death.*

He had no idea how he would breach the heavy metal door until he saw a package on the floor. The M-60 machine gun! He took the gun, and popped the breech and then opened the ammo box. A quick burst from the gun would take care of any locks. It would also alert the whole neighborhood. It was a pretty drastic solution but the only one he could come up with.

He released the machine gun's bolt and listened to it slam home. Phillip braced himself with a wide stance. He knew what kind of kick an M-60 could give when you tried to hand-hold it and with an injured arm it would be even more hard-hitting. He raised the gun and pointed it at the door's locks. Just as he began to squeeze the trigger the doorknob slowly turned.

Phillip froze as the door opened and a bruised and slightly bleeding Gus appeared saying, "Come in."

Phillip let out a long gasp. "My God, we're going to kill ourselves. Sheriff Ross won't have to do a thing," Phillip said sardonically.

Phillip quickly opened the machine gun's breech and removed the ammunition belt. He pulled back the bolt and ejected the one round in the chamber and slipped it into his pocket, then put the machine gun on the floor.

Phillip moved Gus to a chair. "Sit here until I'm through," he said. He then rapidly circled the room using his good arm to look in every cabinet.

"Here it is," he said as he found a simple video recorder and monitor with cables running into the ceiling. "It's timed to take a photo every three seconds," he said to no one in particular.

Phillip ejected the videotape and stuffed it into his backpack. He took a tape from a nearby shelf dated the week before and inserted it into the machine. It would take days before they realized they were missing a tape from tonight.

"Ready to move out?" he asked Gus. Gus said nothing, simply stood up as if he hadn't really fallen ten feet face-first into a concrete floor.

This guy is a machine, Phillip thought.

They re-installed the ceiling tiles, wiped up the blood on the floor, locked the door, rearranged the trophy cases so the area would look undisturbed and then gathered their tools, machine gun and ammo. The two then moved back to the room from where they had entered. They cleaned up the debris on the floor from the hole in the ceiling.

"I'll pull you up when I get on the roof," said Gus. Phillip nodded knowing there were no other options. Deftly, Gus reached down for Phillip's uninjured arm and once again lugged him to the roof.

Once on top, Phillip bent over and replaced the ceiling tile. "We leave the place with a half dead dog, a hole in the roof and furniture moved around and I think they won't notice. The fall must have shaken my brain," Phillip muttered.

They sat on the armory's roof. "Okay, Gus, I've had faith. Now how do we get down?"

Gus smiled and said, "Watch, oh, ye of little faith."

Phillip was taken aback. He had never thought that Gus might have learned from the same Bible he did.

Gus crouched low and moved to the edge of the roof. About six feet away were the branches of a giant aged elm tree. Gus got a running start and without hesitation leaped off of the roof. He slammed into the main branch and after falling about five feet grabbed a secure hold on one of the massive branches.

This is like some kind of Fear Factor, Phillip thought, reflecting on a popular television reality show where contestants are faced with frightening physical challenges but always protected with a safety line. Tonight there were no safety lines.

Expertly, Gus shinnied down the trunk to the ground. Picking up the fallen aluminum ladder, he unfolded and propped it against the wall and climbed up to the top. Phillip handed down the pack of tools and machine gun to him. Gus descended and held the ladder. Phillip slowly edged his way over the wall and came down. They noiselessly moved to cover behind the large trees that dotted the lawn. All as smoothly as if it had been planned.

Phillip pulled out his cell phone and called Anna for their extraction.

"Coming." was the only response he heard as she answered and then quickly hung up. In two minutes she would be parked outside but they would all be vulnerable until they withdrew.

Moments later, Anna, sans headlights, arrived and the men scurried to retrieve the ladder and move it to the SUV. Just as they lifted it and began to pivot to face the truck, the other end swung toward the armory and crashed into the wall, sending a clatter that pierced the silence of the night.

"Damn it," Phillip whispered, "so much for stealth," and then noticed Gus was transfixed on the sky. When he looked up, he saw the reason. Looking down on them in full bright, red splendor was a large, glowing Bloodmoon.

The men rapidly inserted the ladder on a blanket in the back to muffle the clang of aluminum on metal and jumped in. Anna sped away just as lights began to flicker on in a neighbor's house.

The small commotion did not disturb the sleeping neighborhood except for one. Directly across the street, an old man was settled in his frayed easy chair where he had fallen asleep watching the late-night cable pornography channel. He had seen the movie before and that, plus numerous shots of whiskey, had allowed him to slip into an uncomfortable slumber, light enough that the interruption of the evening's silence awoke him.

He stumbled to the window and parted the Venetian blinds. Nothing happened in Stilwell, surely not this late at night. This was something he had to see.

He watched the activity across the street and then found his way to the telephone. Dialing the number for the police, he swelled with pride that it was his vigilance that was going to alert the authorities to whatever wrongdoing was going on. *Who knows*, he thought, *I might get in the paper.*

"You can bet there will be a call to the police within minutes," Phillip said.

"I'm afraid you're right. If they saw my car it won't be long before they come to see me," Anna said. "Everyone knows everyone else's cars in this town.

"Gus, what happened to you? And Phillip? You're both bleeding," Anna said.

"I just took a fall," Gus waved it off.

"We're kind of clumsy for thieves," Phillip said as he and Gus wiped off their "camouflage".

Anna rolled her eyes.

The darkened vehicle found its way back to the store and the team slipped into the office.

"How much time do you think we have?" Phillip asked once they had settled into the lightproof office.

"Not much. If the neighbors called the police, the Sheriff's office will probably be notified and they'll all be looking. We've got to be the prime suspects for any kind of disturbance around here right now," Anna said.

Suddenly, they heard a door rattle. Stunned, they looked at each other and then quickly flicked off the light. Gus dropped to the floor, opened the door and crawled out to a point he could see the front door.

Sure enough, a uniformed officer stood motionless outside, shining the beam of his flashlight around the inside of the store through the window. It wasn't clear what force he was with but it was obvious he was a cop.

Gus backed into the office and then whispered to the other two, "You're right, that's the law."

"I'll bet they're at your house as well, Anna," Phillip said. "I'm glad we got Austin out of here."

Gus waited a few minutes and then checked the entrance again. "Well, he's gone. I don't know where but he's not in front anymore," Gus said as he returned to the darkened office. "Phillip, you must show me how the gun works."

"Oh, yeah. Wouldn't do you must good without that." Phillip took the weapon and began to demonstrate how the breech was opened and the belt ammunition was fed into the gun as well as how to aim and fire the weapon.

"I'm not going to show you how to field strip it or anything like that because I know it's only going to be used once," Phillip said with one eyebrow raised.

Gus, who was watching carefully, nodded. After the instruction was completed Phillip slammed the breech shut and looked at Anna.

"What's next?" Phillip asked.

"Next is fixing you two," she said. Before he could protest, Anna had pulled up a chair and motioned for them to sit. Anna began to place bandages and antiseptic on the cuts on Gus' head and to wrap Phillip's arm.

"You're holding your shoulder. Did you hurt it?

"Anna, it means nothing. Only getting back means anything," Gus said. "What must we do next?"

"Just a minute," Anna said as she packed up the first aid kit and turned on a lamp. She gently opened the book that held the instruction for the magic ceremony.

"Let's see, first pray at the sacred place of your ancestors. We've done that. Next is to go to that place just before the sun rises and conduct the ceremony. Sunrise is 6:34 a.m. and we need to be set up to go so that we finish just as the sun shows itself."

"It's after midnight. We have about five hours to make sure we've got the stuff we need and are in our places. That's going to be tough with the cops looking for us. You know they'll stop us if they see us," said Phillip.

"We don't have much of a choice, do we?" Anna replied.

"No, I guess not."

"After we're through, I'll go by and get Austin and my car and we'll get out of town. That is, if you're not here, Gus," Phillip said, half apologetically.

"I understand," Gus replied.

CHAPTER SEVENTEEN

Austin's mouth sprang open and he sucked in a quick breath. Before he could unleash it into an ear-shattering scream, the intruder's hand smashed through the screen and covered his mouth so hard not a peep could escape.

Two strong arms grabbed the child and jerked him from his bed through the window leaving a trail of bedding dangling from the window and the torn screen jutting from the window like the rigid flag planted on the moon, ever erect regardless that there was no breeze. The man snatched him under his arm and sprinted out of the backyard.

As he ran, Austin squirmed and tried to free himself but the man's grip and his hand over his mouth were just too strong. He could hear his abductor's labored breathing as they reached the waiting sedan. Quickly he was put in the back seat and the door slammed shut. Austin tried to get out but there were no door handles on the inside. He thought of climbing to the front seat but a metal screen blocked his way. The car moved forward and Austin began to cry.

"Don't cry, Austin. It will just make things worse. Just be strong and things will be better soon. This is for your own good."

Sheriff Ross reached over, clumsily picked up the ringing telephone at the same time knocking his glass ashtray from the bedside table. "What?" he barked into the phone.

"Sheriff, this is the dispatcher at Stilwell P.D.. Thought you'd like to know. We just got a prowler call for that area over by the armory. The caller sounded a little looped but who knows, could be your guys."

Ross sat up in bed and turned on the lamp. He had spent the evening consuming nearly three six packs of beer and was still a captive in the stupor that had not yet cleared. "Did anyone see them? Was Anna Whitebear with them?"

"I don't know. The caller reported a car, didn't know what kind it was. He said he saw two men loading something in it and then taking off with no headlights," the policeman said. "But like I say, he sounded a little sloshed. We have to follow up with it but you don't. Just thought you'd want to know. Our chief said we needed to show, you know, inter-force cooperation and all."

"Yeah, thanks for the call," Ross said with a thick tongue and put down the phone. *Was this just a drunk's call or was it worth waking his boys up and bringing them in?* Ross wasn't sure.

He looked at the clock. It was 11:30 p.m.. *Hell, just seven-and-a-half more hours and the day would begin. They couldn't get too far in that amount of time. Besides, the city police were looking for them. Nevertheless . . .*

Sheriff Ross threw his lanky legs over the side of the bed and sat for a moment trying to clear his head and weigh his options.

The small office was becoming claustrophobic with all three people crammed into its small confines. It finally became too much for Phillip.

"I'm going into the store," he announced. "Don't worry, I'll hide myself so I can't be seen from the outside. I just need some space."

"Let me know when you want back in," Anna said and flipped the lights off as Phillip slipped out of the office. She shut the door and turned the light back on.

"Gus," Anna said once they were alone, "I want to apologize to you for something. What happened at the cemetery. I mean, when I kissed you, I don't know what came over me. I know in your mind you're married and that's very real to you."

"Anna, you don't have to apologize," Gus started.

Anna raised her hand but did not look directly into his eyes. "No, I do. I don't know how but I feel connected to you. I have since I first saw you. These emotions I have for you can't have just sprung up. They have to have come from somewhere, some experience. I don't yet know when or where but I will know, someday.

"Until then I can only tell you that I want the best for you and I'll do everything I can to return you to your time," Anna said, her eyes filling with tears as she lowered them.

Gus rose and walked to Anna. Gently, he took her hand and she slowly lifted her face to look into his blue eyes. She saw, for the first time, what deep pools of pain they were.

"Anna, we're two of a kind," he said with a slight caring smile. "You've never said so but I sense that your heart is heavy from the loss of one you loved. You have lost. And I am yet to lose. We are both carrying the pain of having a dear one taken from us. It is that kindred suffering that is drawing us together. But this is not our time. Do you understand?" he asked softly.

"Of course, Gus," Anna said. "And you're right. Thank you for putting it into perspective. God bless you."

Anna smiled. "I think I'll go check on Phillip." She slipped out of the office and found Phillip sitting on the floor behind a counter.

"Are you okay, Phillip?" she asked as she settled down beside him.

"I'm fine, Anna. I'm sorry we've drug you into this mess. It was to be such a simple weekend," he said.

Anna laughed quietly. "I guess this is a lot different from the life you lead, isn't it? I mean, I'm sure you have a very ordered and safe life."

"Yes, yes I do. And I've worked hard for that. I had some rough times in the beginning. My parents were divorced and when I was in college my mother had a very difficult time financially," he said. "I watched her struggle and wrestle with the problems of a single parent and all I did was add to her problems by being in college.

"I don't want that for Austin. I want a 'ordered and safe' life as you say."

"Well, then I need to apologize to you because you got wound up in this," she said.

"Not at all," Phillip said quickly. "I came here to learn about the Cherokee Tribe and it's turned into a great adventure for me and Austin. No one will ever believe it but it's a splendid escapade, nevertheless. With all due respect

I don't think anybody is going anyplace in time but if I can really help this guy some other way then all of this will have been worth it," Phillip said.

"Maybe we better go back in the office. Leaving Gus alone is dangerous. He may come up with something else he wants to take with him," Anna smiled.

They went to the office door and tapped. Gus opened the door. The two slipped in. "Now I'm okay. I'm ready to go," Phillip said.

Anna meticulously laid out the items that were called for to conduct the ceremony. She had managed to find almost everything, including the eagle feather. Everything but the turtle. Where was she supposed to find a turtle at this time of night? There wasn't time to trap one. And yet, Ester had said she must have it.

I've got to find one somewhere, she thought. She just didn't know where.

CHAPTER EIGHTEEN

The ring of Anna's phone shattered the hushed stillness in the store. Catching everyone by surprise, concerned looks were exchanged as she reached for the receiver. Only one person knew she would be here.

"Yes?" she answered tentatively.

"Anna, it's Donna," said the caller breathlessly. "Something terrible has happened! Someone broke in the house and took Austin!"

"What? How?" Anna snapped.

"They cut the screen and then he must have woke up because it looks like they just grabbed through and jerked him out."

"Who was it? Do you know?"

Anna hesitated but she knew she had to ask, that Phillip would ask, "Any sign of a struggle?"

Donna understood immediately what she meant. "No, no blood or anything like that. Denny has been outside the window with a flashlight and he found some boot prints. He thinks it was a pretty big man by the looks of the prints. "I was going to call the police but I thought I better call you first."

"When did it happen?" Anna asked.

"About fifteen minutes ago, I think. I didn't hear it at first because of our old dishwasher. It's so old and loud but we're used to it, you know. Denny just woke up like his sixth sense had heard it. We've been looking all over for the child but he's gone."

"Just a minute" she said, putting her hand over the receiver.

She turned to relay the information to the two men. Panic showed in Phillip's eyes as she unfolded the events.

"We've got to go look for him," Gus said.

"Do you want to call the police?" Anna asked apprehensively.

"We can't. They'd just arrest us for eluding them and then not do any-thing to find Austin. We've got to find him," Phillip said. "For all we know, they're the ones who have him. It's a perfect way to flush us out."

"What about the ceremony?" Anna asked.

Grimly, Gus said, "It will have to wait," knowing full well it would hap-pen on time or not at all.

Anna spoke into the phone. "Donna, I'll get back to you but you must call me on my cell phone if you find out anything. Don't tell anyone yet until we've figured out what to do," she said and hung up the receiver.

Anna turned to the two men and spoke with an air of authority, "There has to be a reason why someone would take Austin. Ransom doesn't make any sense. You're on the run and they don't know where to find you to make ransom demands."

"I think they know more than you think. How else could they know where Austin was?" Phillip asked.

"Phillip, this is a small town. Someone could have seen him in the car with Donna or watched them go into the house. Who knows? Maybe one of the neighbors said something," Anna shot back. "Or second, they want to flush you out, as you pointed out, so they can take care of you. I just don't understand why they would put such a priority on you and take a chance on drawing attention to themselves. You're, pardon me, no one important. Just a guy from the city who will be going home soon. I can't see how you're much of a threat to them.

"Have you spoken to anyone else about the trouble you're having here? Anyone outside Stilwell?" Anna asked.

"No — well, I did call a friend of mine in Oklahoma City. I thought he might be able to help," Phillip said sheepishly.

"Out of curiosity, just who did you call?"

"Nelson Gay."

"The state Attorney General?" Anna asked incredulously.

"Yeah, he's a friend of mine. I thought he might be able to help."

"So you said. Where did you call him from?" Anna probed.

"The motel," Phillip answered.

"That's it, of course! They've gotten their hands on the telephone records. No wonder they want you stopped. You can bring a lot of unwanted attention down on them. But Phillip, they don't just want you to leave town. Now, I'll bet they want you dead," Anna said.

"Yeah," Sheriff Ross answered when his cell phone rang.

"He called Nelson Gay all right," a deputy's voice said. "I went and checked the records at the hotel, like you asked. It was the Attorney General's number for sure."

"Man, I'd sure like to know what was said," Ross said. "Okay, thanks."

He punched in the home phone of his contact, the civil servant in Oklahoma City. He was pretty sure the civil servant could come up with some idea of the conversation that took place. There was no answer only the inanimate recording that invited the caller to leave a message. He tried several more numbers none of which provided an answer.

This ain't good. All of a sudden my source has dried up. It's like he's dropped off the planet.

"That's too bad," Ross said to himself. "Now I'll have to take serious steps." Ross pushed the end call button and then dialed another number.

The voice on the other end answered with a terse, "What is it?"

"I've got a problem here but I can handle it," Ross said. He knew if he tried to hide it, Harley would find out and then no telling what would happen. He quickly outlined the situation and revealed that Phillip had called the state's Attorney General.

"You stupid son-of-a-bitch. Now you've got the state on our ass all because you think you're a real sheriff. You're the reason we're getting heat. You stupid bastard, you better make that go away now or you're going to go away," his boss shouted.

"Calm down. I'll handle it! I just wanted you to know," Sheriff Ross said. "I'm handling it right now." He heard no response and looked to see the line was dead.

"I have the kid," the man said over the cell phone. "It wasn't a problem."

"Good," came the response. "Be careful with him. Have you let them know yet?"

"No, not yet. I'll call them as soon as I can. I need to get to a secure place first."

"Good. I don't want them tearing around town trying to find him. They'd be like bulls in a china closet."

"I understand," the man said and then realized he had lost his cell phone connection.

CHAPTER NINETEEN

"I have Austin. He's safe and unharmed," the gravelly voice said.

"Where is he, you son-of-a-bitch?" Phillip demanded. "I'll kill you, you bastard!"

"Calm down, asshole. He's fine. You can get him back if you'll go to Oak Grove Cemetery. Do you know where it is?" the voice said.

"What do you want?" Phillip demanded.

"I want you to do what I say. Without question. Do you understand?" the voice said harshly.

Phillip struggled to get control of himself. "Yes, I know where Oak Grove is. When do we meet?"

"In an hour. No later. I can't guarantee his safety after that," the voice said. "And Michaels—don't get cute and try to bring a piece or anybody else. Come alone and unarmed."

Suddenly, the line went dead and Phillip could only stare at the receiver as it emitted its irritating whine.

"He wants me to be at the cemetery in an hour, alone," Phillip said.

"You can't go alone. That's what they want and they're using Austin as bait. That's if they even really have him," Anna said.

"Doesn't matter. I have to go," he said.

Anna began to object and then she caught Gus' glance that warned her from continuing. "All right, let's go. We can use my truck. Maybe they won't be looking for it. We'll drop you off and then we'll leave." Anna had no intention of leaving Phillip alone.

Phillip said nothing. Anna and Gus began to organize the items to go into the truck. Blankets, pots and a variety of objects that could be used in the ceremony, if they got to conduct it.

Phillip didn't notice as Gus brought out the machine gun and ammunition they had stolen, wrapped in a blanket and slipped them into the stack.

Suddenly Anna stood and wiped her forehead. "I've got to get gas. I just remembered I'm almost out. You two stay here and get ready and I'll be back in a few minutes."

"Don't you want us to go with you?" Phillip asked.

"No, it's just more risk. If I run into the sheriff he can only get me. We shouldn't be together unless we absolutely have to."

Anna got into the SUV and turned out of the alley and onto the street. She drove around the town until she came to a ramshackle convenience store.

Pulling up to the pump, she looked about and then rapidly got out, swiped her credit card and began to fuel the SUV. She watched as the gallons slowly ticked away on the gas pump.

A battered 1972 Chevrolet rambled into the lane next to her. She didn't have to look to know it was filled with men probably on their way back from the Rebel Club after having too much to drink. She ignored the comments that were coming from inside the car, hoping she would finish filling her truck before they could get bolder.

"Hey, baby. Why don't you come with us and party?" said one of the men. "We'll show you a good time. Me first," he said but all four of the men broke out with crude laughter.

Anna refused to respond or make eye contact. What she didn't need at this moment was an incident. She decided she had enough gas and getting out of there now was more important than a full tank. She withdrew the nozzle and twisted to replace it only to turn into one of the men just inches from her. He was now standing between her and the pump.

"I got a big hose for you, honey," he slurred. He was huge with 16-inch arms hanging from a shirt that had no sleeves.

"Get out of my way, you drunk or I'll call the cops," she said with authority.

"You ain't calling nobody, baby," the drunk said and grabbed her arm with a vice-like grip, his other hand going for her breast. She noticed he was not only missing a tooth but had only a hole in his head where his right ear should have been.

Anna instinctively raised her fist and swung at the man landing a very unfeminine blow to his jaw. Even with her small size, it had a distinct thud when it hit the delicate joint of the man's jaw.

"Argg, you bitch!" he yelled and grabbed for her hair. He pulled her head down and was preparing to deliver a knee to her face. Anna saw a perfect target and let go with another hard punch, this time to the man's groin.

He released her hair and bent over retching. She turned in the narrow corridor between her car and the pump island and was confronted by another man, an equally nasty looking character that had a scraggly beard. With lightning speed, he grabbed her by the throat and began to squeeze. "You lousy slut," he muttered.

She struggled to move under the man's grip but she couldn't budge. Anna didn't think she had many options. She was gasping for breath. In a moment the other man would recover and she would have no chance against two of the brutes. The police weren't an option. Phillip and Gus weren't an option. She couldn't involve anyone else and she had to move quickly before this fool killed her.

She grabbed the pump nozzle that had fallen and pointed it toward the bearded man and squeezed hard. A heavy stream of premium fuel spewed into the man's face. He immediately released her and reached for his eyes, screaming with pain.

Anna quickly twisted around to make sure another of the group wasn't coming up on her. She dropped the hose and jumped into the SUV. The engine roared to life and she sped out of the parking lot with her gas cap dangling from the car.

Arriving back at the store, she doused the SUV's headlights as soon as she hit the alley. She backed into her space with the truck's back doors facing the store's rear entrance. She entered to find the men waiting by the gear.

"What happened to you?" Phillip said in dismay. At first she wondered what had given her away then she realized her appearance had radically changed since she had left twenty minutes before. Her hair was disheveled, her face and neck were bruised and her clothing was torn.

"What the hell went on out there? You look like a wreck and you smell like gasoline," Phillip asked with concern.

"Just a little local color," Anna said casually but her voice was still shaking.

The men stared at her but decided to drop the questioning.

"I'm going to go wash my face and hands and then we've got to head out. He wanted you there in an hour, didn't he," she asked referring to the kidnapper. Phillip nodded.

She came out of the bathroom feeling a little better, looking a lot better and not smelling like a gas tank. They all boarded the truck and began their trip to Oak Grove Cemetery.

CHAPTER TWENTY

Sheriff Ross folded his oversized form into the patrol car and, once situated behind the wheel, started the engine, immediately reaching for the two-way radio's microphone. "Porter, this is the Sheriff, over," he said.

The response was a little slow in coming. "Yes, sir," said Deputy Porter, the duty officer.

"What the hell's wrong there? You asleep? Your shift ain't over until 6 a.m., Mister," Ross barked.

"Nothing, Sheriff. I was just getting a cup of coffee across the room. Sorry it took me a second," Porter responded, straightening himself in the chair and removing his feet from the desk where he had been napping.

"All right, I want you to call everyone in. Everyone, even those who have the day off. I want 'em in in thirty minutes. We've got to get these strangers under control and I mean now. I think they broke into the armory and are probably armed and definitely dangerous," Ross said.

"Well, sure, Sheriff, I'll get right on it," Porter said.

"And Porter? That means you, too. You can pull a double today."

"Yes, sir," Porter said trying to keep the frustration out of his tone.

They slowed at the junction, alerted by the cemetery's directional sign and a mailbox that was leaning so far it looked like it had already been the recipient of a failed turn, and exited Highway 59 then began down the two-lane asphalt road that led to Oak Grove Cemetery. They maneuvered the three quarters of a mile to the burial ground with the headlights piercing a tunnel through the arching trees and overgrown plants on the side of the road.

The road dipped and went through a wash that had only a trickle from the stream. The dark, unlit, alternately gravel and asphalt road finally stopped at the cemetery gate.

As they approached, the graveyard looked deserted. There was no sign anyone else was there.

"I guess we're the first ones here, huh?" Anna said as the SUV crept forward.

"Maybe, maybe not. Stay down as low as you can and don't make yourself a target," Phillip said.

As they pulled into the area that was home to the burial ground, Gus said to Anna, who was driving, "Back into that thicket of trees. It will provide plenty of concealment."

"No, you two get out of here. Come back in an hour," Phillip said quickly.

"Sorry, Phillip, we're not leaving so you might as well accept it," Anna said forcefully.

Phillip looked at Gus and there was no mistaking his intent. He was staying.

"Okay," Phillip said with a sigh. "Just stay out of sight. This thing can be blown real easily." Deep down Phillip was relieved to have his friends backing him up. It wasn't that he didn't think he could handle it; it was just that he couldn't afford a screw up. He wasn't as cock-sure as he always was in his ability to pull the exchange off.

Gus and Phillip got out to guide Anna in. She nestled the truck among the trees and then looked at Gus as if to ask, *is this okay?*

"Don't block the door by this tree. We may need to get out quickly," Phillip interjected as he pointed to the obstruction at the back door. Anna backed the truck even farther into the trees not noticing that as she freed the back door, she had blocked her own door.

Phillip helped Gus camouflage the vehicle. He was amazed that when they finished no visible trace of SUV existed, even if you were looking directly at it.

"Let me see if we're really alone. Keep down," Phillip said. He walked around using his flashlight to check the road for tracks and then returned to the truck. "Looks like we're the only ones who have been here in the last few hours. "Anna, you stay here. I'm going to position myself out where the guy can see me."

"Take this pistol," she said, offering a nickel-plated .38. Her nickel-plated.38.

He looked at her in surprise and shook his head. "I can't take a chance. He said no weapons. I can't do anything else that might jeopardize Austin," he said.

"Don't be silly. It may be the only thing that saves Austin if this all goes south. You're not dealing with honorable men, Phillip. You'd better use every advantage you can get," she said.

Phillip paused and then reached for the .38, stuffing it in the back of the waistband of his trousers.

He walked to the center of the dirt road with the cemetery gate on his left. To his right was a bluff on which sat a small frame house with a few animals and a couple of old junk cars.

He moved 25 feet out in front of the hidden truck in the open area directly in front of the cemetery. "I'll wait for him here. Gus, you take cover. Maybe you can help me somehow if I get in trouble."

Gus nodded and walked into the cemetery and toward the back of the field to find a hiding position behind a tombstone.

Phillip stood in the warm summer night wondering if he would ever see his son again and glad he had taken Anna's .38.

Mosquitoes began to nibble at his neck and the minutes slowed to a dismal crawl; suddenly a set of headlights came into view.

CHAPTER TWENTY-ONE

The loud ring of the telephone pierced the deep sleep and emotional dream of Nelson Gay. He literally jumped straight up in bed. His wife sat up almost at the same time. Nelson grabbed the receiver and said breathlessly, "Hello?"

"Sorry, General, but we have more worrisome news about the situation in Stilwell," Jack Oates said. "I just got a call from Director David. He was told I was the Duty Officer tonight. Word coming out is that our boy Michaels has gotten crosswise, big time, with some of the county's rough characters. They're searching for him all over Adair County."

"Do they know we're plugged in?" Gay asked.

After a pause, Oates said, "Could be. And that means they'll try to kill him."

"But he's got his kid with him!" Gay exclaimed.

"Yes sir, but they don't care. They won't want any witnesses or people drawing attention to them. They'll kill him, too."

Suddenly, Phillip saw a beam of light flash through the trees and then immediately disappear. The brake lights glowed and then the headlights were doused, replaced by dim parking lights.

He strained to discern any movement and then began to make out the image of a car. It came slowly toward him. All too soon he recognized the vehicle and it sent a chill down his back. It was a Sheriff's Department cruiser.

The automobile ground to a stop only ten feet from him. Slowly, the door opened and a well-built deputy carefully stepped out, half-in, half-out of the vehicle. Even in that position, he towered over the car.

"Where's my son?" Phillip demanded.

"I have him and you'll get him. I just want to explain something," Deputy Cole said.

"I don't want an explanation. I want my son. Now!"

"Okay, okay," Cole said and opened the back door. "Austin, your dad's here. You can go to him now."

Phillip could see Austin scramble out of the back seat and as soon as he spotted his father, come flying to him, still in the pajamas he had donned at Donna Still's.

"Daddy! Daddy!" he screamed.

Phillip grabbed him and quickly said, "It's okay now, everything's okay," as he rapidly scanned the boy's body to look for any sign of injury.

"Okay, now can we talk?" asked the deputy moving toward Phillip.

Phillip moved Austin behind him then reached back, pulled the .38 from his belt and pointed it at the man. "We'll talk when you put your hands in the air."

The deputy immediately raised his hands. "Oh, wait a minute. Hold on here. There are a lot of things you don't understand, Michaels. Don't get yourself in more trouble than you're in already." Phillip was unmoved.

Deputy Cole walked closer, his hands imperceptibly lowering as he approached. "You're not going to shoot anyone, Michaels," he sneered. "You might have been a Marine once but now you're just a rich, middle-aged establishment guy." He kept coming.

"You think so, you asshole? Just keep coming and see. When you took my son, I said to hell with the establishment," Phillip barked.

The man was now five feet away and getting closer. Phillip shifted from foot to foot.

Finally, the deputy was face-to-face. He reached over and grasped the pistol with a large hand and twisted it away all the time looking Phillip in the eye.

I just got disarmed without a fight. What the hell is wrong with me?

"Listen, you thick bastard. I'm trying to tell you. I'm not one of Ross's men. I'm an agent for the OSBI working undercover. My name is Agent Page Sutor," the deputy said.

"Yeah, right."

"It is right. We've been watching Ross for months."

"Then how come you haven't arrested him?" Phillip asked skeptically.

"We have enough evidence but we were waiting to try to bust the entire network. It's taken me months to work my way into his confidence. Your little entry onto the scene screwed everything up. Calling the Attorney General was real bright. It nearly blew an operation that we've been working on since February."

"Why did you kidnap Austin?" Philip asked.

"He bought me an ice cream cone, Daddy," Austin quickly interjected in the man's defense.

"Ross' men had already planned to grab him. If I hadn't gotten him first, he might not be alive now," Sutor said. "Look, you asked the AG for help and I'm here. He said to tell you Delta Epsilon 1171. Said you'd know what that meant. Use your head, for God's sake."

Gradually, Phillip began to relax his clenched fist. That was his initiation number in the college fraternity to which he and Gay belonged. Only Gay would have known that. "Well, do you have an ID?"

"Come on, Michaels, Do you think I'd be carrying an ID when I'm undercover?

"No, I guess not," Phillip said, accepting that the man was who he claimed to be.

At that moment Gus emerged from the cemetery and walked toward the two men.

"Agent Sutor, I think you know my friend Gus.

"Gus, this man is an undercover agent. He's going to help us."

The quiet of the cemetery was interrupted when the radio in the cruiser cracked to life. "All units converge on Oak Grove Cemetery. Suspects are armed and dangerous. Exercise extreme caution and maintain radio silence. Ross out."

"Now you're going to have to trust me," Agent Sutor said looking worried. "They'll be swarming all over here in just a few minutes."

"Let's get out of here," Phillip said.

"Forget that. There's only one way out and that's this road we're on. And you can bet it will be blocked before we could get to the end of it," Agent Sutor, formerly known as Deputy Cole, said.

"Gus, would you take Austin back to Anna, then we need to figure out what we're going to do," Phillip said.

Gus looked at him and said only, "We'd better hurry."

CHAPTER TWENTY-TWO

Gus quickly returned. The man stood with Phillip as his eyes locked in a moment of understanding that can only exist among battle-tested warriors.

"How many will there be?" Phillip asked calmly.

Never blinking Agent Sutor said, "Five, maybe ten and all well-armed. They won't be able to get the reserve deputies in. I'm not sure he wants them anyway. He doesn't control them the way he does the regular troops. They'll be here in three minutes."

"They'll be channeled in by the road, don't you think?"

"Yeah. They're too arrogant and too simple-minded to deploy before they get to the gate," the agent answered.

There was a moment's silence and then Phillip, looking at Gus, said, "You position yourself there," and pointed to a small bluff, "and hide in that ditch. I'll set up here and we'll have them in crossfire if it gets that far. Plus you," pointing to Agent Sutor, "can cut off the escape route if they try to flank us.

"And turn your car so it blocks the road."

Both men recognized that Phillip knew what he was talking about and grunted their agreement.

"Can you supply some weapons?" Gus asked Agent Sutor.

"Yeah, I can," he said as he pointed to the car and the shotgun hanging on the screen. He went to the car and returned with the shotgun and a 30-30 rifle. "Here, Gus, you take this rifle. I'll take the shotgun and you've got your own gun," he said pointing to Phillip's Smith and Wesson.

"Don't fire on them unless they fire on us," Phillip said. "If anybody gets hurt on their side I want it to be a case of self-defense." *God, how did I get into this mess*, he thought.

"What we want is to get out of here. If any of us can get to one of the deputy's cars, haul out of here. Maybe they'll give chase and it'll buy us some time and get them away from Anna and Austin," Phillip said.

Quickly realizing that Gus could not possibly steal a car he continued, "And Gus, keep an eye on me so if I can grab one you can jump in with me."

Swiftly both men took their weapons and moved into the assigned position. Phillip hurried to Anna's SUV and leaned into the window.

"Anna, I can't let you and Austin leave right now. We think the Sheriff is on his way out here and he'd intercept you sure as the world, then he'd have a couple of hostages. You're hidden well and no one will even know you're here. Just stay low and if any shooting starts, wait until it's over and it's safe to leave. They don't know you're here and believe it or not, you and Austin are safer this way," he said.

"I can take care of myself, Phillip. You just worry about you and Gus. Are you sure we can't just get out of here?"

"I'm sure. That deputy is an undercover agent and he heard on his radio that they were right down the road," he said. "We're pretty well boxed in. We'll try to find a way to steal their cars and draw them away from here and if we do, then we'll meet up later. If not, we'll just have to defend ourselves here," Phillip said.

"What the hell you talking about? Why is one of my cars at the cemetery?" Sheriff Ross demanded.

"I don't know, boss. All I know is we got a call from the old guy who lives out there. He says that one of our cars is parked not far from his house and one of our officers is out talking to a couple of men he didn't know. I've found everyone else. It has to be Cole," Deputy Kelly said.

"Cole. Figures. I never trusted him. I should have known not to hire someone I haven't known for at least five years," Ross said. "Okay, we're only a few minutes from the `20'. We're going to finish this. Call the old guy back and tell him he'd best quietly evacuate that house until we're through out there. Ross out."

The voice on the two-way crackled. "Sheriff Ross, this is Chief Conley," said the Chief of the Stilwell Police Department. "What's going on? We've been monitoring your radio traffic and it's obvious that you're bringing all your deputies together. Is something going on I need to know about?"

"Naw, Chief, we're just checking out a lead on a couple of fugitives. Doesn't concern your department," Ross said, trying to sound nonchalant.

"Just where are these fugitives? Are they the ones you've been looking for? Anything that happens in Stilwell is my department's concern," Conley said, his voice rising.

"This is a county matter, Conley. It's outside of the city limits so it's out of your jurisdiction," Ross said. "Ross, out."

An old battered pickup pulled up in front of the home next to Anna Whitebear's house. A grizzled looking James Ledbetter, just recently released from Stilwell Memorial Hospital, crept to the side door that opened into the garage. Within a few moments he had jimmied the lock and gained entry. As soon as his eyes adjusted to the darkness he flipped on a heavy flashlight he had brought and there it was, just as he'd been told. The green Cadillac.

Trying to stifle his groans from his recent injuries, he bent down and attempted to slide under the car but his bulk would not allow it. Cursing, he managed to unlock the trunk by hot wiring the dash and the trunk lid obediently raised itself. He reached in and loosened the jack and then brought it out. Doing this was more difficult and noisy than he had anticipated while trying to hold the flashlight. He installed the jack in the proper slot and raised the rear of the car high enough that he could wriggle under it.

Quickly and deftly, like a person who had done it before, he made tiny punctures in the brake and the fuel lines.

Once the car was driven, especially at high speeds on the Interstate, it wouldn't take long for the fuel to find its way to the hot exhaust. The ensuing explosion would destroy the car as if a rocket-propelled grenade had hit it.

If that didn't work then the brakes would fail from the loss of brake fluid. The beauty of both of the methods was that no clues were left as to the cause of the crash. In a fiery crash the first things to burn were the hoses and thin lines. *That sheriff is pretty smart. If he don't get them, they'll die on the way home*, he thought.

Either way, the city slicker, his kid and that son-of-a-bitch that beat him up would never make it back to Oklahoma City.

Anna sat with Austin in the hidden SUV and tried to keep a composed demeanor. Even though she was childless, she knew that young ones could sense tension when adults were nervous. *Lord, what this child had been through and it's not over yet.*

"We're going to have us some fun in a little while, Austin. It'll be a good time. But whatever happens, I want you to promise me you'll stay down on the floor. Stay real low, okay?" she said.

"What's going to happen?" he asked curiously.

"Has your Daddy ever taken you to Frontier City?" Anna asked, referring to an Oklahoma City theme park. Austin nodded. "Well, it'll be sort of like that, where they have the play gunfights. Lots of noise and play guns going off. It'll be fun. But as a scout," Anna hesitated. "You are a real scout now, aren't you?"

Austin was spellbound and promptly said, "Yes, Gus made me one."

"I thought so. Well, as a scout, you must go down low when it all starts and not come up to look until it's quiet. No noise. Just like before, remember?"

Austin nodded with his mouth wide open.

"Remember, you won't look no matter what until it's quiet. Now, let me tell you a story."

Anna had no idea what story to tell but she began with one of the old Cherokee legends of how the Arrowhead berries were formed by the Great Spirit. Austin paid rapt attention and soon had settled into a relaxed position in the back of the SUV where Anna had rigged a pallet for him to lie on.

"Anna," Austin said, surprising her by calling her by name, "that's a pretty necklace. Where did you get it?"

Anna was taken aback by the unexpected compliment from a six-year-old and unconsciously reached up and touched her neck. She had forgotten she had a necklace on. She smiled gently. "This is a special necklace that has been in my family for many generations," she said softly. "It was crafted out of silver and inlaid with semi-precious stones.

"My grandfather gave it to me. He said it had mystical powers and he made me promise I would protect it and keep it safe."

"What is that thing in the center?" Austin asked.

Anna looked down and said, "Oh, that's a sacred Cherokee symbol. It's a turtle..." She stopped in mid-sentence.

The four-car convoy neared the turnoff to Oak Grove Cemetery. The Sheriff switched off his flashing lights and the others followed suit. He slowed to a stop and pulled over on the side of the road. The rest of the cars did the same, moving like a snake slithering to the gravel. Ross got out and stood in the highway where the deputies could see him.

"All right, listen up. We're not going to creep in there. We're going in balls-to-the-wall. If he ain't standing out where we can see him, we'll form a circle in front of the cemetery so we can have a field of fire in any way. First move, everyone out of the cruisers and be ready to shoot. Use your car as cover. I'll try to talk him and his buddies out but these boys are dangerous so as soon as you see one of them, you're authorized deadly force to stop him. In other words, nail their asses. Any questions?"

"Sheriff, we heard that Cole was in there. What do we do about him?" a deputy asked.

"He's a co-conspirator. A goddam traitor. Same deal for him. Nail his ass," the Sheriff responded. The darkness hid the uncomfortable glances the deputies exchanged. They all got their payoff money from the drugs that Ross distributed and they couldn't turn on him without turning on themselves. *But killing a deputy? One of them? That didn't seem right.*

"Let's move out," Ross said and got into his cruiser, turned on his flashing light display and pulled onto the road that led to the cemetery, leaving a blinding plume of dust to swallow the other cars as they tried to follow.

All three men could sense the sheriff's gang was coming. Even though it was late at night, the clouds from the speeding cars rose above the trees like an ascending cloud. Within moments the roar of the engines could be heard and the flashing lights of the cruisers, all designed to intimidate, reflected through the woods.

Ross was the first to arrive. Not expecting to be blocked by one of his own cruisers, he swerved, almost up-ending his vehicle, and nipped the front of the agent's squad car, spinning his car around.

The second car, blinded by the dust thrown up by Ross', tried to stop when the blocking cruiser became visible but in the soft dirt was unable to get traction and crashed into the side of the car.

The remaining cars saw the danger and stopped well short of the accident. The deputies dismounted and worked their way to the cemetery site. By this time Ross had positioned himself behind his car and was bellowing through a bullhorn.

"We know you're here, Michaels. And we know that Cole, or whatever your name is, is with you as well as your mute friend. You might as well give yourself up. You're already charged with suspicion of burglary, breaking and entering, eluding a police officer and attempted escape. You don't need to add more charges to it. We know you're armed, so come out with your hands where I can see them," Ross said.

There was no response to Ross' demands.

"Okay, boys, spread out and start combing the area. Start with this section here," Ross ordered and held his long arms out forming a triangle in front of them.

Reluctantly, the six deputies began to advance toward the cemetery. It was clear that they intended to sweep the area in sections. It was just a matter of time until they uncovered each of them including Anna and Austin. If they tried to move, they'd be spotted and if they stayed, they would eventually be discovered.

The deputies were focused on the section in which Gus was hiding. Phillip noticed that one deputy was closing in on Gus' hidden position. *Get ready*, he told himself, *Gus won't hesitate to shoot him and then the battle will be on.* Phillip tried to watch intently without giving away his location but all of a sudden he could no longer see the deputy.

Gus had nestled down behind one of the largest of the 200 tombstones that dotted the cemetery toward the back edge of the parcel. He had covered himself with grass and leaves and had a good field of fire ahead of him.

Gus was good at this. He'd done it many times before, most recently while scouting the Yankee troops in Kansas. Once he settled in, he wouldn't move.

He could see the deputies congregate in the clearing in front of the cemetery and listen to Sheriff Ross give a speech. He couldn't make out the warnings that Ross made over the bullhorn and wasn't worried until he saw the men start sweeping the cemetery. They began to walk toward his hiding place, each man spread about ten feet apart. Several had flashlights and would arc the beam in front of them. Each carried a rifle or shotgun.

One deputy, however, seemed to be angling away from the group. He was stumbling, obviously being guided by the tombstones and was unaware he was losing contact with his colleagues. First, he made his way to a small, aged, rough-hewn mausoleum and, after examining it carefully, began to walk south again.

He moved closer to Gus' position. Gus hoped he would bypass him, moving through his location and then turning to return a different way.

The deputy was gently cursing as he stepped in small gopher holes and his clothes got caught in briars. He continued to walk until he was almost on top of Gus. Without a sound Gus reached up and grabbed his ankle, twisting it and causing the man to fall quickly to the ground.

Anna was watching the activity from the SUV. The deputies gave no indication they had any suspicion there was a vehicle hidden in the thicket of trees.

Once she realized, thanks to Austin, that she had the turtle necklace, she had taken it off and placed it in the leather pouch with the other ceremonial items. She unconsciously looked in her leather pouch to reassure herself it was still there. At first she didn't see it and then she was sure the necklace wasn't there at all. Frantically, she emptied the contents on the seat next to her. She couldn't turn on the interior light so she bent close to the items to inventory them. The necklace was not to be seen.

She craned her neck to see if it had dropped out of the car. She saw a faint glint only a foot or two from the door. It was the necklace. She flipped the switch that disabled her interior lights and decided to carefully open the door. The deputies had started off in the opposite direction so it was likely she could get it before they returned.

She cautiously pulled the door latch and started to open the door when it was abruptly and solidly stopped. She looked out and realized there was a tree blocking the door.

The deputy fell hard. Before he could utter a sound, Gus had put his hand over his mouth. He didn't want to kill this deputy but he would if that's what it took to escape. The man seemed to struggle just briefly, and then his eyes swelled and he tried to let out a blood-curdling scream but Gus was too strong and his hand would not let the sound escape. Gus could not understand the man's behavior. He was not causing him so much pain that he should react that way, even if he was frightened.

Suddenly, Gus saw the reason for the deputy's behavior. From under the man's back slithered a four- foot western massasauga rattlesnake. The snake was one of the seven species of poisonous snakes indigenous to this area and the man had fallen on it just moments before it had crawled into Gus' hiding place.

The other deputies had turned and were moving back to the clearing. Gus quickly took the unconscious man's shirt off and found the bite mark on his upper arm. He made a tourniquet from the man's belt and cut off the blood supply in the arm to block the venom from getting to his heart. *Maybe he could come back later or maybe one of the other deputies would find him before it was too late. If not, that was war*, he thought.

Gus put on the deputy's shirt and hat and began walking to appear as if he was trying to catch up with the others searching.

The posse of deputies swept through the cemetery and found nothing and then began to return to the center of the area only to re-launch into another area. It was hard to recognize the deputies in any detail even though by now Phillip's night vision was sharp. Yet in the darkness Phillip noticed something different about the row as they returned. One of the deputies was tall and had a familiar way in his walk.

My God, it's Gus. He's wearing a deputy's uniform! Phillip thought.

Methodically, Gus angled to the left of the line and eventually disappeared in the woods. *I don't know exactly what he has in mind but I know it'll make sense*, Phillip thought as he saw the scout fade into the foliage. *We may be able to pull this off without anyone getting hurt. If I'm going to make my move I'd better do it before they start searching this way.* Phillip slipped backwards for nearly 25 feet and then turned and low crawled for another ten feet, then rose and began to scurry deeper into the forest.

"Nothing that way, sheriff. We checked it real close," said one of the deputies as they re-formed in the clearing.

"Sweep up by that old house. And be sure and look under it," Ross said.

It was the house that was providing cover for Agent Sutor. Sutor saw what was happening and quickly surmised the deputies' plan.

The deputies formed a skirmish line and began to advance. To reach the area they had to climb the bluff. The six-foot steep incline caused chaos as they slid and scraped to get to the top.

Agent Sutor had but one option and that was to try to maneuver to the flanks and be missed by the pursuers. He waited until the lawmen were in disarray and then sprinted toward the surrounding wooded area.

While it may have been missed by the struggling deputies, the movement caught Sheriff Ross' eye and he didn't wait to issue an order before he began to fire his shotgun, pumping and firing the weapon as fast as he could. The deputies reacted and began shooting at anything that moved.

"There that bastard is," screamed Sheriff Ross.

Sutor ran hard but suddenly felt a searing pain in his leg before it buckled and pitched him head-first into the rocky ground. By now the deputies had scrambled up the bluff, spotted their target and were pouring massive amounts of fire in his direction. Whatever reticence they had in killing a fellow deputy had dissipated with the first exchange of bullets.

Sutor crawled as fast as he could behind a tree whose branches were already splintering from bullet impact. He was losing blood fast and felt his strength ebbing from him. He cried out with pain as he tried to fashion a tourniquet to stop the flow from his leg. He had to do something fast. The other deputies were closing on him and there was no doubt what they'd do without any witnesses. As far as they were concerned, he was now just another rogue cop trying to kill police officers.

Gus was trying to get to one of the cars in hope that Phillip could make it to him and they could lead the sheriff's men out of the area. When the firing started he froze, then moved to where he could see what was happening. It was clear that Sutor was about to be taken down.

To fire on the advancing deputies would only expose Gus to return fire. There had to be a way to divert their attention. When the answer came it was not his first choice but it was as good an option as he was going to get.

Phillip had positioned himself at the end of the road where Anna and Austin were. Not so close as to draw attention to the hidden SUV but close enough to allow him to protect them, if he had to. Now his location was more of a detriment than an advantage. The only way he could draw the deputies away from Sutor was to open fire, unnecessarily bringing them into his area where they might discover Anna and Austin.

Maybe I can maneuver away from the SUV and then draw their attention by shooting at them. It sounded pretty weak to Phillip but he couldn't think of another idea and time was running out fast for Sutor.

Suddenly a sheriff's car came crashing down the road. Its lights were off and the driver was accelerating and then braking causing the car to buck like an angry mustang. The car swerved around Agent Sutor's car and began heading erratically for Phillip. It was as if the car had gone berserk. Just as it looked as if it would run over Phillip, it veered around and started heading toward the deputies with the driver's side door flapping like a loose glove.

By now the crowd of deputies saw the squad car and were momentarily unsure of what to do. When they realized the car had no intention of stopping they abandoned the pursuit of Sutor and started to fire at the rampaging cruiser. Whoever was behind the steering wheel was being riddled with bullets.

Suddenly, Sheriff Ross felt a burning sensation in his arm. He looked down and saw he had been hit.

Who was driving that car? Phillip asked himself. Then it hit him. *Incredible as it seemed, it had to be Gus. Gus! He didn't even know how to start a car. Could he have picked up enough by watching Phillip to drive and aim that car?*

The echo of blowing tires filtered through the explosion sounds of bullets being fired but still, the cruiser continued on. It slammed one deputy to the ground and then under the force of a shredding tire, swerved ninety degrees and headed toward the other deputies.

The men scattered, some falling as they ran to evade the wildly careening car. Suddenly, the vehicle hit a plow rut and reversed course, spewing dirt from its rear tires. It plowed through the line of deputies and came to rest with a loud crash and shards of flying wood in the corner of the home just hours earlier occupied by the old man.

The deputies ran to the wrecked car and began searching for the driver. "Hey, there's no one here. He must have bailed out!" a deputy yelled to the men.

Immediately, they turned and began combing the ground looking for the driver.

Anna was distracted from her effort to regain her necklace by the commotion and the rampaging car. She watched carefully as it swerved and turned and ran amok through the deputies. *If the situation hadn't been so damn desperate, it would have been funny to watch the cops scatter like a flock of chickens.* She knew it was somehow Gus behind the wheel.

She saw the car stop and the deputies, all of them mad as hell, start searching the field for the driver. In just a few moments they would be on top of Gus and it was doubtful he'd get out alive.

There wasn't much she could do. But there was one thing.

Gus had been low crawling trying to get to the treeline since he threw himself out of the car. He hadn't made it and the deputies, with Sheriff Ross in the lead, were getting closer. His stolen uniform was in tatters and he didn't think he could pull off the masquerade of being a deputy a second time.

He watched as two deputies began to narrow the distance to him. He had re-injured his shoulder when he hit the ground and wasn't sure he could mount much of a resistance if they didn't just shoot him on the spot.

Just as the deputies were within ten feet, a light began blinking from a clump of trees on his right and was accompanied by the rapid clack that only a machine gun could produce. *It was Anna!*

The shots were far from accurate but the recognizable sound and tell-tale flashes drove the deputies to ground, scratching for cover. The gun continued to fire short bursts until it stopped with what was clearly the sound of a bolt going home to an empty chamber. The gun was jammed. After a few moments of silence, the deputies began to raise their heads and look around. Slowly, they rose to full height.

"Two of you men go over and see what that was all about," Sheriff Ross yelled and two of the force peeled off the line and started moving to the small clump of trees.

Anna pulled at the breech. It was clear something was wrong with the machine gun. She had no idea what the problem was and was pretty sure she couldn't fix it.

She looked back at Austin who was laughing and having a great time at the "play" shootout.

"Shoot some more, Anna," he yelled.

In front of her were a couple of deputies cautiously closing in on the SUV. She couldn't run. They might shoot and hit Austin and she sure wasn't going to leave him by himself.

"Get down in the floor, Austin," she ordered. If they started shooting, and they had every reason to believe she was armed and dangerous, she didn't want Austin to get hit. It looked like there was no place to go.

Phillip took a deep breath. All of his options were played out. Sutor was down. Gus was exposed. Anna had given up her position and he wasn't sure if he pulled the trigger he wouldn't be signing each of their death warrants.

Suddenly, the sky erupted with the whumping of rotor blades. The entire area was bathed in the glow of two million candlelight from two helicopter searchlights.

Everyone immediately looked up only to be blinded by the ferocious glare and then quickly lowered their eyes and tried to regain their night vision.

Anna looked up at the sound. What was it? Then the memory of her beloved grandfather appeared to her.

"Look to the sky," she said repeating her grandfather's warning. "The sky will protect you."

"Thank you *i-du-du*," she whispered.

"Finally," Agent Sutor exclaimed.

"Cease fire! Cease fire! This is the Oklahoma State Bureau of Investigation," a voice from the helicopter's loud speaker said. "Sheriff Ross, tell your men to gather in the center of the area illuminated by the spotlight and put down their weapons."

The two small scout helicopters were joined by a larger Huey-type helicopter that hovered off to the side and discharged four heavily armed men who rappelled to the ground in just seconds. Two more large choppers followed, repeating the process.

Gus watched and was overwhelmed. He had been a victim of information overload for the last five days and had done his best to deal with it but this was beyond any realm of comprehension or understanding.

The meaning, however, was not lost on Ross. He knew that his men were now outnumbered and had lost fire superiority. He had no question as to the reason the OSBI was there. He figured Phillip's call was behind that. Ross moved backwards until he was on the edge of the circle and just outside the circles of high-powered light being generated by the helicopters' torchlights.

Somehow, he slipped past the OSBI and stealthily moved through the treeline until he reached the last patrol car on the road leading to the exit road. He got in and started the car and with the lights out began to carefully drive it backwards to the end of the road where it met the highway.

The deputies began to slowly filter into the circle with arms raised. Members of the OSBI assault team quickly disarmed and took them into custody while other members of the team began to scour the area for remaining deputies.

Ross hit the highway and continued to drive with his lights off. He didn't want to be spotted by the helicopters and right now all cop cars were under suspicion. He could keep tabs on the OSBI by monitoring the police radio. As soon as they figured out he had the car, and he'd know because of the radio, he'd dump the patrol car and steal another vehicle.

Sheriff Ross knew he couldn't get far with a gunshot wound. Not when the bullet was still in his arm. He could go to the Stilwell hospital and get emergency treatment and be in an out in 30 minutes. He'd be gone before they even knew the OSBI was looking for him.

He often brought prisoners to the hospital for treatment and the staff knew him well. And while they might be surprised, it would seem believable if he had a gunshot wound in the line of duty. They wouldn't make him wait. It was early enough that the crew on duty would be a skeleton one and it wouldn't raise a lot of attention.

CHAPTER TWENTY-THREE

The three stood motionless and watched as the last of the taillights disappeared into the woods. The OSBI agents had herded the deputies into the remaining operable sheriff cruisers and convoyed them out to detention facilities in Oklahoma City. Rapidly, the sound of intruders faded until Oak Grove Cemetery was once again soundless and serene.

Anna turned to the men and said, "Look," and pointed to a clearing in the canopy. Glowing above them was a full Bloodmoon.

She looked at her watch. "There's still time. Sunrise isn't for another 30 minutes. But we better hurry," she said and looked at Gus. "If you still want to try it."

Gus looked at her and once again muttered what Anna believed was coming to be his mantra, "I have no choice."

"Very well. I'll get the ceremonial items," she said and hurriedly walked to her SUV, quietly opening the back doors so as to not disturb a sleeping Austin. She returned with a plethora of blankets, pots and other obviously sacred ceremonial paraphernalia. She also carried two large packages wrapped in cloth; one was long and one was square and they were both observably very heavy. She set all of the items down and then lifted the two hefty packages and handed them to Gus. "Now, you're ready." He took the items and gave her a slight nod.

As they turned to enter they realized that Oak Grove Cemetery, strangely enough, had taken on an appearance that neither Anna nor Gus or Phillip had noticed before. It sat like an illustration from a gothic horror tale. Ahead stood a tall but long dead tree, a towering silent sentry with its massive dead limbs extended out as if they were reaching for them.

Draped with other live century-old trees and a metal fence that announced its visitors with a loud, eerie screech, it presided over its hallowed residents with a foreboding that would have frightened the most hearty.

"Huh. You're sure you want to do this, Gus?" Phillip asked rhetorically.

The three made their way through the squeaky gate to the point designated by the written legend, to the grave of Gus' oldest ancestor. Anna began to lay out the items specified including two eagle tail feathers.

Phillip and Gus watched in admiration at the reverent way she handled the objects. Suddenly almost as an afterthought, Phillip asked, "Gus, how did you get that car started?"

"I watched you. Making it go was not hard but making it go where I wanted it to was. My cousin had a horse like that. Not well trained," Gus replied.

Phillip smiled and then became solemn. "Gus, if this ceremony works, and Anna's almost got me thinking it will, we won't see each other again. You know I'll always be in your debt for what you did for Austin."

Gus grinned. "Perhaps it's time that I tell you my family name," he said and waited to make sure he had Phillip's attention. "It is the same as your ancestors. It's Rider. Charles Austin Augustus Rider."

Phillip's brow furrowed and his mouth fell slightly open.

"So, you see Phillip, even if this works and I can go to my time, my spirit will be with you and your family. That's where you can repay the debt—within your family."

The implication of Gus' words stunned Philip so seriously, he could hardly respond. "Now it makes sense," Phillip said cryptically. Gus looked at him curiously. "I couldn't understand in the beginning why I felt so obligated to help you. Austin picked right up on it. I had these feelings of loyalty and responsibility when I found you and I didn't know why. Now I do. You're actually part of my own family," Phillip said.

Suddenly, Anna summoned them in a worried tone to the ceremonial circle she had made. She placed them in specific spots around the ring. "Gus, are you sure? I've learned that your heart will stop during this ceremony. If something goes wrong, it may not start again. Are you sure you want to take this risk? It could be your life," Anna asked.

"Yes, Anna. I'm sure for all the reasons you know," Gus said without hesitation.

Anna stared at Gus for a second and then said abruptly as she handed Phillip a small piece of paper, "Here, Phillip, these are the words you must speak. I will tell you when. I just don't know. We may be too late already. The text is very vague about the exact time the rite is supposed to take place. I don't know if you're supposed to make it end as the sun is rising or before it clears the horizon. Plus, introducing the extra objects. They may go back, they may not. In fact, their presence may jeopardize the entire ritual. I just don't know," Anna fretted.

"Anna, I have faith in you and I have faith in the elders. Just do what your heart tells you," Gus said reassuringly.

Anna began to put on ceremonial attire. She put a bracelet on her right wrist and a shawl of finely woven materials around her shoulders. A small fire was lit. It ignited easily. Once started, Anna laid a chip of cedar on it and used one of the eagle tail feathers to dust each of them with smoke.

She began to speak and then stopped in mid-sentence. She heard a strange sound in the distance. The others didn't hear it at first and then, after seeing her concentration, began to listen themselves. It was a dull primal sound, a mix of animal and human. It came from the woods but was impossible to determine exactly from which direction.

"What the hell is that?" Phillip whispered.

Neither Gus nor Anna replied but stayed glued to the sound. Unconsciously, they moved closer together. The hallowed ground they had begun to take for granted seemed to be speaking to them.

The sound appeared to be coming from the south end of the cemetery. At the same time the wooded area began to flicker as if someone had installed strings of Christmas lights in the treeline. The flecks of illumination were stronger than fireflies and seemed to pulse rather than sparkle. There seemed to be a form emerging. Phillip could not make out the figure.

But Anna could.

"Sheriff! What happened to you?" asked the hospital admitting nurse as he walked in holding his arm.

"Oh, bad guy tried to put me out of commission but he's the one who got taken out. Can you fix me up in a hurry? I've got to get back and finish the booking," Sheriff Ross asked.

"Of course. I'll take care of you myself," said Rhonda Goodenough as she ushered him into one of the treatment rooms.

Poor Sheriff Ross, she thought. *Never appreciated. Always in harm's way, doing for others. Maybe he needs to be helped.*

Rhonda had just recently been transferred to the midnight to eight shift. She was sure it was a result of the report the other nurse had filed on her. But it just might be a blessing after all.

She took Sheriff Ross and helped him onto an aluminum table in the nearest treatment room. "I'll get you prepped and then I'll call the doctor. That's a gunshot wound and he'll have to remove the bullet," she said. "I'll be right back.

Ross lay on the cold table plotting what his next step would be. He would leave the hospital and go to his home and get his stash of cash, comprised of small payoffs for protection and what he had been able to skim from the prostitutes, nearly $70,000. Then he'd beat it out of town before Harley or the OSBI could get their hands on him.

Rhonda scurried to the break room and removed the syringe from her lunch sack and returned.

This time she would make no mistake. "This is a little local anesthetic," she said. "It will numb the area." She quickly removed her syringe and injected the insulin under the Sheriff's arm.

Within minutes, Sheriff Ross' eyes began to cloud over and his pulse became erratic and accelerated. His skin became pale and moist and his tongue was thick. He looked panic as his body began to play tricks on him.

"I'll call the doctor now," Rhonda said sweetly. She picked up the phone and pushed the intercom, "Code Blue Team report to treatment room." She repeated the camouflaged emergency call.

Slowly, a petite figure materialized from the darkness. As it came closer and moved out of the early morning mist, Anna recognized the form but didn't know why it was here. She wasn't even sure if the person was actually there or if it was some kind of apparition.

"*O-si-yo*, Ester," Anna said gently.

The image of Ester Shinnyfeld said nothing but continued to move closer to them. This time she was not the strange looking, ill-dressed demented person that Anna had experienced earlier in the day. Instead, she was dressed in bright traditional Cherokee clothing, full black hair twisted tightly into braids and a radiance in her face that Anna had rarely seen in any of the elders.

Gus and Phillip were spellbound. It was as if a spirit were visiting them.

Ester stopped several feet from the small group and stood silently for a moment.

"Who is the traveler?" she asked.

"I am," answered Gus, his voice nervous and uncomfortable.

"Do you know that your heart may stop?"

"I know. If it is the will of the elders then it will stop," Gus replied. "But I will not abandon my friends, my family or my nation."

"So be it. Anna Whitebear, do not forget my words," she said and began to recede into the forest. Once she was no longer visible, the flickering lights died away and the three were once again alone.

Anna was first to speak. "I guess we'd better get started before I get so freaked out I won't be able to perform the ceremony."

Yet again they took their positions.

Then at the very moment before Anna was to begin the mystical incantations horror struck her. She turned white faced with a look of alarm.

Both of the men saw the distress. "What is it?" Phillip asked.

"Now I know why she came. I understand! We've got to stop! We can't go yet. It won't work," she screamed and tore out toward the SUV, still nestled in the thicket.

Within moments the door to the room flew open and the on-duty physician and a male orderly came running into the room trailing a 'Crash Cart'. They immediately began frantic efforts to resuscitate the patient as Rhonda Goodenough looked on with what appeared to be genuine concern.

Anna didn't have the necklace on. She had to have the turtle.

Phillip and Gus watched in dismay as she fell to her knees frantically scratching through the ground. Suddenly she raised her hand in triumph and ran back to them. Regaining her composure, she paused for a moment to allow the solemnity to return. Gus and Phillip regained their posture of meditation, both sorely aware that time was ticking away. They could get caught by the sunrise too soon. That meant not only would Gus not be transported but could also very well lose his life.

Obviously unruffled by the interruption, Anna began the incantations, first with a voice that had a district quiver but then one that grew in intensity. "This fire is to the image of *gadugi*, for us to come together and work for the benefit of our families, communities and nation. We call on our ancestors to protect us and to embrace us safely in their arms," she continued. "Take the chosen one from this home and allow him to travel to the place of need."

Even with the small flickering light of the campfire, Phillip could see she was indeed becoming a part of the ceremony. He looked at Gus who stood rigidly with the smoke curling around, almost clinging to him as tightly as he clung to the two packages Anna had given him. He was visibly in a deep state of ataraxia and, at least in his mind, was being transported somewhere other than where he was. Phillip wondered if his heart had stopped yet. The ritual was beginning to affect Phillip as well. When he started his part of the chant, which was to summon the magical powers to deliver Gus to his ancestors, he felt this overwhelming need to cry, as if all the pain of his people had suddenly been visited on him, a people that just days ago he knew little of.

This must be what it's like to be on peyote flashed through his mind. Suddenly, he understood. He wasn't just reciting words from a book. He was trying to communicate with Gus' ancestors and, for the first time, he fully grasped that he was a Rider descendant and those forbearers were his as well.

He felt lightheaded and the haze seemed to overtake the small group. He could see Anna but just barely and Gus was almost covered with smoke, only his head visible.

Anna began to sing a plaintive song in Cherokee. Phillip couldn't understand any of it but the melody was enchanting. He looked down at the script he was given and it was illuminated with the beams of light from the rising sun. But Phillip saw only tiny snakes on the paper. In horror he dropped the document and found himself falling right behind it. It was the last thing he remembered.

Gus marveled at the way the words Anna was singing melodically echoed in his head. They seemed to engulf him. They were entrancing and his vision was clouding.

Soon he could see only the murky smoke. It surrounded him and he felt as if he were inside a cloud.

He could make out something but it was unclear what it was. Then it became discernible. The face of his father and grandfather appeared and then gave way to the beautiful face of his Mary Ann. Beside her emerged the image of T.L. and they stood together smiling at him, beckoning him home. He felt nothing but happiness and contentment. His mind began to whirl and he was soon absorbed into the blackness.

Phillip opened his eyes and, for a moment, didn't know where he was. The cries of early morning birds caused him to sit up and look around. Across from him was a dazed-looking Anna Whitebear.

"Is he gone?" she asked as she looked around and without waiting for an answer said, "My God, it worked."

"I don't know. I don't see him. I don't know what happened to me. All I remember is the song you were singing," Phillip said and quickly uttered, "Austin!" He jumped to his feet and ran to the SUV, his heart pounding. He opened up the back hatch to find the little boy sitting up and rubbing his eyes.

"I'm hungry, Daddy," Austin said.

"Me too, son. Me too," Phillip chuckled. "Let's get some breakfast."

There was a clattering as the receiver was jostled from its base. "Hello?" the groggy voice said.

"Senator?" asked the Attorney General.

"Yes?" the voice said apprehensively.

"This is Nelson Gay. I'm sorry to wake you so early but I thought you should know that we completed an extensive police operation in the Stilwell area early this morning."

"Not at all, Mr. Attorney General. I've been up for some time. What kind of police operation, may I ask?" the senator answered.

"It looks as if we've uncovered and arrested a number of high visibility criminals. Although he's eluded capture so far, the Sheriff of Adair County is also implicated. We're putting out an All Points Bulletin for him. We'll get him soon."

There was a pause on the other end. Gay swore he could hear a mouth open in disbelief. Before the senator could respond Gay continued.

"I know you can appreciate the need for absolute secrecy in an operation such as this and that's why you haven't been advised of the activities even though they occurred in your district. In case there was a leak, we wanted you to be above suspicion."

"Is that so?" said the senator. He was beginning to recover from the information. Before he could say anything else, Gay interrupted.

"Senator, because you have been such a tremendous help to our office in the past and I know you will continue to be, I've taken the liberty of including you in our press release as one of the people instrumental in this arrest. We'll have a news conference today and we'll release it then," the Attorney General said.

"Well, Mr. Attorney General, that's mighty thoughtful of you. When exactly is this news conference?"

"Probably mid-afternoon, in time for the six o'clock news. That will give you plenty of time to get there and my staff will brief you on the details. And Senator, you know how much I appreciate your support. Now and in the past."

"I'll look forward to seeing you and learning about these successful arrests," the senator said conspiratorially. "Thank you for including me."

Once they were all loaded, they turned the SUV toward the highway. Other than a Gordian knot of tracks and the wrecked sheriff's vehicles there was no indication that anything had happened.

Anna drove down the road. Their first stop was at the closest fast food restaurant they could find. Surprised at how hungry they were, the three devoured their breakfasts.

During a break in the eating, Phillip asked Anna, "How'd you manage that machine gun? I didn't think you knew anything about it."

"I didn't but I'd watched you show Gus how to load it and well, when they were coming right at you and Gus, I decided I'd be damned if I was going to sit there and let them execute you. I tried to hold it down on the top of the truck but the thing vibrated so much it was bouncing all around. I was lucky if I hit anything," she said.

"Actually, I don't think you did hit anything but it sure had the desired effect. Without it they would have been on me and Gus before the OSBI showed up," Phillip said. "I've got to remember how much people learn by watching me do things," and cast an eye toward Austin.

The trio left the restaurant and went by the motel to pick up their belongings. Phillip dressed Austin and then checked out. Then, they drove to Anna's house. As they pulled in they were surprised to be greeted by several men and two highway patrol cars in her driveway.

Standing in the front yard and striding over to meet them was Nelson Gay. Austin was holding his father's hand tightly.

"Boy, am I happy to see you," Gay said as he shook Phillip's free hand. "The OSBI thought you were right behind them when they left the cemetery. When I got here about an hour ago and no one had seen you, we all began to get worried."

"You saved our bacon, Nelson. How'd you know we were almost done for?" Phillip asked.

"The Stilwell Chief of Police, Chief Conley, called and alerted us. He's been quietly assisting in the investigation of Ross. Didn't look like there was much time to spare," Gay said.

"I thought we were toast. How is Agent Sutor?" Phillip asked.

"He's going to be fine. It nicked the bone but they think they can still keep him on active duty," Gay answered. "Not so for the sheriff, however.

We just got a call that he was in the Stilwell hospital. Came in to be treated for a gun shot and died of insulin shock. They didn't even know he was a diabetic."

Anna walked up from the cab. "Excuse me, Mr. Gay, I'm Anna Whitebear and this is my house. May I ask why you're going though my garage?"

"I'm sorry, of course, Ms. Whitebear. We found out that Phillip's car was at your house. You see, the sheriff's deputies are falling over themselves to sell Ross out. So much for honor among thieves. Apparently, he had some plans for you, Phillip, once you got on the highway; that is, if you got past him."

Phillip looked stunned.

"Oh, yeah," Gay said nodding. "We found your brake lines and your gas line had been tampered with. Apparently, he'd given one of his boys orders to make sure you wouldn't get back to Oklahoma City in one piece. A fine fellow named Ledbetter. Ever heard of him?"

"Yeah, I've heard of him," Phillip said.

"We're going to take the car in for evidence but you and Austin can ride back to Oklahoma City with me in a highway patrol car. Would you like that, Austin?"

"Yes!" Austin exclaimed, totally revitalized after being fed.

"Good! Mr. Oates will show you around. Jack, would you give young Austin a tour?" Oates put out his hand and Austin eagerly grabbed it.

"Come with me, Austin, and I'll show you what the police car looks like. Maybe even let you make the lights flash!" He and an excited Austin walked toward the car.

Sensing that Anna and Phillip had things to say to each other, Gay said, "We'll be ready to leave in a few minutes." He quickly walked over to the assembled policemen.

Anna and Phillip began to wander toward her front door. "Well, Phillip, this has to have been a lot more than you bargained for. For just coming to a simple ceremony for your ancestor, you got sucked into a situation where you got beat up, your son kidnapped and you were shot at. Welcome to Stilwell. That's a pretty exceptional introduction to your Cherokee heritage I'd say," Anna said smiling.

Phillip laughed to himself. "You've got that right. I did get more than I bargained for. You know, I'd really forgotten what small towns were like."

"What do you mean?" Anna asked.

"Oh, there have just been a number of times that people I didn't know — and had no reason to know — made a special effort to help me and Austin. To be honest, you forget that kind of treatment exists when you get caught up on the hustle and bustle of a city. I've been embarrassed more than once by the kindness I've received by the locals. You know, I grew up in a small town and it all started coming back to me. Pretty decent folks here."

"I'm glad you got to experience that at least. I'm sorry you didn't get to learn much about the Cherokee Nation," she said.

"Oh, I learned a lot. I had no idea of the complexity of their history and existence. I guess I just thought they were a band of nomadic people who lagged behind the times."

"Do you still feel that way?"

"No, of course not," Phillip said. "I know there's still a lot to learn. But by the time Austin is grown, he'll have a firm grasp in his heritage."

"I hope you won't wait for Austin to pick up the thread," Anna said.

"What do you mean?" Phillip asked.

"Well, it's just that we see so many people come here to find out their Cherokee heritage—to fill in a blank in their genealogy—and then recede back into their normal lives. It's almost a vicarious journey into the struggles and adventures of a people they don't know, have only heard of," Anna said.

"What's wrong with that, Anna? People have a right to find out their history," Phillip said.

"Of course they do," Anna said, her face softening. "But, once you come into someone's life you've sort of got an obligation to stay a part of it, don't you think?

"I probably wouldn't be so demanding if I hadn't had a dream last week. It worries me because if it's true, there are some rough times ahead for us in the Cherokee Nation. We're going to need all the help we can get."

"What did your dream say you'd be doing in all of this chaos that supposedly is going to befall the Cherokees."

"It didn't say. But I suspect I'll get a visit soon from my grandfather. He'll tell me, if I can figure out what he's saying." She smiled.

"Anna, I wouldn't just leave you and Stilwell and the Cherokees after what we've been through. I fully intend to remain a part of what goes on here,"

Phillip said. "I'm still not sure I believe what happened to us. But I guess, as an old friend of ours was prone to say, I don't have much choice!"

The two hugged each other just as Nelson Gay walked up.

"Phillip, I need a few moments," Gay announced seriously.

"Sure."

"Let's go over here. There's someone who needs to talk to you." The two strode over to a middle-aged man dressed in a suit and tie.

"Phillip Michaels, meet Special-Agent-in-Charge Kennedy. He's the head of the FBI in Oklahoma City," Gay said. "I'm afraid there's a problem."

Phillip looked from one to the other. At first, he thought his fraternity brother was having a joke with him but he quickly realized he was deadly serious.

"What is it?" Phillip asked, his blood pressure rising.

"Mr. Michaels, our interviews with Ross' men indicate there was a burglary at the National Guard Armory and you and an accomplice were the prime suspects. We've contacted the National Guard staff and they have confirmed there was, in fact, a break-in and that a machine gun and some ammunition was taken," SAC Kennedy explained. "Mr. Michaels, are you aware that burglary of a federal property, such as the National Guard Armory, is a federal offense punishable by a prison sentence and a stiff fine?"

Phillip's worst fears were being realized. How in the world could he explain his way out of this? *Oh, my friend needed the weapon so he could go back in time to win a Civil War battle? Where is my friend? He's gone back to 1864. And the machine gun? It's back there, too. Oh, my God, what will I do now?*

Phillip stood silently.

"Mr. Michaels, I know you've been instrumental in these arrests so I'm giving you this courtesy. If you're in anyway involved in this burglary, then I suggest you get legal counsel. It will take us several more hours to amass enough evidence to make an arrest on probable cause," SAC Kennedy said.

"Thank you, Agent Kennedy," Phillip said in a daze.

Kennedy turned and walked away. Phillip looked at Nelson Gay.

"What the hell do I do?"

"Phillip, these are the Feds. I can't do anything to help you at this stage. If you don't have a real good alibi, you better call Ben Ratliff. He's the best criminal lawyer I know. Tell him you're my friend. But man, I'd do it as soon as we get back to Oklahoma City," Nelson Gay said, "because if they can pin anything on you, they will have done it by tomorrow morning."

"We've got big problems," Harley said when his boss answered the phone.

The line was silent.

"The heat is all over the place. That stupid Ross has brought the OSBI down on us. And I don't know if they know about the shipment from Maldonado," he continued breathlessly.

"I see. Postpone the shipment. Pay Maldonado a restocking fee if necessary. Shut down the operation. Send the employees out of the country for six months. Get Ross out today. I don't want any chance for him to talk. I want every trace that any of you were ever there completely and totally erased," the boss said emphatically.

Harley listened and then asked tentatively, "Okay. What do you want me to do?"

The voice that answered was a gentle, concerned one. "Well, Harley, I want you to come visit me as soon as you have carried out my instructions," the boss said, using his name for the first time since hiring him. "But not today. I have a press conference to attend."

"Yes, sir," Harley said and hung up the phone.

The senator from Stilwell also hung up the phone, sat back and began to plan Harley's penalty for failing to follow orders.

The office was on the top floor of the tallest building in Oklahoma City. The view from the reception area was spectacular. One could see all the way to Edmond, a suburb nearly twenty miles away from downtown. Phillip declined the pretty receptionist's repeated offers of refreshments. It was as if she would receive demerits if he were spotted sans coffee.

Phillip was dry but not thirsty. Nor could he enjoy the panorama that unfolded before him. He seemed to be in a fog. Everything he had ever worked for was passing before him and he couldn't believe this was happening to him. Suddenly, Ben Ratliff came dashing through the door. "Hi. You must be Phillip," he said extending his hand. "I'm sorry I'm late but court was running behind and I couldn't leave until I filed this last motion. Hope you haven't been waiting long," he said.

Ratliff was mid-forties with a full head of prematurely graying hair. A handsome man, he was beginning to show the extra pounds that age brought.

"Come on in, Phillip and let's talk," he said as he opened the door to his office. Ratliff motioned for Phillip to sit on a couch that was part of a comfortable seating arrangement. He took a chair next to the couch. "Okay, start from the beginning. You covered some of it on the phone. Why were you in Stilwell? When did you go? That kind of thing," he said as he punched the record button on a small recorder.

Phillip began the fantastic story. Ratliff never asked a question or interrupted him. He just sat and listened. Sometimes he seemed to be staring right through him. Phillip would alternate from becoming highly animated to speaking softly and in disbelief. He told of Gus, the sheriff, of Anna and the pursuit that kept him dodging the law.

After almost an hour and a half, he stopped and raised his hands. "That's the story, believe it or not."

Ratliff looked at him for a long minute. He reached for the recorder, flipped open its small door and removed the tape cassette. Then, he threw it in a trashcan by his desk. "Do you think I'm an idiot?" he said, eyes narrowed as he glared at Phillip. "More accurately, do you think there's a jury in the *Twilight Zone* who would believe you? Even if this were the truth, how in the world could I possibly present it to a jury? We might have a chance at an insanity plea. And I wouldn't even consider taking this case, friend of Nelson Gay or not, without the results of a psychological examination," Ratliff said.

"Look, Ben, I know it sounds nuts and it doesn't surprise me that you don't believe me, but if the Feds charge me then it will be today. Will you at least represent me long enough for me to get out on bail?" he asked.

"No. I can't take a case I can't win. And nobody can win this one," Ratliff said.

"Then at least recommend some other attorney."

"I'm sorry, Phillip, but I can't think of anyone, except enemies, that I would feel right about asking. And referring you, with your story, is not what one would do to a fellow attorney whom they wanted to keep as a friend. Your best bet is looking in the Yellow Pages. Sorry." Ratliff stood signaling the meeting was over.

Phillip rose slowly and left the office pretty sure life as he knew it was never going to be the same. He had no lawyer, no story and no defense. Pretty soon he wouldn't have an architect's license. He was going to go to jail.

He drove to his office and tried to put the situation out of his mind by working. That was not successful. He couldn't concentrate and when people talked to him, he couldn't pay attention.

He looked at his watch and it was four o'clock. *What the hell?* he thought, *I can't get any work done; I may as well take a walk and try to think.* He locked his desk and rose to leave.

He took the elevator down to the labyrinth of tunnels that honeycombed Oklahoma City's downtown and began walking, hoping it might help clear his head. He passed restaurants and shops full of people all enjoying themselves. He yearned to be one of them. Free of worries. Bright futures ahead. Even though he had been in the tunnels frequently, his mind wandered for the first time thinking about what it would be like to work all day underground.

At first he ambled down the tube then, without realizing it, worked himself into a hurried pace. He wasn't paying attention to his location. He began to tire and became disoriented and lost. His chest was tight and his breathing was labored. Saliva glands were pumping liquid into his mouth. He wondered if he were having a heart attack. He remembered his doctor's warning. His mouth was so full he had to empty it someplace. He looked around and seeing no one, spat into a nearby trashcan. He leaned against the wall, panting. A few passersby looked at him strangely. Finally, a woman stopped and said, "Sir, are you all right?"

"I'm fine, thank you. Just catching my breath," he answered haltingly, still leaning against the side of the tunnel.

She smiled sympathetically and walked away. Phillip mused at how caring Oklahomans were. *If this were the New York subway, people would just step over you if you were lying on the floor. Wonder how they'll treat me in prison.*

Slowly, he began to feel better. His mind seemed to be clearing enough that maybe, he could come up with some kind of strategy to deal with this crisis. Then he saw a bar and thought of stopping in and getting shit-faced. *That would hardly help your situation*, he thought. *When you sobered up you'd still be in jail.*

Just as he decided to pass it up he looked inside and saw Brian Starnes. Starnes had once been a car salesman for a foreign car dealership Phillip had designed. Tiring of selling high-priced cars to arrogant rich people, he had left the dealership, gone back to law school and last year, gotten appointed as a Special Judge.

It's a long shot but maybe Brian can give me some advice, he thought. He entered the bar and announced himself to the judge, trying to stay upbeat and not give away what he was feeling. "Know where a guy can buy a Porsche Carrera?"

Surprised, Starnes greeted him warmly and invited him to sit down. Phillip watched for an opportunity to break through the small talk and tell Starnes about his problem, but the judge wanted to talk about old times.

"Say, Brian, I was going to ask you ..." Phillip would say only to be interrupted with another tale of car dealer days.

Suddenly, Phillip's cell phone began to vibrate on his belt. He could see it was his office calling. He excused himself and pushed the talk button. It was his secretary.

"Mr. Michaels, there are two men to see you," his receptionist said nervously. Then she whispered, "They say they're the FBI."

Phillip's heart leaped to his throat in panic and then just as quickly dropped to his stomach. He knew who it was.

His first thought was to order her to tell them he was gone for the day. Buy himself a little more time. Then the fallacy of that alternative flashed in front of him. They weren't going to go away. He would just be setting himself up to be arrested in front of his wife and child.

"The FBI, huh? Okay. I'll come back. It'll take about fifteen minutes," he said wearily and punched the end button, holstering his phone.

"What did you want to ask, Phillip?" the judge asked, now all ears.

"Nothing, Brian. It was good to see you," he said and shook his hand weakly. *You'll find out in plenty of time,* he thought.

Sure enough, when he arrived back at the office he immediately recognized one of the men. It was Special Agent-in- Charge Kennedy whom he had met earlier. Agent Kennedy quickly introduced the other man, another agent but Phillip wasn't paying attention and his name went past him.

"Let's go in my office," Phillip said mechanically and all three entered. He knew his face was pale and ashen. Phillip reflexively offered them chairs but both men declined. He had no illusions why they were here and they were making it clear it wasn't a social call.

"I guess you expected us, huh?" Kennedy said with a solemn look.

"Yeah, I guess so. Just not so soon," replied Phillip.

"Well, this case surprised us. It wound to an end quickly. After our conversation this morning I felt this was a task I should perform personally."

How nice of you, Phillip thought mockingly. *His life was over.*

"I know you've been through a lot so I wanted to come by and inform you that you've been cleared of the burglary," SAC Kennedy said.

Phillip was flabbergasted. "How? How was I cleared?" he asked trying not to sound too incredulous.

"We confirmed your whereabouts from Mrs. Whitebear and Agent Sutor. She established you were with her constantly from yesterday afternoon until early this morning," he said. Phillip knew what Kennedy was thinking but wasn't going to worry if it looked like he had been engaged in extramarital activity. "Then, this afternoon the missing weapon was found over 100 miles away by a couple of kids playing on the banks of Cabin Creek by a little town called Strang. That's quite a distance from your location. It appears, from a call the Stilwell Police received, that the burglary occurred about eleven p.m..

"Agent Sutor says he met you at the cemetery after midnight. You couldn't have made it up that far to Cabin Creek and back, if you were with Mrs. Whitebear and Agent Sutor. We know when the incident at the cemetery started so the times just don't work out," Kennedy said.

"I see. Well, it's good to know that I'm no longer a suspect," Phillip mumbled, still a little dazed. He had questions but was afraid to ask them. He would just leave well enough alone.

The two men turned to leave. They shook hands and walked to the door and then at the last moment, Agent Kennedy turned toward Phillip. "It was bizarre."

Phillip drained of emotion, looked at him quizzically.

"I mean the machine gun. The serial numbers matched the stolen gun but it was all oxidized and the parts were all frozen together. It looked as if it had been in the mud for a hundred years but, of course, it was just stolen last night. Bizarre," Agent Kennedy said as he shook his head and left the office.

CHAPTER TWENTY-FOUR

Phillip Michaels' Home
Oklahoma City

Phillip sat up in bed sweating and breathing hard. He looked to his left and Carri was sleeping soundly, a soft purr coming from her lips. He reached over and turned on his bedside lamp and stared at the wall.

I'll just take a moment to settle down and then I'll go back to sleep.

He sat up for a minute taking in deep breaths and waiting for the pounding in his heart to subside. Finally, he stood and half-stumbled into the bathroom and ran a glass of water from the tap. Drinking it wetted his parched throat. He headed back toward the bed.

He sat on his side of the mattress. Carri turned over and opened her eyes. "What is it, honey?" she asked.

"I'm sorry I woke you. I just had this incredible dream. I don't remember anything about it but it must have been a doozie because I'm drenched with sweat and my throat was dry as a bone. My heart was beating like I've been running a marathon," he said. "Go back to sleep, sweetheart. I'm fine."

Carri patted him on his arm and rolled over to return to sleep.

Phillip, instead, got up and walked to the kitchen. Once there, he decided he really didn't want anything to eat. He went back to the bed and stretched out. Just as he reached to turn out the lamp, he noticed a scribbled word on the small pad he kept by the phone on the table. There were two words scrawled on the pad, *gadugi* and Cherokee.

Gadugi? What in the world does that mean? He took the paper and lay in bed staring at the words, turning them sideways and upside-down trying to make sense of them.

Gadugi must be some kind of Cherokee word. It has Cherokee by it. But why would I write it? I don't know anything about the Cherokee Tribe.

His memory flashed to a recent telephone call he had received. *Guess I better take that lady up on her offer and go to Stilwell Sunday for that ceremony. It might be kind of interesting. I can find out what gadugi means then. Maybe I'll take Austin.*

Phillip Michaels extended his arm, turned off the lamp and went back to sleep.

EPILOGUE

In the annals of the Civil War in the Trans-Mississippi West campaign there was a series of battles centering on an obscure site in northeast Oklahoma—then known as "Indian Territory"—called Cabin Creek.

Accounts of clashes in the west are often sketchy, perhaps because most were small unit skirmishes rather than full-fledged large battles. But for some unknown reason there was an extensive record left of the final engagement at Cabin Creek. It was noted that after a succession of defeats at that location, the Confederate troops, comprised of Cherokees and Texans, were victorious over a much superior Union force. Even with the large amount of information available regarding the fighting, the reason for this victory has never been revealed.

Caught while crossing Cabin Creek, the Federal wagon train, comprised of over a thousand Union soldiers, was attacked just as they arrived on the far shore and were literally pushed back into the creek. Rumors, never proven, assert that the Union commander, drunk at the time, fled in a state of panic leaving his troops to escape on their own abandoning the animals and supplies to the attacking Confederates. Tons of goods were captured and, while the control of the West fell to the North at the Battle of Pea Ridge a few months later, they, nevertheless, supplied the Confederates in that area for months to come and allowed them to continue the struggle until the end of the war. Their famous leader, Brigadier General Stand Watie, became the last Confederate general to surrender in the War Between the States.

Unofficial accounts speak of an incredible volume of fire from the Confederate lines that caused some Union veterans to recall "the rainstorm of bullets at Shiloh." Given that most Southern soldiers were equipped with old style, slow firing rifles it is inexplicable how the gunfire was massed so effectively. Some speculate the Confederates had perfected a rapid-fire rifle capable of a rate of sustained fire in the range of thousands of rounds per minute. However, proof of any such weapon's existence has never been found.

During the ensuing years, many descendants of the veterans of the battle spread throughout Oklahoma but most remained in the area still known as the Cherokee Nation.

One such case was of C.A.A. Rider who survived the war and later was elected to the Cherokee National Council, the unicameral congress of the Cherokee Nation. His name can still be found on official documents of that era.

His descendents would become active in state affairs, even serving in elective offices throughout the 20th century working to build the state that he helped settle.

And today, the Cherokee Nation still exists, thriving, meeting its challenges and looking toward a future of opportunity for its citizens and their descendants.

Acknowledgements

Thanks to Oklahoma Attorney General Drew Edmondson, himself a native of eastern Oklahoma, for advice on the state's legal system; Cousin and former second-generation Treasurer of the Cherokee Nation Jay Hannah for in-depth knowledge of the region and the history of the Cherokees; The good people of Stilwell, Oklahoma, a town with a proud place in Cherokee history and whose residents welcome visitors in a far friendlier way than is portrayed in this novel.

Cherokee artists David Scott for his encyclopedic knowledge of Cherokee language and history and P.J.Gilliam Stewart for sharing her Cherokee icons with me.

To Butch Roat, the finest automobile service advisor I've ever known who educated me on the operation of modern auto engines; Well-known Cherokee novelist Robert Conley for his critical eye on many of the portions dealing with Cherokee mysticism.

To Kristy Ventimiglia for her eagle-eyed proofreading and Branden Hart for his computer mastery.

And finally, to respected Cherokee activist Betty Starr Barker for her unceasing support and for making me feel at home in Stilwell.

Author's Note

One summer evening, as the sun slowly blended into the horizon in one of Oklahoma's spectacular sunsets, I found myself standing at the deserted site of the Battle of Cabin Creek. Heavily shaded by long-standing trees, my cousin and I slowly and quietly walked to each point around the hallowed circle and read the markers that identified the different military units facing each other, both Union and Confederate.

The sounds of day had faded and an eerie stillness had settled across the field of battle, so long ago cleansed of its carnage. It was then that my cousin Jay, a professional grade historian said softly, "Most of them fell here" indicating we were standing in the heart of the killing field. At that moment I was struck by a profoundly powerful connection to those men, my direct ancestors, who so long ago in the flower of their youth faced death only 30 yards away.

The import of that instant will never leave me and we softly uttered a prayer of appreciation for the lives that fate had dealt us…a result of the heroism of our ancestors who confronted danger and death in pursuit of a cause they felt was just. I knew then that I could never write about those people or their time again without in some way acknowledging them.

Thus, while this is a novel about time travel it is also a story about the Cherokee, their land, their history and their trials and tribulations. The careful reader will find in this text many family names that belonged to the leaders of the Cherokee Nation during the period in which the story takes place. While this is a complete work of fiction and the characters were created from whole cloth, I have woven actual Cherokee surnames into the story to honor them, their memory and their sacrifices.

They are remembered and respected, for it was the way in which they led their lives that has allowed me to exist, grow and flourish.

—GBA
January 2006

Printed in the United States

Printed in the United States
70291LV00004B/142-357